To my dear friend Sue Lowings, a very fine writer indeed.

kelly harte

guilty
feet

RED
DRESS
INK
TM

First edition April 2003

GUILTY FEET

A Red Dress Ink novel

ISBN 0-373-25026-6

Visit Red Dress Ink at www.reddressink.com

Printed in U.S.A.

ACKNOWLEDGMENTS

A big thanks to Colin Larkin for unwittingly giving me the idea, even though he sussed me immediately when I tried a "Sarah Daly" on him and thought writing the book was a mistake at the time. Joanna Harris for thinking it was a good idea and also for letting me use her name. Martin Harris for being pleased for me. Christian Harris, the "Dive Master," for keeping in touch with his old mum so well as he sensibly avoids "real life" with the lovely Pip in Thailand. Sue Lowings for being the best possible friend and a limitless source of help, advice and encouragement in the writing department. Judy Currie for her ancestors, and for being around when I needed her. David Ashcroft for the Web site he promises to create, and for looking after Fluffy so well. Sam Bell (who looks years younger than she really is) for keeping me on the straight and narrow so very nicely and for using words like *Yikes!* Juliet Burton for all her time, patience and good-natured support. Also Tom, Dan and Carmen for never giving me a hard time, and finally to the other Tom, whose only vice is, erm, plastic bags.

chapter 1

I had no sense of the significance of that day while I was actually living it. That only came with hindsight. At the time I was too busy being depressed about my life, and my job situation wasn't helping much. There were just fifteen of us left in the office by then. And things must have been bad because even the fact that Rob (thirty-one-year-old, good-looking company marketing director) was having extra-marital relations with Susan (his dumpy, forty-seven year-old PA) failed to raise as much as an eyebrow—let alone a smirk or a smutty comment.

If anyone could even be bothered to speak at all, the major topic of speculation was how long it would be before the company folded. A few of us thought we might struggle on till the end of the month, but Sid, the ever-gloomy and ludicrously youthful office technical genius, had put it around only that morning that we wouldn't make it till the end of the day. Mostly we sat staring at our computers, though, pretending to look for new business leads while wishing we'd been wise enough to accept the voluntary redundancies that had been on offer a few weeks ago. Either that or we circulated not very funny/very rude e-mails to anyone we could think of. And when we got bored with that we let the devil do whatever else he does with idle hands, and in my case, *mind*.

This involved a great deal of brooding about Dan, and Aisling Carter, and wondering what I could do to get my own back on the lying bastard and scheming slapper. I was still finding it hard to get my head round the fact that they were together, especially after all that Dan had said about her in the past.

On her looks: 'All right if you like Barbie dolls, I suppose.'

On her voice: 'Sounds like a Siamese cat on heat.'

On her name: 'Sneaky.' (Looks like *Aisling* when it is written and sounds like *Ashling* when it is spoken.)

On her character: 'The biggest name-dropper in the whole of Leeds.'

We'd laughed about that a lot. It had been 'Kate' (Moss) this, and 'Denise' (van Outen) that, or 'Jamie' (Astin) the other. And, OK, so she might have come into contact with a few famous people in the course of her sickeningly glamorous work, but to hear her talk you'd think they were all her very close friends—friends that never quite found their way to her flat in Leeds...

The flat she'd moved into just beneath ours, a couple of months before I left Dan.

And had made it so obvious that she fancied Dan it had been almost funny at the time.

'Can you do me a huge favour and help me move my sofa,

please, Dan?' Four times to my knowledge she tried that one on, and it wasn't as if the sofa didn't have castors!

'Would you be an angel and show me how my central heating system works again, please, Dan?' In the middle of summer.

'Could you water my plants while I'm away, *pleeease*, Dan?' Jetting off here, there and everywhere with her highly paid PR job that everyone knew she'd only got because her god-mother owned the company.

Jammy, devious cow.

And now Dan *doted* on her, according to Libby, who lived in the flat upstairs from Dan and kept me informed about what was going on. Only I was beginning to wish that she didn't, because talking to her, hearing how happy Dan was with Aisling, had made me a little bit crazy. I kept getting vengeful thoughts in my head, really wild and wicked ideas that would probably have come to nothing if I'd had some-thing else to distract me just long enough for me to realise how mad those ideas really were. A new man, perhaps, or a job that involved actual *work*.

I'd been employed for Pisus UK for just over a year. It was a fast-growing e-business agency at the time I joined, and competition for staff had been hot. They'd offered to double my former salary and I'd naturally bitten their hand off. With nothing but admin experience before, I reached the dizzy heights of manager in charge of several extremely prestigious accounts within a month. It was all very exciting for a very short time, but like almost everything else remotely con-nected to the Internet things had since taken a serious dive. And as a part of our job was to build and maintain company websites we were right there in the thick of things.

I was luckier than most, in a way. While most of the com-pany's clients had slunk away like flies in winter, I'd managed to persuade a number of mine to hang on in there. I spoke to them all every day, and while being as honest as I possibly could I was also trying to be optimistic. Because, despite Sid's latest dismal prediction, I was one of the end-of-the-month hopefuls.

But not hopeful enough to stop me looking for work elsewhere. Which is why I tapped out a quick e-mail to Cass, asking if she knew of any jobs going. It made me feel a bit guilty about my clients, but I was a lot more concerned about not having an income. I didn't care what job I did, how lowly, how dull, just so long as it paid enough to cover my rent and my phone bill. Food and electricity I could probably manage without.

Writing the e-mail distracted me for about two minutes, but I was soon back in sombre brooding mode, thinking of Dan and wondering how it had all gone wrong with us. I even got out his dog-eared photo again, the one which I'd taken last New Year's Eve in the kitchen. He'd been cooking for us, and the event was so rare I told him it needed recording for posterity. He looked hot and harassed in the picture, but still pretty gorgeous, with that dark hair that always seemed to need trimming, and a secret smile that said if the food didn't work out then there was always the afters to look forward to.

We'd been together just over two years when I left. And looking back now, almost nine weeks on, I still couldn't explain what had happened with us. It was as if one minute we were blissfully happy and the next we loathed one another. There must have been an in-between stage, I suppose, but that part was all an unhappy blur. I just remembered the good bits now and the insult stage. Or rather one particular whopping great insult.

'If you're not very careful,' he'd told me stingingly the night before I packed my belongings and left the flat, 'you'll turn into your mother.'

Only those who know my mother could possibly understand how cruel that particular slur had been on my character, and he left me no option. But it still wasn't supposed to have been the end. Dan was *supposed* to have called Cass to find out where I was. (She had my permission to tell him.) And if he didn't want to do that, well, he knew where I worked. Some flowers would have been nice, with a note telling me how much he missed me. But most of all I wanted an apology for saying such a terrible thing.

Only nothing happened at all. Not a single word. And so who, after all that, could blame me for choosing to lick my wounds in a bit of luxury? For taking on an expensive flat that just happened to be well beyond my normal means? Cass did, of course, but then Cass has always taken the safe option. She was one of the sensible ones who had refused to be seduced by silly salaries from a boring but safe admin job with a firm of accountants.

Which was exactly what I was after now, as a matter of fact. So I checked the wording I'd used in my e-mail and sent it off quickly, and then, in an attempt to look busy, I decided to check my Hotmail account. Only my mother used that address—a hangover from a trip to India four years before, when she'd insisted on buying a PC so we could stay in touch (which really meant keeping an eye on me and what I was up to). For some reason it had remained her favourite form of communication, which made sense with my brother, who lived in Los Angeles now, but not with someone who'd ended up living only twenty miles from the family home.

And heaven help me if I missed a message.

There were two. The first was titled: *Help is at hand!*

Spoke to Barbara Dick yesterday and she tells me Nicola is getting married next June to a hospital registrar with a very bright future. I told her about your job situation and she sug-

gested you get in touch with Nicola. What are friends for? And if a recruitment consultant can't help, well then, who can?

Not in a million years.

Nic Dick (how could her parents have done that to her?) wasn't my friend and never had been. She was my mother's friend's daughter, who'd never forgiven me for getting off with her boyfriend at a party when we were seventeen. I hadn't even fancied him much, but the cider affected my judgement. I'd drunk far too much, I'm afraid, and anyway he was the one who made the first move, not me...

She'd titled the second e-mail *P.S.*

And don't worry about what you did to Nicola all those years ago. She's a Born Again Christian now and those sort of people don't hold grudges.

That didn't ring true at all. Especially the Born Again bit. Call me cynical, but I couldn't help thinking she must have a motive for getting religious all of a sudden. She'd made my life hell during the final school year and I don't believe that people can change *that* much.

It was just as I was about to shut down, without answering my mother's mail because I was so mad with her for telling the Dicks about my latest troubles, when I thought how nice it would be to be someone else for a while. Someone who wasn't just about to lose her job. Who wasn't living beyond her means. Whose mother didn't humiliate her. Whose life was actually going somewhere. Whose former boyfriend wasn't a lying hypocrite.

My finger hovered over the mouse, with the arrow directed at the *exit* symbol, when it suddenly occurred to me that I could be. Someone else, I mean—and I could start with a brand-new Hotmail address. In whatever name that just happened to take my fancy.

The idea took hold of my imagination quickly, and within a couple of minutes one idea had just led to another...

I couldn't have done what I ended up doing if Dan hadn't been a writer. He works mostly for the music press, and has had a couple of books published about fairly obscure (fairly obscure to me, anyway) recording artists from the dim and distant past. The books were well received by those in the know, and although they didn't sell very well he had been recently commissioned to write something with more mass-market appeal. I'd learnt this from Libby along with everything else. She didn't know what or who the book was about—Dan said it was all a bit hush-hush at the moment—but she did know that he'd had a pretty good advance and was taking time out from his usual work. So it must be important.

The point about him being that kind of writer is that he had a fairly public e-mail address. He liked getting feedback from readers and made a point of publishing the address for this very purpose. He got his fair share of 'wacko mail', as he called it, but enough constructive stuff, he insisted, to make it worthwhile.

And the main point of that point is that there was absolutely no reason he should guess that it was *me* writing to him.

To start with I came up with very silly and outlandish names: Poppy Pickles and Jacosta Whitherspoon, to name but two. Fortunately, silly and outlandish-sounding people (including Poppy and Jacosta) had got there already, so I ended up with a fairly straightforward name for my new account. Which is just as well or I might have looked like one of the wackos and my fiendish plan might never have got off the ground.

I eventually opted for Sarah Daly, which sounded so pleasant and normal that I felt immediately comfortable with it.

It did require switching the first and last names around, but 'dalysarah@hotmail' seemed to have just the right ring about it to me.

I spent ages composing Sarah's first message to Dan. It had to sound authentic, interesting, and really worth replying to. Especially now that he was taking time out of his regular work. There was a very good chance that he was so immersed in his book—and Aisling—that he might not even bother to check his mail, but it was definitely worth a try.

Luckily I used to proofread his work before he filed it, so I already had a pretty good idea what I could write about. I might be a bit out of date, of course, but that needn't matter. Magazines often ended up being read a long time after they went to press. So I plucked out the last one I could remember proofing and based my message on that.

> *Dear Dan*
>
> *I don't usually write to people I don't know, but since you publish your e-mail address I assume you won't mind too much. I recently read something you wrote about Bob Dylan and it struck a chord, so to speak. I might not be of his generation but my parents are, and hearing his stuff in my formative years left a big impression on me. What I liked about your article, though, was the fact that you're obviously not one of those people that sees him as some sort of god (like my parents did—still do, in fact).*

Just the thought of my parents worshipping Dylan made me laugh out loud. They were both light opera freaks, had been even when everyone else was getting excited about the Beatles, and till this day remained stalwarts of the local Gilbert and Sullivan Society. I couldn't be certain they'd even heard of Bob Dylan. Nobody in the office seemed to notice my outburst, or if they did they couldn't be bothered to comment on it or ask what I'd found so funny, so I got back into Sarah mode.

I'd said what I did because I knew Dan had this thing about people who considered Dylan to be some kind of minor deity. It was meant to provide a connection between the e-mailer and e-mailee, but it still didn't mean he had to reply. Unfortunately I'd already used up the full extent of my Dylan knowledge, but after thinking about it for a while I came up with what I hoped was the clincher, something he could rarely resist...

I know there are a lot of books written about him, but I won-der if you would mind recommending a particularly good one that I could give to my parents for Christmas. Something au-thoritative but not too fawning. Something that shows the man with all his flaws as well as the artist.

Thanks and best wishes

Sarah Daly

I read and re-read it several times before clicking onto the *send* symbol, and then I read the sent copy again and regret-ted it. Sarah sounded so—I don't know—silly and naïve? And I'm not sure I would have bothered writing back to her, even if she did ask me for a recommendation.

But there was no getting it back, and no harm really done. And although it wasn't exactly wicked, or wild or very venge-ful, writing to Dan, trying to fool him into believing that I was somebody else, wasting some of his precious time, made me feel better than I had in ages.

I resolved to dig out some of the articles I'd kept of Dan's that evening, and the two books he'd written on people whose names I couldn't recall at that moment. I would fa-miliarise myself with his work, turn myself into a music fan.

And if Sarah let me down I would go in with the big guns next time. I'd invent someone else, a Tara or a Tiffany, who'd be sassy and knowledgeable and opinionated. Because, although I still didn't really know why, I was determined to start some regular bogus correspondence with Dan.

It started to rain as I left the office, and I hadn't brought an umbrella or coat with me. I was wearing one of the expensive suits I'd splashed out on after receiving my first big pay cheque, and because I might never be able to afford anything half so nice ever again I didn't want to get it wet. So I darted into the Italian, which was handily placed just down the road. It served the best cappuccino in Leeds, and during the past year at Pisus UK it had become my local.

Though it didn't close till six o'clock, the place usually started to wind down at five, and with a bit of luck Marco would have time to flirt with me. Since my break-up with Dan I often went there for this very purpose. It was a bit of cheap therapy, really, having a big hunky Leeds Italian calling me 'Bella Joanna' and begging me to go out with him. I guessed most women over sixteen and under forty-five received the exact same treatment, but as long as he didn't do it when I was around I felt pretty special for a while.

Giovanna, Marco's mother, was singing 'Volaré' when I entered the café. It was such a big cliché of a song and she sang it so often that at first I thought she was a pretend Italian. Especially since she had very pale skin and corn-coloured hair, which she always swept into an elegant plait at the back of her head. But it turned out that I was wrong. She was completely authentic, first generation, moved here from Milan when she was just nineteen. When she wasn't singing 'Volaré', she liked to talk a lot in a rather loud, still heavily accented voice that used to alarm me. It made her sound fierce, but in fact she is anything but.

Over the time I'd been going in there I'd learnt quite a lot about her life. I now knew that Marco's father was an Englishman whom she'd met and fallen madly in love with when she was working here as an au pair.

'*Ciao bella!*' Marco cried, as he emerged from the kitchen behind the counter. By now Giovanna had stopped singing 'Volaré' and was asking me how things were going at Pisus as the big old-fashioned and noisy, all singing and dancing coffee machine frothed up my cappuccino.

Marco came round from behind the counter and squeezed the breath out of me. I'd asked him once about his father and he told me that he 'wouldn't piss on the bastard if he caught fire.' Which gave me a pretty good indication about his feelings for the man who'd turned out to be married and had abandoned both mother and child when they needed him most. It seemed the world was full of lying, deceiving and bullshitting bastards!

'I expected to be out of a job by now,' I said when he let me go, 'but it looks like we've weathered the storm for another day.'

Giovanna patted my hand as she placed my cappuccino on the counter. 'You mustn't worry, Joanna. A pretty, clever girl like-a you will soon-a find work.' Then she threw up her arms in a gesture of dismissive flamboyance. 'Anyway, you waste-a your time in that office. With looks like-a yours you should-a be in the movies!'

I could see where her son had learnt some of his lines.

'Thanks, Giovanna,' I said with a wide, silly grin. 'And I don't know about that but I do feel quite cheerful today. Quite optimistic.'

Marco beamed as he picked up the huge cup and saucer and took it to a table near the window. The place looked as if they'd had the theme-makers in but, just like Giovanna, the café's decor was completely authentic—chrome and sky-blue Formica Fifties kitsch. It was perhaps fortunate that someone like Giovanna had taken over the café all those years ago, when she'd been left in the lurch by her English lover. She wasn't the type for fussy new fads. She was of the if-it's-not-broken-why-fix-it school and, fashions being what they are, the café's decor was once again the very height of cool.

Marco sat down opposite me. He was a dangerously handsome man, but because I knew him so well, and because he really wasn't my type, I couldn't bring myself to fancy him. Unlike his mother, he had dark hair and skin, like Italians are supposed to, but he spoke with a marked Leeds accent. His toothpaste-ad smile matched impossibly white shirts, and I kept meaning to ask Giovanna what her secret was—not about her son's teeth but the whiteness of her wash, which I was fairly certain she would be responsible for. My own so-called whites varied from just a little bit 'off' to something closer to silvery grey.

'Joanna,' he said, lowering his voice so his mother couldn't hear him. There were only two other people in at the moment, and sound carried well over chrome and Formica.

'Yes, Marco,' I whispered back, moving closer to him across the table to join in the conspiracy game.

'I have to go away soon for a while, and I wondered if you would like to fill in for me here.'

I was completely taken aback. 'It's good of you, Marco, but I don't want to tread on anyone's toes.' I knew that he already had people who helped out in the café when he took time off.

'It's OK,' he said. 'I've already checked and no one's available. And it's you that would be doing me a favour.'

'But I might not be available till the end of the month.' I was still hanging on to my hope of Pisus surviving that long.

'I understand and it doesn't matter. I can go any time. I just need someone who's, well…flexible. I'll only be away a week, but I'd be happy to keep you on till you found something else.'

I could do flexible, I supposed as I spooned chocolate-covered froth off my coffee. And I couldn't afford to have gaps between jobs. I glanced up at Marco and he looked so anxious that I began to wonder what this was really about. Why was he whispering? What didn't he want Giovanna to know about?

'OK,' I said, 'you've got a deal.' I looked over at his mother, who was humming something melancholy now, not her usual style at all. 'I take it you don't want me to mention anything yet to Giovanna?'

He looked a bit shifty, then he grinned. 'Like-a Mamma says,' he said, doing the accent, 'you are clever as well as pretty, Joanna. But don't worry, she's going to love the idea.'

chapter 2

Dan Baxter groaned aloud when he heard the knock at his door. He glanced at his wristwatch and was surprised to find it was seven-thirty. He'd been working since six that morning and had only stopped twice for coffee and once for a corned beef sandwich. Suddenly he was aware how hungry and thirsty he was.

He frowned as he looked back at the computer screen and considered ignoring the knock. It was more or less time to wind things up, but he'd sooner work through the night than answer the door to who he guessed was out there. The knock sounded again, more forcefully now, and he knew he would have to answer it. If it really was who he thought it would be he was pretty certain she wouldn't give up.

It *was* who he'd thought it would be. Libby, standing there with a large covered tray. She'd been playing Mother quite a lot since he started the book, but if this was food she'd brought with her then she was stepping the role up a pace.

She looked as if she'd just come out of the shower, all pink and shiny and make-up-free. The ends of her curly shoulder-length hair were damp, and at first glance she looked almost attractive. She didn't usually wear it loose, and just for a moment he was reminded of Jo, whose hair was curly and shoulder-length, but just a different colour.

Libby was wearing a pale turquoise fleece zipped up to the neck and, from what he could see beneath the tray, something dark that covered the whole of her legs. She didn't look as if she'd come to try and seduce him, he thought, and then immediately felt guilty for entertaining this idea again. Nothing she'd done so far had given him cause to suppose she was trying to be anything but a friend. It was just an odd feeling he got now and then.

She beamed at him now and, sliding one hand beneath the tray to support it, she used the other to lift the blue and white teatowel a little at the corner. The aroma of something delicious wafted temptingly up.

'Lemon chicken,' she trilled, nudging past him into the hallway.

She was already laying *two* places at the kitchen table by the time he caught up with her, and this time he groaned inwardly. Hungry and grateful he might very well be, but he definitely wasn't in the mood for company. Not Libby's. Not anyone's. She set the tray down in the middle of the table and whipped away the covering with the panache of a magician at a children's party.

It did look good, though. Chicken with rice and roast vegetables.

He shrugged resignedly, and when she produced wine from a carrier bag he hadn't noticed she'd brought with her, he found a corkscrew and took two wineglasses out of the cupboard. The fact that he had any clean glasses available was down to Libby as well. Last night she'd insisted on tidying up the flat, and although he'd found it embarrassing having someone he didn't know very well cleaning up after him she'd refused to take no for an answer. And she'd done such a good job he could hardly complain.

'How did it go today?' she asked him brightly as he poured out the already chilled Australian Chevin Blanc. She was seated by now, smiling and expectant.

'Not bad.' He shrugged. She was talking about the book that he'd been commissioned to write, which involved a very tough deadline indeed, and he took the opportunity to slide in a pretty strong hint. 'I've only got three weeks left to finish it, which is going to be tight.'

'How come you're being so secretive about it all?' she asked, ignoring the hint as she flicked her hair in a distinctly flirty manner.

He sat down and carefully drew his chair back a bit, so there wouldn't be any knee contact under the table.

'I'm not being secretive,' he lied. The fact was that he was being very secretive indeed, and for what he considered a very good reason. If it got out that he was doing a quick cut-and-paste job on VantagePoint, the latest five-minute-wonder boy band, then he was very much afraid that his professional credibility might be harmed. 'I just don't like talking about my work very much,' he added lamely.

'Why did you tell Aisling about it, then?'

Dan, who'd just tucked into the first delicious mouthful of chicken, took a moment to reply. He'd forgotten how prickly she could be.

'I didn't tell her,' he eventually said, truthfully now. 'I left a letter from the publisher out and she read it.' Luckily there had been very little detail in that particular letter, but he was still mad with Aisling for being so nosy—and madder still for passing the information on to Libby.

She seemed pleased by this explanation. 'That's not really on, is it?' she said. 'Reading your private mail, I mean.'

'It's more than "not really on",' he said with feeling. 'I'd call it bloody rude.'

Libby agreed with a nod and, relaxing now, finally picked up her own knife and fork.

'I didn't realise you were such a good cook,' Dan said, because it was true and because he was keen to change the subject.

'I do a great curry as well,' Libby replied eagerly. 'Made from real spices. Not one of those awful ready-made things that come in jars.'

He felt as if he was supposed to say that he'd love to try it one of these days, but he didn't want to encourage her.

'How's the job going, by the way?' he said instead, conversationally. He couldn't actually remember what it was she did, but that didn't matter. It was about keeping the focus on her. She had a habit of trying to wheedle information from him of a personal nature and he wasn't in the mood for talking about himself.

'OK,' she said, 'though I've just been moved to a different department and I don't like my new boss very much. Her idea of managing people is to push them around.'

'That's what's good about my line of work,' he said. 'Not much direct contact with people.'

She looked concerned about this.

'But don't you feel a bit isolated at times?'

He shook his head firmly. 'Never.'

'It must have been strange when Joanna moved out, though,' she said in that wheedling tone that instantly put Dan back on his guard.

He put his knife and fork down and knocked back half of the wine in his glass.

'Yeah, sure. We'd been together for quite a long time, and the flat did seem pretty empty for a while, but I'm used to it now.' And, yes, he *was* getting used to it, but it didn't mean that he liked it, and it certainly didn't mean that he wanted to discuss the matter with someone he wasn't even sure that he liked very much.

'You don't still miss her, then?'

'Look,' he said, more sharply than he'd intended, 'I'm sorry, but I'm tired and I'd rather not get into this just now.' In fact all he wanted to do was finish the food, do his word count, check his e-mails, maybe play some music, and get some shut-eye. So he very much hoped she wasn't planning on staying long.

'I was only testing the water,' she said sulkily. 'It's just that I've heard she's seeing someone else now, and I didn't want to say anything if I thought it was going to upset you.'

It felt as if he'd been kicked in the stomach, and although he wanted to know who this 'someone else' was, no way was he going to ask the question. He managed a feeble shrug.

'Well, good luck to her. Time one of us took the plunge, I suppose.'

She was watching him closely—trying to see behind the words, he suspected—and he wondered how he was going to get through the rest of the meal now that his appetite had disappeared. He wished more than ever that she'd just go away and leave him alone, but that was clearly not going to happen.

'Why don't you tell me something about yourself?' he said in desperation. He realised suddenly that he knew practically nothing about his neighbour of over a year, and although he found it hard to conjure up very much interest in Libby, listening to her had to be better than having to field her intrusive line of questioning. 'You're not from Leeds, are you?'

She frowned at this, but he continued to make eye contact with her until she answered the question.

'No,' she eventually said. 'I'm from London originally, but I prefer the North.'

It was hard work, but he managed to keep her talking about herself while he struggled to clear most of his plate. She failed to mention any men in her life, but he didn't push her on that particular subject for fear of the conversation turning to *relationships*.

When he finally put his knife and fork together, he took a sneaky glance at his watch and noted that it was twenty past eight.

'Would you like some more wine before we clear up?' Libby said as he reached over the table for her plate. Despite the fact that she'd done most of the talking, she'd still finished her food long before him.

'Not for me, thanks.' One glass had been quite enough for Dan. He was very tired and another glass would probably knock him straight out.

'You don't mind if I have another, do you?' she asked him, ever so sweetly.

'Well, I do have some things to get on with before I can shut down my computer...'

But she was already pouring it.

'Don't worry,' she said. 'Five minutes and I'll be on my way, I promise.' She picked up the glass by its stem and smiled, showing her slightly overlapping front teeth and a bit of roast aubergine skin that was stuck between them.

'I wanted to ask your advice,' she said.

'Fire away,' he replied, thinking that if she wasn't gone by half past eight then he'd have to remind her that her time was up.

'I've got a small collection of vintage vinyl,' she went on coyly after a pause, 'and I wondered if you'd be able to value it for me.'

He looked at her without understanding for a moment.

'Are we talking *records* here?'

She nodded. 'They were my father's.'

She hadn't mentioned her family before, and he assumed by her comment that her father was dead.

'What sort of records are you talking about?'

'LPs and singles, mostly from the Sixties and Seventies. Pretty good stuff, I think. I could go and get some of them now, if you like.'

But Dan shook his head firmly. 'Not tonight, Libby. I'd be happy to look another time, but...'

'That's fine,' she said, ever so slightly prickly again. 'I quite understand.'

'Maybe over the weekend,' he said. 'I don't know too much about actual values, but I could probably point you in the right direction.'

She seemed quite content with that, and after knocking back the contents of her glass got up from the table.

'Don't worry about the washing up,' she insisted as she moved round the table beside him. 'You go and see to your work, and when I've cleared up I'll just slip out of the door. I won't disturb you.'

He wasn't that happy about leaving her there in the kitchen, but he couldn't just frog-march her out of the flat.

'Thanks then, Libby,' he said, somewhat over-enthusiastically in his relief to be getting away. 'It was a brilliant meal and I'm very grateful.'

'My pleasure.' She smiled, and then, before he knew what was happening, she reached up and kissed him. Only a peck on his cheek, but it was the way she looked at him as she planted the peck that he found so disconcerting. It was just a bit too intense and lingering, as if she was trying to tell him something he definitely didn't want to hear.

'Goodnight, Libby,' he said, and moved rather too fast out of the kitchen. He kept his computer in the bedroom, and as he closed the door behind him he had the mad idea of putting a chair up against the doorknob. He told himself that he was being ridiculous, that she was hardly going to force herself on him, and even if she did he wasn't such a wimp that he'd have to give in. He knew it was daft, but he still let out a long sigh of relief when he finally heard the click of the front door closing behind her.

At last he felt able to run his word count, which was excellent: 7,483 words. Not bad for one day, even if few of the words were actually his. The important thing was that he was well on target to meeting his deadline. It was more about deadline than content with this particular book, and that was one of the things that bothered him. It was essential to get it on the shelves fast, before the boy band peaked, and it was hard to square that with his love of good and enduring music.

He stretched his arms over his head and realised that was exactly what he needed now—some good and enduring music. He got up and went into the sitting room. It still looked so bleak in there without Jo's things cluttering up the place—just the green sofa and a badly sprung leatherette armchair, a coffee table covered in white glass rings, his precious Martin D41 guitar, and one mother of a CD collection.

They took up the whole of the back wall in purpose-made floor-to-ceiling (and the room had very high ceilings) strips of pine shelving. There must be getting on for four thousand now, he realised, and he was fast running out of space. The CDs were in rough alphabetical order, by artist. From A Certain Ratio to ZZ Top, but not yet in dictionary or encyclopaedic form. He'd acquired such a large collection in such a relatively short time through his work. Record companies sent out piles of CDs to anyone who wrote about music in the hope of receiving a good review. Most of them had only ever been played once or twice, but there were some that he'd played nearly to death.

It was one of these that he took from the 'H' section now. John Lee Hooker's best, in Dan's opinion, his five-star 1989 album *The Healer*. Its unique Latin-bluesy fusion found its way deep into his soul, and from the title track—a superb duet with Carlos Santana—he derived some mysterious comfort.

One of the few good things about being on his own was that he could play what he wanted, when he wanted, and as loud as he wanted. When Jo had lived there she'd insisted he put earphones on if he wanted to play anything that she didn't like very much. And even that had sometimes annoyed her, particularly near the end. She had been forever complaining that he cared more about music than he did about her, but he realised now that it had been just one of many excuses for having simply gone off him.

Why else would she have left without any attempt at an explanation?

A sudden image of Jo came uninvited into his head—Jo with somebody else—and he shook it quickly. He did a quick U-turn out of this particular road to self-pity and turned the sound up just a tad higher, as a small act of belated defiance. Fortunately, the building was old, with thick walls and presumably ceilings. He'd occasionally heard the soft thump of drum and bass coming from Aisling's flat below, but he'd never yet heard a sound from Libby's upstairs. He'd assumed she didn't go in for music much, so it was a big surprise to learn that she had a collection of vinyl.

He returned to his bedroom to check his e-mails—the last job before he shut down his computer for the night. There were only six messages waiting for his attention, so it shouldn't take long. Two were deleted immediately as junk, and two others—from magazine editors looking for contributions—could wait until tomorrow. But there was one from Steve that required a little more thought.

Steve was an old friend he'd kept in touch with from school in the Midlands. He lived in London these days, but he definitely had a soft spot for Leeds, which he'd been visiting on and off ever since Dan got his first job on a newspaper there. The job had lasted nearly five years, until he felt confident enough to go it alone and write full time about music. And because he'd settled into the life pretty well he'd seen no reason to move on from the city.

It must be over six months since Steve had last made his way up north, and now he was asking if he could come and stay at the weekend, but Dan wasn't too sure about this. There was the book to think about, and then there'd be explanations to give about Jo. He decided to sleep on that one as well, but—since he wasn't accomplishing much—he made up his mind to reply to his favourite wacko.

Jedski, as he called himself, had been e-mailing Dan since he first started publishing his address. He had no idea what he looked like, of course, but pictured him with long, thinning lank hair, and Crypt Factory tattoos all over his skinny arms. He was obsessed with the band and wrote at least twice a week as part of his tireless campaign for More 'Factory' Respect. He didn't believe they got their due in the general musical press, and no amount of Dan directing him to the specialist publications seemed to get him off his back.

His e-mail today was entitled: *Country Bloody Music.*

> Dan the Man
> *I see the NME did a big piece on some bird called Faith Hill this week now I ask you how come they give that much space to a talentless minority act that no ones ever heard about*

and still ignore Factory there's definitely a conspiracy going on
here and I'll get to the bottom of it if it's the last thing I do.
    J

Dan smiled and whipped off a quick reply. Jedski didn't go in
for punctuation any more than he went in for logic, and he
decided to respond in kind for a change. He couldn't be bothered to point out that Faith Hill had sold millions of albums
in the last year while Crypt Factory had sold about twelve.

   You might be right Jedski it's more about looks these days
   and beautiful women increase circulation.
      D

He was just about to open an untitled e-mail from someone called dalysarah when the telephone started ringing. He
reached for the receiver, already guessing who it would be.

'So,' said his mother, 'how are things with you?'

'Can't complain. You and Dad OK?'

'Good, thanks. Your dad's got one of his meetings tonight
but he said to send his love. And what about Jo? I haven't spoken to her for ages.'

Dan felt his face colour, as if he was a boy again and just
about to be caught out in a lie. He was glad his mother
couldn't see him or she'd have sussed him in a moment.

'She's fine. Down at the gym, as usual. She's become ad-
dicted.'

Thank God he'd invented that bloody gym. It was the only
plausible explanation for Jo's constant absences from the flat.
Why he hadn't told his mother the truth yet he didn't know.
To begin with he'd hoped it might still work out, that she'd
come back, so rather than go into all sorts of unnecessary explanations he'd come up with the gym story. Of course if his
mother had only known Jo as well as he did she'd have re-

alised it wasn't a very likely tale. Joanna Hurst loathed all forms of physical exercise and she never stuck to anything for longer than a couple of weeks.

'She must be very fit by now, and toned as well.'

'Yeah, I suppose she is,' he mumbled.

'It might not be a bad idea if you joined her. All that sitting around every day—you could do with some exercise.'

'Maybe,' he said uncomfortably, wishing she'd get off the subject. Thankfully, she did.

'Talking of which, how's the work going? Earning enough to pay the rent?'

He hadn't told her about the book for the same reason he hadn't told anyone else.

'I'm doing fine, Mum.'

'Good. Well bring Jo down to see us whenever you can. I know what busy lives you lead, so if I don't see you before it's definitely still on for Christmas, I hope?'

'Wouldn't miss it for the world.'

'Wonderful. Well, that's it, then, I think. Give my love to Jo and get her to ring me some time. I miss our little chats about you.'

'Will do, Mum. Take care.'

He felt guilty as he replaced the receiver. He was going to have to tell her the truth about Jo soon, especially now that she was with someone else and Christmas was only a few weeks away.

He sighed and looked back to his screen. He opened the untitled e-mail and after frowning at the contents for a minute or two knocked off another quick reply.

chapter 3

I didn't know what to make of Dan's reply to Sarah, which was waiting for me the following morning. As it turned out I'd been too tired to do all the reading I'd planned, and had decided to leave it till I knew how Sarah had performed. Which wasn't very well by the look of the response that she'd got from Dan.

It wasn't at all what I'd expected. It didn't sound like Dan at all, in fact, and for a brief moment I even entertained the absurd possibility that I'd accidentally e-mailed someone who was trying to double-bluff me, who was posing as Dan.

Sarah, it began. Not 'Dear' Sarah, and somehow I quite liked that. The fact that he didn't bandy his 'Dears' around all that freely. It was the only bit I did like, though.

Just be grateful your parents have good musical taste (my mother had an unhealthy fixation on George Michael when I was growing up), although I'll admit they do seem to be stuck in a time warp. But why shatter their harmless illusions? I recommend you buy them something for their garden, if they've got one, that is.

Dan

It sounded so...cynical and condescending. (Had Aisling done this to him?) As if he thought Sarah a fool and wasn't about to suffer her gladly. And, yes, all right, I know I thought she'd sounded a bit silly and naïve myself, but I felt quite defensive about her now. She'd only asked him for a bit of advice, after all! She didn't deserve a snotty reply. I also felt protective towards Jean, Dan's mother—so what if she had been a George Michael fan? I really like Jean. She was just so easy to get along with, so genuine. Not like my mother, whose first question whenever she met anyone new was not 'How do you do?' but '*What* do you do?' She judged everyone on their job title, and if it didn't come up to scratch in her eyes then that was it as far as she was concerned. There could be no redeeming themselves after that.

She could never quite get her head round what Dan did for a living, and for that reason she was unable to take him seriously. I think she preferred to believe he was just my flatmate rather than my boyfriend, and when I told her I'd left she kept up the pretence. 'About time you had a place of your own, darling. You were never going to meet anyone nice when you were sharing a place with another man.'

Hopeless.

I felt guilty for not having been in touch with Jean, and a bit hurt that she hadn't tried to make contact with me. On the other hand, though, how would she know where I was?

I'd briefly considered dropping her a line, but decided against it in the end. I didn't want to make things awkward for her now that Dan was going out with Aisling.

Nothing was happening in the office, so I decided to compose a response to Dan. In draft form. I didn't want to be goaded into shooting directly from the hip, as I was very tempted to do. I needed to consider this long and hard. So I did. I considered it so long and hard that it wasn't until just after four o'clock that I actually clicked on *send*.

In the meantime Sid had told me that something was definitely brewing. I guessed he was trying to make up for getting his predictions so wrong yesterday and didn't take very much notice of him. Then Susan, dumpy forty-seven-year-old bit-on-the-side of Rob, thirty-one, stirred things up a bit by bursting into tears and storming out of the building. Rob left himself half an hour later, and that all had to mean *something*.

And later still, at about two o'clock, several strange men in expensive suits had appeared in Reception. They'd asked to be shown to the MD's office and there they remained as I sent off my e-mail.

Dan, it began. (I'd changed my mind by now, and if Sarah wasn't 'Dear' to him then he wasn't 'Dear' to Sarah.)

> *What's wrong with George Michael?*
> *Give me 'Careless Whispers' sooner than 'Blowin' in the Wind' any old day of the week.*

I didn't even bother to sign off.

Of course the stress and uncertainty of the past few weeks could not be ruled out as a possible reason for my inability to express myself better, but the fact is I was really fed up. The tension was thick in the office now, and Sid, who kept hovering around my desk like the grim reaper, had 'I told you so' written all over his child-like face.

And he was right. At exactly four-fifty (I'd been watching my watch for over an hour) the company MD appeared with the expensively suited men and announced that we should all clear our desks immediately. He didn't even bother to use the word 'regret', and there was certainly no mention of monies due.

I considered enquiring whether I might take my computer in lieu of remuneration, but quite honestly I didn't have the bottle. One glance at the stony-faced Suits and any hint of bravado vanished immediately.

Still, I could do one final check on my e-mails, I supposed. Maybe Cass would have replied to my pathetic pleas by now with an offer that I couldn't refuse.

She hadn't. But when I did a last-minute visit to my Hotmail account, to see if my mother had sent me any more glad tidings (she hadn't either), I checked Sarah's mail too. And found a reply from Dan.

I was startled by the speed of his response, but I didn't have time to read it now so I printed it off and slipped it into my bag.

We were actually escorted out of the building by the Suits. And as we gathered, hunch-shouldered in the persistent drizzle, we half hoped, I suspect, that someone might come up with a plan. I had flashes of putting myself forward as leader. Of giving a speech so full of passion that they'd all be putty in my hands. I'd suggest the old tying ourselves to the railings trick (if there were any railings), or storming the building, holding hostages if necessary, until some bugger agreed to pay our wages.

Only I didn't, of course. I imagine everyone entertained the same kind of mad idea, briefly, but in the end they didn't do or say anything either. It was just a fact of life these days. Tech companies folded and there wasn't a damn thing we could do about it.

They don't come much more steady than my father. He'd worked for British Gas for thirty-three years, and even he had been affected. He'd taken out a technology-based ISA only three months ago and so far it had quartered in value. My mother never stopped griping about it, making Dad feel an inadequate, reckless fool for doing what she'd encouraged him to do when it looked as if they might make a fast buck.

At least I'd only lost a couple of weeks' wages.

Since no one even suggested we went for a farewell drink together, we eventually began to disperse from our collective stupor. Staff had come and gone so frequently at Pisus UK that I didn't know any of them all that well, and to be honest it wasn't going to break my heart knowing I'd never see any of them again. With the possible exception of the Child Sid, that is.

I sought him out from the disconsolate, disbanding throng and gave him a Marco-style hug. He seemed pretty stunned, but not unhappy.

'Do you fancy getting something to eat?' he said, and it didn't seem too bad an idea.

'Kentucky Fried Chicken or Burger King?'

'How about going mad and doing Pizza Express?'

When I hesitated, thinking about my already overstretched budget, Sid seemed to read my mind and insisted on paying. And I hesitated no longer.

He had a Soho and I had a Caprina—fancy names for very small, but very good pizzas. We'd managed to put away the best part of a bottle of their finest house red by the time they were placed in front of us. And I'm not very good with red wine on an empty stomach.

I could hear myself slurring as I asked Sid if that was his real name. And I knew I was in a bad way when he said that it wasn't, that his real name was hard to pronounce at the best of times and that I had no chance in my particular state. I hadn't really taken it on board before, but it suddenly clicked that Sid's dark hair and eyes were due to the fact that he had Asian blood in his veins. But it was his age I was really curious about.

'How old are you?' I asked, carefully now, after I swallowed a morsel of my Caprina.

He didn't smile very much, didn't Sid, but he managed one now.

'How old do you think?'

I put my knife and fork down and considered this. I also considered the fact that everyone seemed to eat their pizzas sissy-style in Pizza Express, with knives and forks, instead of the usual tear and finger method. And, because I didn't like to draw attention to myself, I was doing the same.

'I presume you're over school-leaving age,' I ventured, 'and you've worked for Pisus UK for nearly six months, so you've got to be sixteen and a half, I suppose.'

'I might find that quite insulting if I didn't know you were drunk.'

'I might find *that* insulting if I didn't know you were as well,' I replied, quick as a flash. 'Well, go on,' I said, 'put me out of my misery.'

He gave me what my mother called an old-fashioned look.

'I'll be twenty-two in January, but when I tell my dad I'm out of work I might not make my birthday.'

'That's a bit unfair,' I said. 'It isn't your fault the company folded.'

'My dad will think differently. He'll say if I was as good at my job as I tell him I am I could have saved it.'

'Has he always been that unreasonable?' I asked, feeling a bit sorry for Sid now. Maybe having an unreasonable father was the reason he always looked so glum.

'The fact is I think I *could* have saved it if I'd been allowed to do what I wanted to do.'

I'm sorry to say that I laughed in his face. 'You've having me on,' I said, when his expression remained poker-straight.

He shook his head. 'I'm serious, Joanna. I went to see the MD soon after I joined the company. I could see what was going wrong and I made suggestions he chose to ignore.' He popped a piece of Soho delicately into his mouth and chewed it solemnly.

He really was serious. Either that or he was a little bit mad.

'I know what you're thinking,' he said when his mouth was empty again. 'But I also know that I'm right. In fact I know I'm *so* right that I'm going to make an offer to the receivers for the company.'

The drink was clearly getting to me. For a minute there I'd thought I heard him say he was...

'I mean it, Joanna, and if it comes off I want you to work for me.'

'Me?'

'I'm not promising anything definite just at the moment, but I might even give you a percentage incentive. I'll have to think about it.'

I suddenly felt quite sober.

'Are you serious?'

'Why not?' He shrugged. 'You're the only account manager that managed to hang on to your clients. You're very good at what you do—you just don't believe it.'

It was true. I didn't believe it.

Sid poured the remaining dribble of wine into our glasses and looked at me. 'Admit it, Joanna. You think you're a fake, don't you?'

I admitted it. For the past year I'd felt like an impostor. I'd been waiting to be found out at any moment and given the boot.

'Then maybe your parents didn't do as good a job on you as mine did on me,' he said. 'My father might be tough but he believes in me, always has, and that's made me believe in myself.'

That put the dampers on things for a while. I started getting morose then—blaming my Gilbert and Sullivan-worshipping parents for destroying my self-belief. It took another bottle of wine to cheer me up again.

When I woke up in the morning—believing that death was a preferable option to how I felt then—I found a note that Sid had written for me on a Pizza Express paper serviette. It was scrunched up on my bedside table and when I straightened it out it became clear to me that I had spent the previous evening in the company of someone suffering from a bad case of Juvenile Delusional Psychosis. (If there was such a condition.)

I, Sid, confirm that Joanna will be first on board (and may be offered a percentage incentive) when I secure ownership of the company formally known as Pisus UK.

I vaguely recalled making him write it, as proof of his offer, but I shuddered now and tossed it aside. I realised that I should be grateful I'd come out of it all relatively unscathed, and that with bit of luck I would never have to see that particular madman again.

I eventually dragged myself out of bed, and when I'd downed two glasses of water I filled the kettle and plugged it in. At least I was feeling like death warmed up in comfort, I thought, looking round my small but shiny and well-equipped kitchen. I wandered into the bijou sitting room, with its French windows that looked over the mud-coloured river. Everything else was in varying depths of gun-metal grey: the sky, the buildings on the other side of the River

Aire—former warehousing, mostly, that, like the one I was
looking out from now, had been converted in recent years.

I thought about opening the window, taking some fresh
air into my lungs, but it all looked so bleak and the air
wouldn't be all that fresh anyway. It was a typical early November Leeds day—the sort that makes you think about
crawling back into bed until April—but, vile as I felt, I knew
I'd have to get on with it. I had about three hundred pounds
in my current account, and the rent (a lot more than that)
was due in ten days, so I needed to call in and see Marco and
find out when I could start work at the café.

I heard the electric kettle switch itself off and went back
into the kitchen and found a teabag. I made two mugs with
the same bag, and when I'd added milk I took the mugs with
me into the diminutive bathroom, putting them down on the
closed toilet seat lid.

By the time I'd finished in the shower the tea was just
about cool enough to knock straight back. I felt a bit better
then, but the wardrobe mirror in my pygmy-sized bedroom
told a very different tale. I looked exactly like someone who'd
drunk far more than was good for them the night before.

I nearly gave in to the temptation of my unmade bed at
that stage, but struggled against it. It took a considerable
amount of make-up and some nifty work with my trusty dif-
fuser to make me look passable—like someone who maybe
just hadn't slept very well, worried as they were about losing their job.

Since I didn't need to put on a suit, I chose something cosy
and comfortable to wear, then changed my mind about that
because cosy and comfortable wasn't the image I wanted to
project—especially to Marco. So I got out my favourite dress,
something I'd found in a charity shop years ago, long before
lovely old clothes were called *vintage*. Beautifully hand-made
from some beige silky-looking fabric back in the Forties, I

think, it had intricate little pleats and cross sections that made it look incredibly expensive. It hung wonderfully, just skimming my knees, and Dan used to love it. I wore it on our very first proper date. We went to a bistro on his side of town, which was a pretty good ploy on his part. It meant we were handily placed for coffee back at his flat, and I never really left after that.

And although the dress was less suitable for a typical November day in Leeds, it made me feel good and that was what mattered.

By now it was five past twelve—which wasn't, I realised, a good time to call at the café. They'd be up to their eyes in spaghetti lunches for people who had jobs and money to pay for them.

I wondered about calling Cass, to do my pleading over the phone, but I was afraid to use it because that was another bill that was due very soon. I decided I'd call at her office on the way to the café instead, the walk would do me good, and because I had time to kill now I might as well put on some music. I didn't have a very big collection of CDs. I'd left all that stuff to Dan. And those that I did have were mostly purloined from his flat on that Saturday afternoon when I did my runner.

He'd gone off to interview some local band who were making waves in the business, apparently, and because I knew I wouldn't have that long I called Cass to help me abscond. She wasn't very happy about it. She liked Dan a lot and thought I should have told him what I was doing, that disappearing like that was mean and childish.

I had to remind her just whose friend she was supposed to be, which was mean and childish too, I suppose, but it did the trick. I stayed with her just over a week, and then, when Dan still didn't call I moved in with my parents. Which was another reason I'd ended up taking a flat beyond the means of someone living under the threat of redundancy—because after a single day I was desperate to get away from my mother.

I didn't take many of his CDs. Just enough to fill a small grey CD box I'd bought from Ikea. About twenty in all, and nothing he'd particularly miss.

I went through them now, wondering which album would work best on my spirits, and paused at the first compilation Dan had ever burned for me in the early days. He'd printed a proper cover for it on his PC and it looked quite professional.

It was made up of my favourite tunes of the time, tracks by the likes of Monaco, Embrace, The La's, and I put it on straight away, on the cheap portable player I'd bought when I moved into the flat. I imagined how disapproving Dan would be if he saw it. He had this thing about 'sound quality', which I never quite understood, but then he could be very up his own bottom about that sort of thing.

It sounded perfectly OK to me as I listened to a snatch of 'There she Goes', and as I idly flipped the CD case over I noticed the dedication at the end of the track list.

For Joanna, it read, *to play 'til her heart's content.*

I searched through the remaining CDs, found the other two compilations he'd put together and went straight to the dedications.

For Joanna, read number two, *so she knows how I feel.*

It had been ages since I'd looked at them, let alone played them, and when I glanced at the track list a quite distinct lump formed in the back of my throat. 'You're My Baby', 'She's the One' and of course, 'Just the Two of Us'...which, despite the lump, made me smile because it was the Doctor Evil version. *Austin Powers—The Spy Who Shagged Me* was the first film we ever saw together, and it was as we were leaving the cinema that Dan asked me to move in with him officially.

The last compilation he'd burned for me marked our first and only real separation during our time together. He had agreed to attend an important music writers' convention in the States, and although he'd been quite looking forward to it the dedication said it all.

It's going to feel like a year...

I changed the CD and the lump in my throat threatened to choke me. The first track was 'Beautiful Day' by 3 Colours Red, which always got to me at the best of times, but it was Al Green's 'Let's Stay Together' that finally had me snivelling.

So why didn't we? Stay together, I mean?

It wasn't as if we stopped fancying each other, I thought miserably. Then I stopped snivelling suddenly when I re-membered that it was Aisling that Dan fancied now. Which quickly turned into a much darker thought. For all I knew he might have fancied her all the time. Since the moment she moved in downstairs.

And that was the real reason he hadn't called me. The lying, cheating...

I turned the player off and sat there fuming for a few min-utes. I felt so angry and frustrated, knowing what I thought I now knew but having no way of knowing for sure. And, worse, not being able to do a damn thing about it.

Unless—

I'd just remembered the e-mail he'd sent to Sarah and got up hurriedly and fetched it from my bag. I had no idea what to expect after her last message to him, but the important thing was that contact was being maintained.

And I got a very nice surprise when I read it. He wasn't only keeping in contact, he was actually doing it pleasantly for a change.

You'd get on well with my mother! it began.

Sorry if I wasn't very helpful at first. If you really want to upset your parents I recommend No Direction Home *by Robert Shelton, though I still think you should leave well alone.*

Nice of you to take the trouble to write to me, by the way. If you read the musical press you must be pretty keen on music. I presume therefore that your tastes are a little bit wider than early eighties teen pop? And, yes, OK, 'Careless Whisper' is a good song. I even remember a line from it—something about guilty feet having no rhythm! Strange, but I quite like it.
Dan

My hangover disappeared in an instant.

'I love you Sarah Daly!' I trilled aloud as I did a little jig of delight. The darling angel had come up trumps. He wanted to know what music she liked. She'd provided the opening I'd been angling for and I wasn't going to let her down.

Then I realised something and stopped jigging about delightedly.

It had occurred to me that I no longer had daily access to a computer.

chapter 4

'But, Cass, I'm desperate,' I said in the same wheedling manner that used to work on Dan. It still did on my father, but never had on my mother or Cass, so why was I bothering?

The firm of accountants she worked for occupied a floor of one of the ugliest buildings in Leeds. A concrete and glass Sixties sore thumb amidst otherwise reasonably attractive buildings. The interior had hardly fared any better. Thin partitions divided what had once been a huge open-plan affair, and what Cass described as her 'office' was in fact an eight-foot-square area of space that didn't even benefit from natural light. The furniture and equipment was generally of the same period as the building, making Cass's stylish iMac computer look as ill at ease as Doric columns on the Pompidou Centre.

I was doing most of the talking while Cass continued to

work with her back to me. I had no idea what she was up to, but from what I could see on the screen it looked so deadly boring that I was almost relieved when she confirmed that there weren't any jobs going at Fowler and Fowler's.

I'd been telling her how badly I needed to have access to the Internet—ten minutes would do—but she wasn't having any of it.

'Find an Internet café,' she said. 'There's bound to be one close by. You can use the phone book to look for one if you like.' She jerked her head in the direction of a battered metal filing cabinet that was stacked with directories.

'I can't afford Internet cafés.'

She shrugged and continued tapping away.

'Book yourself into the library, then. You can have Internet access there for an hour for free.'

I'd already thought of that, as a matter of fact, but since the library was quite a long walk across the city I'd been trying to persuade Cass to let me use her computer. I knew when I was beaten, though.

'Can I call from here?'

'If you must.'

I made a face behind her back and then moved round to the phone on her desk and dialled the number for directory enquiries because I couldn't be bothered to look up the number. When they gave me the information I wanted, I parked my bottom on the edge of her desk and called the library. I was told that they didn't have free space until five o'clock, which wasn't for hours, but since it was a take-it-or-leave-it situation I reluctantly took it.

Cass stopped what she was doing and looked up at me when I'd finished my call.

'God, you look rough,' she said, not pulling her punches.

'Cheers,' I said with a disconsolate shrug.

'Look Jo—' she sighed '—I'm sorry about the job, but it

isn't as if you really are desperate, is it?' (I'd told her I needed to get online to look for work.) 'The job at the Italian will make a perfect filler till something more permanent comes along.'

'I know.' I sighed back, glad now that she was at least showing a little concern. The trouble with Cass Foster is that she is so No-Nonsense, which I put down to the fact that she is one of a very rare breed these days—the eldest of *six* siblings. She just gets on with things herself and expects everyone else to do the same. She was exactly the same at school—one of the sensible ones, not much given to the usual teenage angst and suffering. As I looked at her now, in her M & S baby pink twin-set, with her brown, neatly bobbed hair that made her look as if she was off to a talk on making jam at the WI, I remembered the day that we first got to know one another. We were both in the upper sixth form by then, with our own common room, where we hung out between lessons or sometimes, in my case, when lessons were going on. I was avoiding Geography that day, I think, and ever-diligent Cass was busy revising for our upcoming 'A' level exams.

We'd been in the same class since we were eleven but I'd never really bothered much with her before. We belonged to entirely different groups—hers swotty, mine work-shy—and never the Shania (Shania *Twain*—one of Dan's so-called music-biz jokes) had met. But since none of my lot was around that day when I needed them I decided that Cass would have to do.

I'd just had that bit of trouble with Nicola Dick and her boyfriend. She belonged to yet another group, the 'Glamorous Set'—all five of them blonde, though not one to my knowledge natural. *Appearance* was everything to that particular group, and it didn't begin and end with just looks. Having it known that someone like me had got off with her boyfriend must have been a very bitter pill for Nic to swallow, but I didn't think about it like that at the time, of course.

Cass had listened to my complaints of unfairness with her eyes fastened firmly on her textbook. I hadn't minded that much because I didn't expect her to understand. I just needed to get it all off my chest. How it had been all Jon Braithwaite's fault, how I didn't even fancy him, and how nasty that cow Nic Dick was being to me, especially about my hair.

But she'd clearly been listening because eventually Cass had turned her full, big blue-eyed attention on me and told me not to be such a whinger. More or less, anyway. Her exact words were, 'At least your hair is entirely your own, but if you really believe you're being unfairly treated in this matter tell Nicola so. However, before you do that you might also consider the possibility that if you'd stayed sober none of it might ever have happened. In other words you should accept some of the responsibility and simply put the whole business down to experience.'

No one of my own age had ever spoken to me like that before, and when I got over my shock I actually laughed. It didn't change anything between me and Nicola—we continued to hate each other until we left school—but for some reason Cass and I did engage in a sort of friendship after that. We stayed loyal to our own separate groups, but now and again we would meet up in our respective homes and make sarcastic comments about one another's clothes and widely differing tastes in music.

I think we actually preferred each other's homes. Cass loved the uncluttered peace she said she found in mine and I loved the chaos of hers. We lost touch for a bit when we left school, but one day I bumped into her again in Leeds, discovered she was living there too, and we just sort of picked up where we'd left off.

'Don't you think it's strange how Nicola Dick ended up

doing so well for herself?' I said suddenly now. 'I thought she'd get married before she was twenty to some rich middle-aged bloke who'd keep her in hair dye for the rest of her life.'

Cass was used to my sudden changes of subject and merely shrugged.

'Must be more to her than meets the eye.'

I told her about Nic getting engaged and the Born Again bit.

'I've got to admit that doesn't sound much like the Nic Dick we used to know,' Cass said with a frown. 'He's not a plastic surgeon, is he?' she added, completely serious. 'Maybe it's all about breast augmentation.'

'I wouldn't put it past her,' I said, thinking of Nicola's boyish figure. 'But that still doesn't explain why she's gone all religious.'

'Ah, well,' said Cass, turning back to her screen, 'people can change, I suppose.'

Cass plainly had a kinder view of human nature than I did.

'Better go, then,' I said, buttoning up my coat against the bleak November weather. 'Do you fancy getting together over the weekend?' I added as I picked up my bag.

'Can't,' she said, tapping away again now. 'I'm going home. Mum's organised a family gathering for Saturday night. It's my grandmother's eightieth.'

'Wish her happy birthday from me,' I said, feeling a teeny bit peeved about not being invited. 'And try not to worry about me while you're tucking into the sherry trifle.' (Her mother did the best sherry trifle this side of the Pennines.)

'You can come if you want,' she said, picking up the vibes even though she was working away.

But I had my pride and I refused to be an afterthought.

'Cheers,' I said, 'but I've got stuff to do.'

'Suit yourself,' I heard her say as I turned to leave, and I pulled another face at her back before I left.

Marco was on his own when I went into the café. There was no 'Bella Joanna' today, I noticed. Just an anxious look over his shoulder towards the back kitchen.

It was one of their quiet times when I got there, and Marco came round from behind the counter and directed me to the door again.

'I heard about Pisus,' he whispered urgently. 'So when can you start?'

'I'm overwhelmed by your sympathy for the loss of my job,' I said, automatically lowering my voice to match his.

'Sorry.' He managed a grin. 'But it didn't exactly come out of the blue, now, did it?'

I shrugged. 'Fair enough, I suppose. Would Monday be OK?' It was Thursday now, and I wouldn't mind a couple of days to get my head round this career move of mine.

'Monday's great.' He seemed unusually excited about something and I wondered again what he was up to.

'I take it by all this secrecy that you still haven't told Giovanna about me working here yet?'

He glanced round quickly towards the counter and seemed relieved that his mother hadn't reappeared.

'I didn't want to say anything till you confirmed you could start. I'll tell her later.'

One of his hands was resting on my shoulder, and with the other he opened the door.

Charming, I thought. And I don't even get a chance to show my lovely vintage dress off.

'I'm really sorry, Marco,' I said, 'but much as I'd love to stay and have a cup of your wonderful cappuccino I've got a date with a PC.'

'That's a shame, Joanna,' he said, clearly missing the sarcasm in his haste to get rid of me. He nudged me out of the open door and then frowned. 'You're seeing a policeman now?'

I grinned at him and shook my head. 'Wrong kind of PC.'

'Good,' he said, 'because when I get back I want to take you out.' The old flirty charm was suddenly back and I felt my flagging spirits lift. In fact they lifted so much that I didn't even make my usual excuses.

'We'll have to see about that' were my actual words.

He was so surprised by this change of tack that he seemed to forget all about his mother and followed me outside.

'Then how about a trial kiss?' he said. 'To help you make up your mind.'

It was the middle of the afternoon in the centre of Leeds, and it wasn't the place for kissing, trial or otherwise. But I had to admit I was tempted. It had been ages since I'd had anyone's arms around me, and for some reason I was feeling vaguely reckless.

I think he expected me to laugh at such a suggestion, but he took advantage of my slight hesitation and grabbed me around the waist. And there, in that busy Leeds precinct, he planted his lips firmly on mine. He didn't go as far as tongues, I am happy to say, but it did kind of shake me up. I wasn't sure if that was because it was so unexpected or whether it was the actual kiss that did it, but when he pulled away, grinning at me, I found myself melting a bit.

'I'll call you,' he said with a wink.

And me—well I, didn't say anything at all.

I had to show some identification before I was allowed on the computer, but it seemed a small inconvenience for a free hour's access to the Internet. It had rained lightly on my way to the library and my hair was a ball of frizz by now. I was just glad I was unlikely to see anyone I knew. I was still confused about that kiss, but having talked it over with myself I'd come to the conclusion that nothing had really changed with Marco. He might be a good kisser, but there's more to fancying someone than that—isn't there? And, yes, I was flattered by his attention, because he was very good-looking and he had a fabulous body, but just how shallow is that?

Besides, one thing at a time, I told myself, and it was Dan I was interested in just at the moment.

There were four computers available to the public. Two were currently occupied by a couple of kids dressed in school uniform and one by an elderly woman who was carefully copying something down from the screen by hand. It occurred to me that she would be better printing the information off, but I was the new girl on the block, and certainly didn't want to gain the reputation of a know-all busybody, so I left well alone.

I'd already worked out what Sarah was going to say to Dan in her latest message, so it didn't take long.

Thanks for the recommendation but I've decided to take your original advice. You're right, why would I want to spoil things for them? (My parents, that is.)
I have to admit I don't know all that much about music.

I had to make that clear from the start. I'd decided by now that my idea of turning myself into a knowledgeable music fan overnight was just too unrealistic. Besides which, I was afraid of being sussed as a phoney.

I'm just your average CD-buying customer who knows what she likes and what she likes keeps changing. The music magazines aren't mine, I'm afraid. They belong to my flatmate—

I planned to keep my 'flatmate' fairly anonymous. It could get just too complicated if I had to make up too many new identities—

I just happen to pick them up occasionally.

I was aware that this was a risky admission. That I might lose his interest with comments like that, but on balance it seemed the less dangerous route.

Looks like your mother's music had an effect on you whether you like it or not.

He'd never mentioned that he remembered a line from 'Careless Whisper' to me, and it seemed odd to have learned something new about Dan through a stranger— a stranger to him, anyway. But then that wasn't all I'd learnt about Dan today, I thought, fuming again at his possible deceit.

And finally my trump card. Something to connect Dan with Sarah and make certain that he replied again.

And, talking of lines from songs...

I quoted a lyric and cheekily asked if he had any idea where it came from.

Of course he'd know where it came from. He absolutely loved Coldplay—had been one of the first music writers to draw the public to their attention.

I sent the e-mail gleefully, and then wondered about spending the rest of my hour searching for jobs. However, because

I am all too easily distracted from anything that seems remotely chore-like, I happened to glance at my elderly neighbour and saw that she was still laboriously copying stuff down from the screen. Because I didn't feel quite so new any more, I opened my mouth to explain about the printer when my attention was further drawn to something beyond her grey head.

Between my neighbour and the stairs that led up to the reference part of the library was a glass partition, and through the partition I could clearly see Dan, hurrying up the stairs. My heart did one of those flip things and I automatically ducked behind the old lady, pretending to get something out of my bag.

When I finally glanced up again the staircase was empty, but my heart was still in top gear and racing and I knew I would have to leave the old lady to her long-winded ways. I had to get out of the place, and I had to get out of there fast.

Libby hauled the cardboard box full of vinyl out of her wardrobe and carried it into the living room, ready for Dan to inspect at the weekend.

From the moment she'd learnt what he did for a living she'd felt a connection to him through the collection. It had felt like a sign, and despite the fact that he lived with Joanna she'd sensed it was only a matter of time. She'd heard their arguments and guessed—rightly, as it duly turned out—that their relationship was very much on the rocks.

She was trying to decide if she should call on him now or whether it might be better to leave it tonight. She was certain she was making good progress. Six weeks ago she had hardly spoken to him, and now they were sharing food and wine in his flat. Even so, he was proving to be harder work than she'd expected, which was why she had invented a new boyfriend for Jo. It was obvious Dan wasn't completely over her yet, but if he believed that she had moved on then Libby very much hoped he would feel able to as well.

She made a sudden decision and switched on the TV. It would not do, she considered, to come on too strong at his stage. Dan needed time for the knowledge that Jo was now out of reach to sink in before making her next move. She mustn't wait *too* long, of course. Not with Aisling hanging around. But since she was away at the moment Libby felt she could well afford to hold on for another day.

She'd just flopped into her armchair when the telephone rang and she reached to answer it. She allowed herself to hope it was Dan and turned the sound of the TV down with the remote control. He was one of the few people she'd given her number to, just in case he needed her to get something for him while he was busy writing his book. She'd had to be careful about making friends since arriving in Leeds. Apart from Dan, the only other people who had her number were her office (and they hardly ever rang her at home), and... And then she sighed. And Joanna—

Damn.

'Hello? Libby?'

Despite her disappointment she had a role to play, so she arranged her features into a smile.

'Joanna!' she said, sounding oh, so pleased to hear from her. 'How are things?'

Things must be bad if she was still bothering to ring, Libby thought. Joanna had never shown any interest in her while she was living with Dan. The only reason they were in touch now was because Jo wanted information. She was upset because Dan hadn't bothered to call, stupid cow, and because Libby was afraid that she might contact him the lie about Aisling had just sort of slipped out.

'Oh, you know, not bad,' she said. There was a momentary pause. 'Well, since you ask, that's not entirely true. The company I worked for folded yesterday, so I'm sort of jobless at the moment.'

'That's awful,' Libby managed. 'But last time we spoke you did say things weren't going too well.'

'I know, and it's not too bad I suppose because I've got a fill-in job with a friend. At the Italian. It's a pasta place in Carlton Lane—do you know it?'

Libby didn't—not yet anyway.

'Well, that's good at least.'

'How about you?' Jo asked her then.

'Things aren't going too well where I work at the moment either.' She didn't usually talk about herself, but tonight she was in the mood for a moan.

'I'm sorry,' Jo said, sounding surprised. 'I didn't realise. Where is it you work anyway?'

They'd been talking on the phone for nearly two months and she'd never bothered to ask before.

'Bennett Associates,' Libby said, trying not to sound resentful. 'You know—the tech recruitment firm that Pisus used occasionally.'

'Is that the same recruitment firm where Nicola Dick is a partner?'

'As a matter of fact I've just moved into her department. Is she a friend of yours?' Libby added guardedly.

'Not exactly,' Joanna said. 'Just someone I knew at school. I never really liked her much, if I'm honest.'

'That's OK, then, because I can't stand her myself.'

'I heard she'd gone all religious lately,' Joanna said.

'She's wearing a crucifix, if that's what you mean, but the word is she's only doing it because her fiancé's parents are very devout. I don't believe she's serious about it for a moment.'

'That explains a lot,' Joanna said with a hint of a chuckle in her voice.

Then she finally got round to the real reason for her call.

'How's Dan?' she asked, trying her best to sound casual.

'Fine, I think. Working hard on his book, you know.'

'And, er, Aisling? Are they still together?'

' 'Fraid so,' she said with a sigh, as she twisted the cord of the phone round her fingers.

'Are you sure, Libby? It's just that I saw Dan today and he looked a bit, well—sorry for himself, I suppose.'

'That's just wishful thinking,' Libby answered quickly. Then a worrying thought struck her. 'You didn't speak to him, did you?'

'No. I just got a glimpse of him in the library.'

Libby was greatly relieved. It certainly wouldn't do for the two of them to accidentally meet. She wouldn't want either of them finding out about the little fairy tale she had been spinning. She softened her tone and decided to take the tale up a gear.

'I didn't really want to tell you this,' she said gently, 'but I think Dan's taking her to meet his mother at the weekend.'

There was a groan at the other end of the line.

'So it really is serious, then?'

'Looks like it.'

'Do you think he fancied her before I left?' she eventually said, as if hardly daring to ask it. 'He made out he didn't, but I'm beginning to think he might have been lying.'

Libby enjoyed the enormous sense of power she felt at that moment. It was tempting to tell her what she did not want to hear, but she could afford to be generous under the circumstances.

'No,' Libby said firmly. 'I'm pretty sure that he didn't. But you know what Aisling is like, how pushy she is. I think he only caved in after considerable pressure.'

'Well, that's something, I suppose,' Joanna said with a very relieved sigh indeed. 'And thanks for everything, Libby. You're a real friend.'

And Libby, who didn't often hear those words, managed to hold back a satisfied smirk until she replaced the receiver.

chapter 5

'What on earth are you doing here?' I grunted as I opened the front door to my mother. I'd had a terrible night, hardly slept at all, and I really could have done without her showing up at the flat at eleven-fifteen. And finding me still in my nightwear.

'What a lovely welcome from my only daughter,' she said as she *almost* brushed my cheek with her brightly painted lips on her way past me to the kitchen. She was hauling a large leather shoulder bag onto the narrow work counter when I followed her in.

'Lemon and ginger OK for you?' she asked as she started filling the kettle. She was referring to the one of the variously flavoured teas that she carried around with her everywhere, and when she'd plugged in the kettle she took a small box of the stuff out of her bag.

'I'd rather have coffee,' I said, already resigned to the fact that any plans I might have had for the day were about to change. Not that I had any actual plans, but that wasn't the point. It was her taking the matter for granted which bugged me. Then something occurred to me.

'How come you knew that I wouldn't be working?'

She got two mugs out of the cupboard, checked to see that they were up to her standard of cleanliness, crinkled her nose uncertainly, shrugged, and then turned round to face me.

'I had a call from Barbara last night. Nicola told her what had happened at Pisus.'

'How the hell does she know?' I said, rattled.

'There's no need to be like that,' my mother said calmly as she popped a teabag into one of the mugs. 'She seemed most concerned about you. And it's her business to know about that sort of thing. She used to supply some of the staff, don't forget.' She opened another cupboard and took out a jar of coffee.

I stared at her back as she busied herself in my kitchen and wondered if she really believed that Nicola was concerned about me or whether it was all part of the elaborate game she'd been playing with Barbara Dick for years. It was obvious to me that she disliked the woman as much as I disliked Nic, so why did she always try to make out that they were such lovely, caring people?

She turned back to me, gave my pyjama bottoms and crumpled T-shirt a critical once-over, and rolled her eyes when they came to rest on the orange rat's maze on top of my head.

'I have no idea where that hair of yours came from,' she said unhappily. 'I can't even blame it on your father.'

I let it pass. She was always going on about my hair, suggesting that I had it cut, straightened, dyed... I was used to it. I was more interested in finding out what this visit was all about. I sensed that the big leather bag might be involved, and cast a curious eye over it.

'What's that for?' I said.

'Ah,' she said mysteriously, 'so you've noticed.'

'I could hardly fail to.'

'Family history,' she said in a tone that usually accompanied a nod and a wink.

Just then the kettle clicked off and she poured water into my instant coffee.

'Now, go and get showered and changed and I'll tell you all about it when you're ready. Oh, and put something smart on, darling. I've booked an appointment for us at the records office, but I thought we'd go somewhere nice for an early lunch on the way.'

'The records office?'

'Yes, darling,' she said with a patient sigh. 'The place where they keep all the old records of births and so forth.'

'I know what it is,' I said huffily. 'I was just thinking that there might be better ways of spending the day.'

'Nonsense,' she said dismissively. 'Now, off you go, and don't forget to do something with that hair.'

I took my time, spending ages trying to straighten my hair. And because she would only get annoyed if I ignored her instructions about what to wear, I put on one of my expensive suits—navy blue with a fine pinstripe. Last time we'd been together it had ended in a big row, and as she was clearly making an effort it seemed only fair that I should too. I went to town with my make-up as well. I looked pale after my sleepless night, so I applied the blusher in bucket loads.

I knew I should have been pleased to learn that Aisling had had to work hard on Dan, but it was the idea of her meeting his mother that troubled me. It just made it all seem so final. And, yes, OK, so I'd been thinking about Marco as well, and that kiss, and that maybe I'd like a repeat performance, but it didn't make me feel any less confused about Dan. It still felt like unfinished business.

'At last!' she said when I entered the sitting room to find her with a big blue folder opened up on her lap. She was wearing one of her Versace-style outfits, black with gold-coloured buttons. It looked exactly what it was—a cheap imitation—but nobody had the nerve to tell her that. It was all part of the new image she'd adopted a few months ago, after losing some weight at a slimming club and dyeing her hair a few shades lighter. I think she was aiming at an Ivana Trump look, but the outcome was more whorehouse madam.

'You look nice, darling,' she said, and I waited for the sting in the tail. 'But why don't you put on those lovely earrings I bought for your birthday?'

'Because they make me look like a Christmas tree,' I said, honest for once about her revolting present. I might have been making an effort to please, but I drew the line at being seen in Leeds with a pair of mini-chandeliers dangling from my lobes.

She shook her head, as if she despaired of my lack of good taste. She felt just the same way about my flat. She disapproved of the new minimalist approach I'd adopted since moving there, which was more about making some room in the place than any real statement in decor. She was a trinket sort of woman herself, with a particular penchant for porcelain figurines in period costume, and I think she pitied me for not sharing her sophistication. She patted the sofa next to her now. 'Come and sit down,' she said sympathetically.

I did as she told me and she stabbed a red fingernail at the open file.

'I've joined the local Family History Society,' she said importantly, 'and these are the results of my research so far.'

She flicked through dozens of neat handwritten and photocopied pages of A4 paper and I'll admit I was quite impressed.

'You've never mentioned this before,' I said.

'I didn't think you'd be interested, darling, and besides, I didn't want to say anything until I found something worth mentioning.'

'Where did you get all this stuff from anyway?' I wanted to know.

'Various libraries and records offices—oh, and of course the Internet. The Mormons are marvellous people, you know.'

I looked at her worriedly, thinking of Nicola Dick.

'You're not getting religious as well, are you?'

'Don't be silly, darling. They collect family history records and make them available to anyone who happens to be interested.'

'And this is *your* family history, not Dad's?'

'Of course,' she said tartly. 'I knew your father's parents, don't forget. I can't imagine there'd be anyone of any worth in *their* background. All thieves and vagabonds, I shouldn't wonder.'

'That's not very nice,' I said defensively. Both my dad's parents had died before I was born, but he spoke of them kindly and they looked fairly normal to me in the photos I'd seen. And Dad and his brother—Uncle Bob, a ticket clerk on York's railway station—seemed far too ordinary to have vagabond genes.

'Well, maybe not thieves,' she conceded, 'but certainly peasant stock through and through.'

'But the Thompsons are something special,' I said with my tongue in my cheek. 'Is that what you're saying?'

'Precisely. And don't worry, darling. Don't forget that you're half Thompson too.'

I wasn't sure that I should be so grateful for possessing genes that might have helped turn my mother into such a snob, but I'll admit I was still vaguely curious.

'So what's this thing that's worth mentioning now?' I asked.

'I'll tell you all about it later,' she said as she closed the folder.

'There's still some checking to do before we can be certain, which is why I've made the appointment for us.' And then, as if she was bestowing on me the greatest possible favour, 'I want *you* to help me unearth the missing piece to the puzzle.'

Dan had made it a rule not to answer the phone when he was working to a deadline, but when it rang and rang for ages, stopped and rang for ages again, he began to wonder if it might be urgent.

He'd been keeping his head down for the last day or so, fearing another knock at his door, another unwanted interruption. He'd been wondering if there was a polite way of asking Libby to stay away, but he hadn't come up with anything yet. He really didn't want to offend her, but he was pretty certain by now that her interest in him was more than just friendship. He kept seeing that look on her face after she'd kissed him and it was making him very uncomfortable.

He snatched up the phone to shut it up.

'Dan Baxter.'

'I've been ringing you all morning. What you been up to?'

Dan recognised the voice of his old friend Steve and sighed. He'd forgotten all about his e-mail.

'Sorry, mate, I'm working to a very tight deadline.'

'Which is why you didn't answer my e-mail, I suppose?'

'Forgot all about it, I'm afraid.'

'Well, too late now. I've booked myself a seat on a train and will be with you around ten tonight.'

'What if I'd been away?'

'I'd have asked Jo to put me up.'

'Ah, well, you'd have been in trouble, then, because she doesn't live here any more.'

A short silence, then, 'You're kidding me, right?'

'I'm kidding you, *wrong*.'

Dan ran his free hand through his overgrown hair that Jo always used to trim while he waited for Steve's response.

'Just as well I'm coming up, then,' he said. 'And I want all the gory details. Gotta go now. See you later, OK?'

'OK. But I've got to work during the day while you're here.'

Dan replaced the receiver and decided that having Steve around for a bit wouldn't be so bad after all. At least he'd be there when Libby showed up with her vinyl collection.

He couldn't believe it when two minutes later someone knocked at his door. He glanced at his watch, realised it couldn't be Libby at this time of day and, since his concentration had already been broken, decided he might just as well see who it was.

'Dan!' Aisling said sweetly when he opened the door. 'You're not still mad with me, I hope?'

'You're back, then,' he said, stating the obvious resignedly, letting her close the door behind him as she followed him into the kitchen.

'I was just wondering whether to go into the office, but it doesn't seem worth it now. It is Friday, after all.'

'And it is almost midday,' he said sarcastically. He held up a jar of instant coffee. 'Would you like one, or will it keep you awake?'

'Don't mind if I do,' Aisling said, ignoring the jibe as she looked around the tidy kitchen. 'You had a cleaner in or something?'

'Sort of,' he said. He had no intention of telling her about Libby and her Mrs Mop guise.

She draped herself on one of the kitchen chairs and crossed her legs in a deliberately provocative manner. He couldn't help smiling as he turned away and spooned coffee into a couple of mugs. At least things were completely out in the open between them these days. When Jo was here he genuinely hadn't understood that Aisling fancied him. She couldn't make it any clearer now, but she never took offence when he made it just as clear that she wasn't his type.

'How was the trip?' he asked when he handed her a mug.

'Oh, you know—the usual.'

'Lots of celebrity parties?' he said, and pretended to yawn as he pulled out the spare chair and sat down opposite her.

She sighed and shrugged at the same time. 'It can all get a bit tedious at times.'

She was a bit of a posh bird, was Aisling, with a 'Mummy and Daddy' who despaired of their daughter for choosing to live in a part of Leeds that lacked the essentials in life, such as a nice little patisserie on the street corner. He felt quite relieved that she didn't seem inclined to get into the latest A-list gatherings she had attended, but as she took on a far-off look in her eyes he noticed that there was something different about her.

'What's happened to your hair?' he said, puzzled. Last time he'd seen her he could have sworn it was shoulder-length. Surely hair didn't grow all that fast?

She picked up the ends of her breast-length hair and giggled.

'Hair extensions, silly. Cost me a fortune, but worth it if they fooled you.'

He could see when he looked closely that the hair had an unnatural quality to it at the ends—a bit like doll's hair. He decided it was probably best not to say this, though, and besides, it was time to get serious.

'To answer your question...' he began.

'Which question?'

'The one about being mad with you.'

'Oh, that,' she said, sounding bored. 'I assumed you weren't any more since you've made me some coffee.'

'Well, I am. I don't like people reading my private mail and if you ever do it again I'll ban you from my flat. OK?'

She didn't look remotely chastened.

'I just love it when you're all manly and masterful, Dan,' she said, cupping her face in her hands and fluttering her eyelids.

'I'm serious, Aisling. It wouldn't even have been so bad if you'd left it at being nosy. I just don't see why you had to tell everyone about it.'

'I didn't tell everyone,' she said, defensive now. 'Just Libby. She's always asking about you and I get tired of having nothing to say.'

Dan sighed. It was hard to be mad with Aisling for long, and besides, if what she said was true what harm had she really done? Then something else occurred to him.

'What do you mean, she's always asking about me?'

'You know,' she said with a sigh. ' "How's Dan? What's Dan up to? Have you seen Dan today?" It's the only thing we ever talk about. I think she's trying to find out if you've succumbed to my charms yet, and it's humiliating to have to admit that you haven't.'

And *he* had to admit, if only to himself, that there were times when he might well have succumbed. If she'd been around last night for instance, when he'd heard about Jo being with somebody else—but that was the problem. It would never be for the right reason.

'Like I said before, Ash—you're gorgeous, but you're just not my type.'

'Well, you're not mine either,' she said, uncupping her pretty heart-shaped face. 'But what does that matter?' She shrugged. 'We're both free agents at the moment, so what harm would it do to give it a try?'

'Because then it would be hard to be friends when we found that it didn't work out.'

He was thinking again of Jo now, of course, but at least he didn't have to risk bumping into her every day. He had no idea where she was living now. He'd thought about phoning Cass many times, or trying Jo's office. And now it was all too late. Now she had someone new in her life.

'You might have a point,' he was surprised to hear Aisling say through his thoughts. 'But that doesn't mean I've given up yet,' she added with a grin. She stretched and got up from her seat. 'Better go and unpack, I suppose.'

'What about your coffee?' Dan said as he picked up his own mug and followed her into the hallway.

'You know how I hate that nasty instant stuff you serve up, Dan. My body's a temple, remember?'

He looked at her body as it glided gracefully down the stairs and he had to admit that it was a very fine temple indeed. Smiling still, he went back to his computer and decided to check his e-mails before getting down to work. There were only three waiting for him, but the one that stood out was from dalysarah.

It was becoming a *daily* thing, come to think of it, and he wondered if it was time to discourage her by not replying. Still, might as well read what she had to say, though, he thought.

As well as a quick introduction to Thompson family history, lunch included a lecture on food fat content and a chicken salad without any dressing that cost what would have kept me in burgers for up to a week. Oh, yes, and some deft subject-dodging whenever I asked about my father.

We drove to the records office in my mother's Corsa, and because we had difficulty parking we managed to arrive ten minutes late for the appointment. Which seemed to annoy the woman in charge of the office greatly. Clearly a charm school drop-out, she had a glacial, superior air, and warned us in no uncertain terms that the smooth running of the office was dependent on the courtesy of all its users.

I was sure that this would infuriate my mother, but instead she apologised profusely, ignored the unforgiving tut-tuts, and generally did a very good impersonation of a polite and mild-mannered follower of rules and regulations. There was clearly something about records offices that had a transforming effect on her, and I wished I could bottle whatever it was and feed it to her twice daily.

There were three other people inside the wood-panelled room, all of them so deeply involved in what they were doing that they didn't even glance up at us, the interesting new arrivals. It was the sort of place where you didn't need to be told that whispering was obligatory, and I'm not sure why, but it was at that particular moment that the whole strangeness of the situation struck me.

My mother didn't normally include me in her interests, and if I hadn't been trying so hard to make up for our last falling-out I would already have made further enquiries about her motives. But it seemed a bit late for that now, so I put my suspicions aside for the time being and followed her whispered instructions on handling the equipment. She showed me how to use the cunning little microfiches that looked like photograph negatives and contained enormous amounts of information when magnified on a screen. Once I felt confident with what I was doing, she instructed me to examine the marriage records of a certain parish of Tillingham.

I'd learnt by now that my mother had got back as far as 1841 through the Thompson family tree, to the birth of one Henry Thompson. She had a copy of his baptismal record and it showed that his parents had been Ann, and Henry Thompson Senior. It was Ann that she was particularly interested in. Because although our forebears to this point had been generally disappointing as far as she was concerned—a long list of law-abiding artisans—she'd somehow got it into her head that Ann might have been a member of the aristocrat Fothershaw family of Tillingham. I'd never heard of Tillingham but according to my mother it is a former grand estate on the outskirts of Leeds, now covered in box-like starter homes that were erected in the late Eighties. It didn't matter that the family no longer owned the land, although that would have been a bonus, of course. What seemed to matter most to my mother was proving that she had aristocratic blood in her veins.

She'd as good as admitted to me over lunch that it would be one in the eye for Barbara Dick, who'd apparently been researching her own family history for years and years. The best she'd come up with so far was a bastard child whose father might possibly have been a philandering archbishop.

She was being very guarded about where the idea had come from, and I had my doubts about it all from the start. Certain things just didn't add up to me. Like why a member of the aristocracy would marry a Thompson, for starters. But my mother dismissed such unhelpful scepticism out of hand.

While I was doing the groundwork my mother was finding out what she could about the Fothershaws. Being a prominent family in the area, there was a fair bit about them in the archives, and as if the links were already proven beyond any reasonable doubt she was making copious notes about them. In order, no doubt, to rub Barbara Dick's nose in it later.

It took a long time, but eventually I came upon something. That is, I found the record of a marriage between an Ann Fothershaw and a Henry Thompson, which at first glance seemed promising, though I quickly realised that it couldn't be anything to do with us. Somewhat perplexed by the coincidence, I signalled to my mother and she calmly slipped into the seat beside me and examined the screen. I don't know why, but somehow that calmness bothered me.

She nodded, evidently pleased but just not excited enough. 'Well done,' she said. 'I knew I could rely on you to find it.'

'I've found *something*, all right,' I whispered cautiously, 'but I'm afraid it doesn't prove that we've got Fothershaw blood in our veins.'

'What more proof do you need?' she said, unperturbed.

'Henry Thompson is not an uncommon name,' I said. 'And we know that our Henry—the one that we are absolutely *certain* about—was born in 1841.'

'Yes,' she replied guardedly, 'but so what?'

'This marriage took place in 1797,' I said, prodding my finger at the date on the screen. 'And, assuming Ann was twenty or so when she married, that would put her in her sixties when she gave birth.'

She looked uncomfortable for a moment, but quickly rallied.

'Well, a woman in Italy gave birth at that age recently.'

I glanced at her sideways and it all suddenly felt a bit fishy to me.

'Not without the aid of modern medical science, she didn't.'

She got a bit narky then. 'Typical!' she hissed. 'Most people would be thrilled to know they belonged to an important Yorkshire family, but oh, no, not you.'

And the penny suddenly dropped. I looked at her again and her shifty expression clinched matters.

'You've been surfing the net, haven't you?'

'I don't know what you mean,' she said slyly.

'You looked for links with the name Henry Thompson and any old Ann who happened to belong to an aristocratic family in the area—and this is the best you could come up with.'

When she didn't reply I shook my head and sighed. 'You can't go adding people to the family tree just because it *looks* good.'

'I don't see why not,' she said childishly. 'Nobody needs to know.'

'You mean Barbara Dick doesn't need to know?'

I realised then that what their relationship was all about was outdoing each other. They were rivals in everything— from the juiciest parts in local Gilbert and Sullivan productions to how well their daughters were faring in life. And things definitely weren't going well for my mother in that particular aspect of their rivalry.

'Precisely,' she said. 'She's always boasting about her wayward cleric, and I thought—'

'Why did you bring me in on the act?' I interrupted her.

It was then that she finally squirmed, and I knew the answer to my question.

'I don't believe you!' I said, and I said it in a raised voice.

One thing you can say about my mother is that she knows when the game is up, and the game was definitely up for her now.

'Well, you know what Barbara is like,' she said with a shrug. 'She'd be so green with envy that she might be tempted to check the facts for herself.'

'And find the same discrepancies that I found.'

'But I didn't expect you to notice,' she said matter-of-factly.

'Exactly,' I said. 'I'm just the idiot daughter you could blame it all on if things backfired.'

'Something like that,' she agreed lamely.

Just then the woman in charge of the office came over and glared at me for daring to speak above a whisper. And because I was so furious with my mother, I looked at her defiantly.

'Don't worry,' I said in such a loud voice that everyone else in the office finally looked up. 'We're leaving.'

chapter 6

It was a day of people turning up unexpectedly at my flat. Sid was waiting outside for me when I got back from my long walk from the library, where I'd gone after my mother dropped me off. And he looked even colder than I was and a lot more fed up.

'How long have you been here?' I asked, then frowned at him nervously. 'And how do you know where I live?'

'I brought you back here two nights ago,' he said glumly. 'That's when we arranged for me to pick you up at six o'clock.'

It was all coming back to me now. For some reason I'd agreed to go to his home for dinner. I glanced at my watch and was embarrassed to see it was almost six-thirty.

'Sorry,' I said, wishing that I could get out of it but knowing it was too late for that now. 'Have I got time to change?'

'I'm afraid not. My mother insists on punctuality and dinner will be served at seven sharp.'

At least I had my good suit on, and he was right about me not having time to change. He'd borrowed his mother's car to pick me up, and even though we were going against the tail-end of the rush hour traffic we still didn't arrive at his home till two minutes to seven.

I was surprised by the size of the house, which was subtly lit by discreet outdoor floodlighting. It was one of those Victorian piles that in less leafy areas often get turned into a dozen or so student bedsits. This was clearly a ghetto for the rich, however, and as we turned into the drive I glanced over at Sid with new interest. Maybe he wasn't mad after all. Maybe he did have the wherewithal to purchase companies from receivers. It was one of those passing thoughts that I dismissed almost immediately.

The moment I was introduced to his very unusual family, in fact.

Mr Perrez—Dawood, as he insisted I call him, was a bit like his son—quiet and rather morose—but I began to understand why when I got to know the women of the family over dinner. They were already seated at the dining table when we got there and they were completely exhausting right from the off.

Sid's mother, Jennifer, who surprised me turning out to be Irish, quickly informed me that she was a Feng Shui consultant with a lot of rich clients. She was very flamboyant and a bit eccentric and she was wearing a magnificent red sari that had a few western touches, including a Dolce and Gabbana leather bum-bag strapped around her enormous waist.

The daughters, Darinda, Belle and Marinda (I kept getting Marinda and Darinda mixed up), competed for my attention for much of the evening. It was as if they had been locked up and I was the only outsider they'd seen in years.

For the first half an hour or so they pumped me mercilessly for details of club life, which I felt obliged to exaggerate when my original, honest responses—that I didn't go to clubs very often, that I'd never been offered drugs—seemed such a huge disappointment to them. At fourteen, fifteen and sixteen, they weren't yet allowed to go to clubs, and by the way they were talking I hoped that they never would be.

'Yes, but you *must* have friends who've taken Ecstasy,' persisted Marinda, or possibly Darinda.

It was the names I mixed up, not the faces, which were very different. One was plump, pale and cherubic, while the other, more like her father, was tall and quite dark-skinned. Belle, the youngest, was pale and thin and lived up to her name by being extremely pretty.

'I suppose so,' I said, looking nervously at their father, who didn't appear to be listening.

Jennifer clearly took my lack of experience as reticence.

'Don't be afraid to talk about such matters in front of us,' she said in what remained quite a strong accent as she served up tuna steaks with slices of lime. 'We're a very open family, and if you know of anyone who has come to grief taking drugs so much the better. The girls need to know the downside of experimenting with mind-altering substances.'

The girls turned their wide-eyed attention back on me and I felt honour-bound to come up with something educational.

'Well...' I began.

I told them of a newspaper report I'd read about some tablets that had been laced with rat poison and applied it to an imaginary friend of mine. I called her Nicola, which seemed to enliven my enthusiasm for the tale. I found myself quite good at it, fibbing like that for their own good, but I think a lot of the credit must go to the encouragement I got from my completely captivated young audience.

'There now,' Jennifer said when the story came to an unhappy close, with Nicola slowly recovering on a life support machine though she was never likely to be the same again. 'Let Joanna's story be a lesson to you all.'

I felt as if I'd done a pretty good job, but when I glanced sideways at Sid for some recognition he ignored me. Like his father, he appeared to be giving his entire concentration to his food.

'And what about you, er...Dawood?' I ventured, while the girls started an argument over which of them was the most likely to take drugs when they got the chance. 'What do you do for a living?'

As soon as I said it I could have kicked myself. It was the question my mother asked first, and because of that I'd always made a point in the past of letting people tell me what they did only if they chose to.

'He's a raging capitalist,' Jennifer answered for him—very fondly, though, I thought, as if she had said 'he grows beautiful orchids in his greenhouse.' 'He owns a string of turf accountants, as he still quaintly calls them—betting shops to the rest of the world.'

I was tempted to ask how many, but I didn't want to sound any more like my mother than I already had so I just said, 'That's interesting,' lamely, and, because the girls were still squabbling, I took the opportunity to look around me.

The dining room was very beautiful. It had the typical grand high ceiling of a fine Victorian house, with a huge crystal chandelier that hung from a rose cornice directly above us, but there the period theme ended. The rest of the furnishings were otherwise a shrine to modernism, smooth-lined and clutter-free.

Jennifer had obviously been watching me.

'It all works surprisingly well, doesn't it, Jo?' she mused. 'The old and new cleverly fused in accordance with Feng

Shui principles. I had everything made by Jeffry Saville—you know, the furniture designer and Feng Shui master.'

I didn't know, but it didn't matter because a nod of interest was all that she needed to trigger a lengthy lecture on positive energies and how they can be harnessed in order to create health, happiness and prosperity. She gave a few examples of lives she had changed through her work: a woman who'd met the perfect man; another who landed the job of her dreams; a businessman who sold his company for twice as much as expected. It all sounded just a bit trite to me, but I think I made the right noises. She finished off by suggesting that I seriously consider consulting her myself (special prices for friends of the family) and by giving me half a dozen cards to distribute amongst my contacts.

And throughout the three girls chattered and threw in the odd sarcastic comment that was completely ignored by Jennifer. As were her son and her husband.

The food had been delicious: the tuna followed up by a salad of exotic fresh fruits, some of which I'd never even seen before, let alone tasted. And afterwards we took coffee or herbal tea in the gigantic sitting room. It was two rooms knocked into one, Jennifer explained, and was just about to demonstrate some of the changes she'd made in Feng Shui terms when Sid announced that I had to get home by ten to receive an important phone call.

His father looked relieved and the women of the house deeply disappointed. Marinda (or Darinda) had been pressing me to look at her bedroom, though I think she had an ulterior motive. I suspected she had more questions for me on the outside world, and I was very relived that I wouldn't now be expected to further exhaust my limited imagination.

I bid cheerful farewells and offered my heartfelt thanks for a lovely evening to a sombre Mr Perrez and the still alarmingly lively women in his life, and had hardly ever felt quite so relieved to take my leave from anywhere. It wasn't that I didn't like the family. I did. A lot. It was just that I was afraid of not living up to their expectations of me, and with a few minutes longer I would probably have given myself away as the dull and ordinary person I felt compared to them.

'That's quite a family you have,' I said as we started down the drive, with the females still waving us off from the doorway.

'Sorry,' he said. 'It was unfair to thrust them on you without warning you first. But I was afraid you wouldn't come if I did.'

'But they're terrific—' I began.

'But only in small doses, aye? I don't usually subject people to more than an hour at a time and you managed nearly two.' He turned to me admiringly. 'Who's Nicola, by the way?'

'Ah... So you didn't swallow my story, I take it?'

'I read the same article, but I still felt sorry for Nicola. I take it by the relish you used that she isn't your favourite person?'

'You take it correctly,' I said. Then something suddenly occurred to me. 'Was that some sort of test you were putting me through?'

'As a matter of fact, yes.' He kept his eyes firmly on the road ahead now.

'What sort of test?' I asked carefully. Then a worrying thought. 'You're not thinking of asking me to marry you, are you?'

We were at a traffic light now, and I heard Sid laugh aloud for the very fist time.

'Sorry,' he said when he recovered, 'that was very rude of me.'

Though I was relieved on the whole, it did indeed seem

a bit rude, but I chose not to take offence. 'Well, what was it all about, then?'

We started up again and he returned to normal dour Sid mode.

'I thought if you could cope with them that you could cope with working for me.'

I wasn't sure what he meant, but I took a stab when I remembered the paper serviette that he had written on.

'Are you talking about Pisus UK?'

He nodded. 'I've been on to the receivers and I've got an appointment with them early next week.'

'And I thought it was the wine talking,' I said, which was better than telling him I'd thought he was mad.

He glanced over at me and looked a bit hurt.

'I never allow alcohol to do the talking for me,' he said sternly. 'All I need to know now is if you meant what you said about working for me or whether in your case it really was the wine?'

I didn't need to think about it. Sid might be morose, and childlike, but he could also be an enormously impressive young man. I had every faith in him talking those Suits round to his way of thinking. And with the backing of a father who owned a string of turf accountants, the sky was the limit as far as I could see.

'Well, I've only had one glass tonight, and if you'll allow me that then the answer is a definite yes.'

At ten past ten Dan opened the door to Steve and found that he wasn't alone. He was so stunned to see Libby standing comfortably next to him—as if they were old friends or something—that for a moment he didn't know what to say.

'Well, are you going to leave us out here on this cold landing all night?' Steve finally asked.

'Come on in,' Dan said, standing aside, taking the bag that

Steve shoved in his direction. 'I just didn't know that you two were acquainted.'

'We weren't,' said Steve cheerfully, 'until about five minutes ago.'

They all three moved on to the sitting room, where Dan dumped Steve's bag on the leatherette armchair.

'We met outside,' Libby explained. 'I went down to empty some stuff in the bins and bumped into Steve as he was getting out of his taxi.'

'And when I realised she lived above you,' Steve put in, winking slyly at Dan so Libby couldn't see, 'I asked her in for a coffee. Didn't think you'd mind, since you're neighbours.'

'Of course I don't mind,' Dan managed to lie. 'Coffee all round, then?' Cursing Steve under his breath, he started towards the kitchen but Libby headed him off.

'I'll make it,' she said, 'while you two do some catching up.' She was acting like someone who knew her way round his flat only too well, which annoyed Dan slightly.

'You and she—you know...?' Steve said quietly as soon as Libby closed the door behind her.

'Definitely not.' Dan shook his head firmly.

Steve looked surprised, then pleased. 'Good. You won't mind if I nudge in, then, will you?'

'You fancy *Libby?*'

Steve moved his bag off the chair, noticed the sag in the middle of the seat and flopped on the sofa instead.

'Still into junk shop chic, I see,' he said with a grin. 'And don't sound so shocked,' he said, quietly now. 'She's a good-looking woman. In fact when I saw her outside I thought it was Jo at first. Similar build and hair.'

Dan frowned at this, then realised he'd thought the same thing when she turned up at his door with the food. She even wore the same sort of clothes that Jo wore.

'Fair enough,' he said, sitting on the mock leather arm of

the chair rejected by Steve. The springs had collapsed in the seat and it was long overdue a visit to the local tip.

'She's been telling me a bit about Jo. How she just walked out without a word.'

'I know it sounds bad,' Dan said, hiding his irritation with Libby for discussing his private life with his friend, 'but things hadn't been going well for a while.' This was true, but he still didn't know what had made her leave. Despite racking his brains he hadn't come up with a good enough reason.

'Yeah, maybe.' Steve shrugged, as if he knew all about that as well. 'But just to disappear like that?'

Steve undid his jacket and slipped it off. Dan noticed that he was getting a bit of paunch on him—the result of all that sitting around selling stocks and shares, no doubt. He pulled his own stomach in and, although it was OK at the moment, thought his mother might well have a point about taking some exercise.

'She did what she thought she had to and I'd prefer to leave it at that. And anyway,' he said feigning cheerfulness, 'I want to hear about you.' He lowered his voice. 'Since you're clearly thinking of making a play for Libby, I take it there's no one else at the moment?'

Steve did the male ego-saving thing of trying to appear a bit cagey, but Dan knew him too well for that.

'Go on,' he said, 'admit it. You're as much a sad lonely bastard as I am.'

Steve grinned and conceded with a shrug. 'I'm beginning to wonder what's wrong with me. I haven't been out with a woman in over six months.'

'It isn't all about women,' Dan said, trying to convince himself as much as Steve. Then, because he'd sounded just a hint pompous, 'And we have our work as a solace.'

Steve laughed.

'How's yours going? Libby tells me you're writing another book.'

Christ! Was there anything she hadn't told him? But relax, Dan, he told himself. This is your old mate, here, come for a pleasant weekend.

'Yeah, got to have it finished in less than three weeks, which is why I'll have to carry on working while you're here, I'm afraid.'

At least Steve didn't ask who or what the book was about. He just shrugged and raised a speculative eyebrow towards the door.

'Well, if I play my cards right I might not have to be on my own.'

Libby lapped up Steve's attention while they drank their coffee. Pretty soon they were on to her record collection and, encouraged by Steve, she went up to her flat and brought back a couple of samples. And Dan, who'd seen a lot in his time, had never quite seen anything like it.

'Do you realise how rare these albums are?' he asked when he got over his shock.

'Not really,' Libby said. 'I just know that...erm...my father spent a lot of time acquiring them. I've never had them properly valued, though.'

'Wow!' Steve nearly choked on one of the ginger biscuits Libby had produced from somewhere. 'Well, I know jack shit about vintage vinyl *per se*, but even I know that we're talking a lot of dosh here. A *Revolver* and a *White Album*.' He turned to Dan. 'Any ideas, you music expert you?'

Dan took one of the LPs from Libby.

'Christ!' he said. 'Have you seen this?' He pointed out the serial number to her, and both she and Steve looked at him uncomprehendingly.

'This particular album is like a numbered limited edition

of a print by a famous artist. And the lower number the higher the value.'

Steve moved round behind Libby to look over her shoulder.

'Does this mean what I think it means?' he eventually said.

Dan nodded. 'Five zeros and a nine means that that was the ninth pressing. And last I heard, nought-to-ten pressings were worth five grand plus.'

Steve went back to his seat and for a moment he and Dan just stared at Libby.

'I had no idea,' she said, and the statement had a ring of truth. 'I thought maybe a few hundred, but...'

'And you've got more like this?' Steve wanted to know.

Libby shrugged. 'Well, not the same as these. But I do know that my father was particularly proud of a single. I got the impression it was more important to him than the rest.'

'What is it?' Dan asked. He'd put aside his reservations about Libby now, in his genuine excitement.

Libby shrugged. 'I can't remember what it's called, and it's by a band I've never even heard of.'

'What's their name?' enquired Steve eagerly, sitting on the edge of his seat now.

Libby's forehead puckered. 'I think they're called the Quarrymen.'

There was a short silence as the meaning of her words sank home.

'Not *the* Quarrymen?' Steve said at last. He glanced at Dan, who was almost as stunned as he was. 'Christ, even I know that must be worth an arm and a leg. The Quarrymen was the first band that John Lennon belonged to. I didn't even know that they'd made a record.'

Dan shook his head. 'They didn't. A record company put out a very limited number of discs in 1981. They were taken from old acetate recordings from the Fifties, and there were only twenty-five of them pressed. The last one I heard about changed hands at twelve thousand quid.'

'Surely not!' Libby exclaimed. 'How can it possibly be worth that much?'

'Rarity value,' Dan said, feeling slightly dazed. 'And if there's more like that and these two here I can safely say that you're sitting on a small fortune. More than that, though,' he said, 'you have an incredible collection of mega-rare vinyl.'

It was Steve who suggested that he went with Libby the following day to visit a friend of Dan's who would give her a proper valuation of the entire collection, but although she agreed Dan could sense she did so with some reluctance.

He was surprised how quickly she changed the subject after that.

'Do you know if Aisling's back yet?' she asked him conversationally. At least it sounded conversational, but as she said it she glanced over at Steve, who responded with a flicker of interest.

Dan nodded. 'She got back this morning.'

'Who's Aisling?' Steve asked them both.

'She lives in the flat downstairs,' Libby supplied. 'She's in PR and mixes with lots of famous people—apparently.'

Dan frowned at Libby's animation. He wasn't sure why, but it felt as if she was up to something.

'Young, free and good-looking?' Steve put the question to Dan.

'I suppose so.'

'Well, then, why don't we all go out for a curry or something tomorrow night?' He looked at Libby, who nodded enthusiastic agreement and then looked at Dan.

'I don't think so,' said Dan. 'I've got the book and—'

'You've got to eat,' Libby cut in. 'Besides, you could do with a break—and Steve has come a long way to see you.'

'Right,' said Steve, getting into this now. He glanced at his watch. 'A bit late to call at her flat, I suppose, but we could give her a ring.' He was already on his feet. 'What's her number? I'll try her now.'

'I know it,' Libby said, springing up quickly. She joined Steve at the phone and tapped in the number before Dan could think straight and stop her.

Libby passed the receiver to Steve.

'Hello, Aisling?' he said, grinning stupidly over at Dan. 'You don't know me, but I'm a friend of Dan Baxter...'

I took the printout of Dan's message out of my bag as I got into bed, and when I read it again I was glad that I hadn't allowed Sarah to reply to it yet. There was a definite suggestion that he was beginning to take her e-mails for granted. It was the *Glad tidings Daily Sarah* part that did it. I can imagine how it might seem charming and pleasant to someone who didn't know him that well, but to me it sounded decidedly cocky. So much so that I decided that he would have to wait a couple of days before he heard from her again.

As for the message itself—well, that was OK. Quite promising, really, and I felt pleased with myself for putting that quote in. It had definitely got to him, made him wonder if there was more to little Sarah Daly—who didn't know very much about music—than met the eye.

Strange that you should choose that particular line. It's one of my favourites too.

How old are you, Sarah Daly, and where do you live? Not your address, of course, just which part of the country?

All the best

Dan

Oh, yes, he was interested all right. And as I read and re-read that brief message I shuddered with what felt like a strange mix of pleasure and just a hint of foreboding.

I spotted some creeping cellulite on my left buttock first thing the following morning. I was doing one of my body checks that only happen a) when I've been good about not eating chocolate for a week and am looking for the results of all that denial, and b) when I'm feeling particularly self-critical, which is usually about once a fortnight. I do it in a full-length mirror, in full, cruel daylight, and I always regret it deeply. Even after chocolate-denial periods I am never happy with what I see, so you can imagine the effect such a devastating discovery had when I was already pretty pissed off with myself.

Because it requires a considerable amount of bodily contortion, I don't usually include my rear view in these regular checks, and with the greatest of horror it occurred to me now that this single cellulite-covered buttock was exactly what Dan would have seen every time I'd got out of his bed.

Was it that which had turned him against me?

And why just one buttock anyway? Did it make me a freak? Did it mean that I must forever in future keep it covered up? Or was there some exercise I could employ that would correct the hideous disfigurement?

Or maybe, blessed *maybe*, I was just imagining things and it wasn't cellulite after all, but just some temporary skin-puckering caused by the way I'd been sleeping.

I took a power shower, which was the best thing about my flat, and aimed the fast flow of water directly at the offending buttock for a good five minutes. It was red from the pressure and heat, but when I rushed back to the mirror I could swear there was a slight improvement. Content with this for the time being, I dressed quickly and decided to detox my body for the next twenty-four hours as a precaution. This involved a cup of hot water instead of coffee and a wrinkled apple in place of toast. And to keep me from any temptation I decided to go out for a walk.

It was still only eight o'clock when I set out, which wasn't like me at all. Not at the weekends anyway. I would normally have gone to a club on Friday night after work and slept until at least midday on Saturday. But now, wearing jeans, a floppy jumper and lightweight mac to cover any unsightly bulges, a clingy hat on my head to cover my wayward hair, I witnessed the city coming to life. It wasn't a gradual thing at all. There were already a lot of cars and buses about. But I enjoyed the novelty of having whole pavements to myself for a while. Then, as suddenly as a film scene-change, my body-contact-avoiding radar switched itself on as I found myself weaving through a seething mass of humankind that seemed to have appeared from nowhere.

I really like living in Leeds. It has been hyped as the first twenty-four-hour city in the north, and although I've never stayed awake long enough to test this claim, I've been told by a few of my more energetic friends that it is so. I doubt it can compete with London or New York as yet, but it definitely vies with Manchester for title of Coolest City in the North of England. I'm biased, of course, but I think Leeds just nudged ahead when the first branch of Harvey Nichols outside the capital was opened here a few years ago.

I didn't have a plan as such, so I was quite surprised when I found myself opposite the library at about ten minutes to nine. I wasn't sure quite how this had happened, but since I was there, and since I had time to kill, I might as well see if there was a computer free. Not for any e-mailing purposes, you understand, just to surf the net for a while, check out the on-line recruitment agencies in case Sid's plans came to nothing.

I had to hang around for ten minutes till the place opened, but the rain kept off and I filled in the time by walking up and down the stone steps, about twenty each way, which I was certain was great for buttocks.

I hadn't booked a computer, of course, and was just trusting to luck that there might be one spare. There wasn't, but luck came in a different form, that of a pleasant and helpful librarian who recognised need when she saw it and allowed me five minutes on a machine whose booker was late. It was hardly enough time to search for jobs, but I thought that there must be something I could do with five minutes. Like check out my Hotmail account, for example, to see if there was a message from my nutty mother.

There wasn't, but because I didn't like to feel I was completely wasting the time allotted to me, I decided I might as well check Sarah's account as well. And, since I still had three minutes in hand, Sarah decided to swallow my pride and respond to Dan's message after all.

The fact is I was intrigued as to why he appeared to be so

curious about some cyber stranger at the same time that he was taking Aisling home to meet his mother. And I wasn't sure why, but I had this idea that if I could just pep up his interest in Sarah it would make me feel a whole lot better.

I was also vaguely aware by now that pretending to be someone else in order to deceive my ex-boyfriend was not a particularly healthy state of affairs, but it didn't stop me writing the message.

> *Dear Dan*
> *To answer your questions, I'm twenty-six and I live in London currently, though I grew up in Cornwall.*

I chose Cornwall because it's somewhere that Dan always loved going to when he was a kid—sneaky, ay? Then, because I wasn't supposed to know very much about him.

> *What about you?*

I'd have added some more, but by now a middle-aged man with a nylon shopping bag was breathing down my neck, mumbling something about bookings and rules, so I quickly sent the e-mail and turned my nicest possible smile on him.

'I'm so sorry,' I said, 'but I just needed to check and see if there was a message from my brother who's travelling in South America. Our mother is a little concerned that we haven't heard from him in quite a few weeks.'

It was a whopping great lie and it just came straight out of my mouth without me even turning pink. I think that was because it wasn't me that was doing the lying. It was Sarah.

It wasn't what Libby had expected. Baz Baines, the dealer Dan had recommended to her as the best in Leeds—the expert who would be able to value her collection—operated from a large terraced house in one of the scariest parts of Leeds. It was certainly a no-go area after dark, and she was quite glad to have Steve along with her. Baz had offered to go to her, but she didn't want any connections being made between her address and the collection.

The house stank of pipe smoke and chip fat, and the room where Baz conducted his business was stacked floor-to-ceiling with vinyl. The only other things in the room were a Formica-topped table and, on it, an ancient-looking computer. There was just room on the table for Steve to put down the heavy cardboard box. They'd borrowed Dan's car to transport them over and had been issued clear instructions by him that he was not to be disturbed until six p.m.

Baz was about fifty, Libby guessed, spoke with a broad Welsh accent and dressed like a fading rock star. He wore tight black jeans, a striped, collarless shirt and a stained waistcoat over it. His hair was thin and straggly, grey and far too long.

'So,' he said in a business-like manner that did not involve any preliminary chit-chat, 'let's have a look, shall we?' He took the first album out of the box and handled it like a woman handles a delicate furry animal. With the greatest tenderness and care.

'Jeez,' he said, glancing at Libby. It was all he said until he'd examined the rest, stacking them carefully in two separate piles, one for singles, one for LPs. Then came the question she had thankfully anticipated.

'Have you got any proof of ownership. Receipts or suchlike?'

She shook her head. 'My father didn't bother to keep them, I'm afraid. I don't think he ever planned on selling them so there didn't seem any point.'

Baz didn't respond to this, but looked thoughtfully at the two piles of vinyl.

'Does that make any difference?' Steve said.

'Probably not. It's just useful to have some proof of ownership, especially with a collection this valuable.'

'How much are we talking?' Steve wanted to know, then glanced at Libby apologetically. 'Sorry,' he said. 'I shouldn't be asking the questions.'

'That's OK,' she said, covering her irritation. She would have much preferred it if Dan had come along, but he'd been adamant about getting on with that damn book of his.

Baz did a visible totting up in his head.

'Total?' he said. 'Around thirty grand, give or take a thousand or two.'

'Christ!' said Steve.

'But, like I said, it could take some time to find the right buyers.'

'How would you do that?' Libby asked.

Baz tapped the monitor of his computer.

'I have an Internet site that I do most of my selling through. For which I take twenty per cent commission.'

Libby did her own totting up and arrived at a figure of twenty-four thousand, excluding commission, which was a very satisfying sum.

'OK,' she said. 'Only I prefer to keep my name out of this.'

The two men looked at her—Steve with mild curiosity, Baz with suspicion.

'It's just that I feel a bit guilty about it,' she ventured to explain. 'My father loved his collection and I don't want his friends to find out that I'm selling.'

'Why *are* you selling?' Baz wanted to know.

Libby was beginning to get annoyed. She hadn't expected the third degree.

'If you must know it's because I need the money. Simple as that.'

'Seems fair enough,' Steve said sympathetically.

Baz looked at her for a moment, then shrugged.

'So you want me to go ahead?' he said.

Libby nodded. 'Does that mean I leave them with you?' she said, glancing around at the chaos.

'It's not as bad as it looks,' Baz said unsmilingly. 'I know where everything is. And I'll need them here to catalogue them.'

'I can see that,' she said, 'but this isn't exactly Fort Knox, is it? What happens if you get a break-in?'

'Never had one yet,' Baz said casually. 'But if you're un-happy with security you can come back later and take them away. I can send any buyers directly to you then.'

'No,' she said quickly. Then, because they were both look-ing at her again, she smiled sadly. 'Like I said, I'd sooner not be involved. Too painful, I'm afraid.'

Dan answered Sarah's e-mail immediately. It was the only in-terruption he allowed himself, and he was surprised how much he welcomed the break.

Dear Full-of-Surprises Sarah

Cornwall, ay? Interesting that, as it happens to be one of my favourite places in the world. I used to go there on holiday when I was a kid. They were great times for me. Which part are you from? And what took you from Cornwall to London?

I live in Leeds, and since you know what I do for what is laughingly called 'a living' the only other information that I can think to tell you at the moment is that I'm twenty-eight and I'm currently single.

Dan

He wasn't sure why he'd added the last bit, but he didn't think it would do any harm. He'd been tempted to ask what she looked like as well, but decided that was probably going too far at this stage. Then he questioned what he meant by that. It was as if he was expecting it to move on to another stage, and he didn't really mean that at all.

Did he?

Of course he didn't. He was having enough woman trouble at the moment. What with Libby and Aisling trying to come on to him in their own different ways, and Jo still not out of his head, he could do without any more complications. And yet—

There was no *and yet* about it, he told himself firmly, and then stretched and looked at his watch. Bloody hell! Five-thirty already. Steve would be back any minute, and an hour after that they'd be heading out on the town with Aisling and Libby. Which he still wasn't happy about, but he wasn't sure why.

If Steve had his eye on Libby—and he certainly seemed to—that just left Aisling to handle, and he knew he could do that without much difficulty. It was just an evening out with a few friends, a break from routine which would do him good... So why could he not escape a nagging suspicion that things weren't as clear-cut and straight forward as they should be?

By six o'clock I was feeling bored and sorry for myself again. I'd already phoned a couple of friends, despite my fear of using the phone. They'd suggested I joined them for a night on the town, which had been very tempting, but clubs are expensive, even for those on detox diets, and I had to be sensible now that I no longer knew what the immediate future held.

So in desperation I decided on one last call, and made it to Sid. I asked him if he fancied sharing some hot water with me, and he said a firm no, but that if he was allowed to bring his own food round he wouldn't mind spending some of the evening with me.

He brought a Thai takeaway, which smelt delicious and made me produce gallons of saliva as I watched him eat it in front of me. He offered me some, and I very nearly succumbed, but was saved by a vivid image of my cellulite buttock, which I still hadn't dared look at since the morning.

While I tried not to drool, he ate in silence, and as this was clearly the way he liked to do things I saved the question that had come into my mind till he took his empty plate into the kitchen and dutifully washed it up.

'So, have you got a girlfriend?' I asked as he sat in the armchair at a perfect right angle with my sofa. I was sipping hot water while he was slurping from a bottle of lager he'd brought along with him.

'Not at the moment,' he said cautiously. 'Why?'

'Just wondered,' I said, though the truth is it was a prelude to bringing up the subject of Dan. Sid might look like a child but he was really an almost grown-up man, and he must have an idea how their minds worked.

'You're not thinking of offering to fill the vacancy, I hope?'

I wasn't sure if he was joking or not, or just getting me back for my comment about him proposing to me.

'No, but there's no need to sound quite so horrified at the thought.'

He managed the faintest of smiles. 'If there's one thing I've learnt about women, having spent my life surrounded by them, it's the fact that they don't "just wonder" about anything. There's always something behind a question like that, so you might as well just spit it out.'

He was casually dressed tonight—casual for him, anyway. Smart black trousers, neat sky blue sweater over an open-necked shirt. In terms of clothes he was the male equivalent of Cass.

'It's a fair cop,' I said, impressed by his knowledge of female minds. 'Fact is I want to pick your brains on the thoughts and behaviour of the puppy dogs' tails of the species.'

He looked at me blankly.

'It's what little boys are made of, apparently,' I said.

He smirked. 'As opposed to sugar and spice and all things nice?'

'Precisely.'

'Well, unfortunately I don't think I'm all that well qualified.'

'You're not gay, are you?'

'No,' he said without offence, 'but, like I said, I've just grown up around too many women.'

'There's your dad. He's a man.'

'True. OK,' he said with a sigh. 'Fire away, then, if you must.'

'I've got this friend...' I began.

He held up his hand. 'If you want my opinion then can we drop the bullshit, please? We're talking about you, I take it?'

'If you know so much about women then you should know that you're supposed to go along with their bullshit.' I exaggerated a sigh. 'But OK, fair enough. So long as this doesn't go any further.'

'Where would it go?'

He had a point. Sid didn't know anyone I knew who mattered, so I was as good as anonymous.

'It's about Dan and me,' I said.

Sid looked thoughtful for a moment.

'The bloke that you used to live with? He came to the office a couple of times, didn't he?'

I nodded. 'Things hadn't been going well for a while, and I left when he said I was turning into my mother.'

'And were you?' Sid said.

'Of course not!'

'Then why did he say it?'

'To be mean. Why else?'

'I thought being "mean" was the province of sugar and spice,' he said wryly. 'In my limited experience I find men tend to say things because they believe them to be true. There's not usually an ulterior motive.'

'Well, that's rubbish,' I said a bit hotly, though I wasn't sure how to back it up. So I didn't even try. 'And it's not even what I wanted to talk about.'

'Then get to the point,' he said coolly.

'The *point* is that I've never heard from him again. And he's taking his new girlfriend home to meet his mother this weekend. They're probably all sitting down to one of Jean's fabulous dinners as we speak.'

'Which bit of all that is the problem?'

'All of it, of course!'

'Did you tell him why you were leaving?'

I shook my head.

He glowered at me. 'Not even in a note?'

I shook it again.

'Well, I can only speak personally, but if you left me without explanation you wouldn't hear from me again either. Did you ever call him?'

'No. But...'

'What the hell did you expect, then, you silly cow?'

I looked at him aghast. I don't think anyone but Cass had ever called me that before.

'I expected him to be worried about me. To call one of my friends.' I told him everything else I'd expected, knowing full well that I wouldn't be getting any sympathy now.

And I was right.

'Well, good on him,' Sid said. 'He was obviously fed up with all the shit you were giving him and he did just the right thing.'

'OK,' I said miserably. I didn't have the heart to argue. 'But it can't be right that he's already taking someone else home to his mother, surely? Someone he swore that he didn't fancy.'

Sid shrugged. 'I took you home to meet my parents.'

'This is different,' I said miserably. 'Dan's practically engaged to Aisling, apparently.'

'How do you know all this?' Sid asked with a frown creasing his boyish brow. 'If you're no longer in touch with him, that is.'

'Someone told me.'

'Someone reliable?'

'I think so. Yes,' I said more confidently, 'I'm sure she's reliable.'

'Ah,' said Sid. 'An *all things nice...* Are you sure about her motives?'

'You've got a lousy opinion of women,' I said.

He sipped some lager, then looked me right in the eye.

'No, I haven't,' he said. 'I just understand them better than most. And if you really want my opinion, I think you should ring Dan and tell him what a prat you've been and ask if you could meet for a chat.'

He made it sound so easy, but it just wasn't. I was about to say as much when he suddenly got up and went to the door, where he'd left his coat and a black canvas bag. He was plainly bored with my whingeing.

He brought back the bag and unzipped it on the coffee table.

'I have a spare,' he said as he took out a neat little laptop computer. 'And I'd like you to e-mail your former clients. Explain what's happened and tell them to expect to hear from us again very soon. Tell them they're not to worry about their Internet sites. Say I'll deal with any technical problems till we can sort out Pisus's future.'

'Yes, boss,' I said with a bright-eyed grin. But it wasn't the clients I was thinking about at that moment. It was the knowledge that I now had easy access to Sarah's Hotmail account.

★ ★ ★

The meal had gone well. Good food, lively conversation—mostly about Libby's impending windfall, but that was fine. She was bright and lively and looked surprisingly attractive tonight. She was wearing a cream-coloured dress that reminded Dan of one of Jo's. A favourite of his, as a matter of fact, and what with her copper-coloured hair he found himself strangely drawn to her.

Of course the three pints of lager which Steve had pressed on him might have had a hand in creating the illusion that she looked and behaved like Jo, but he didn't think about that at the time.

When they moved on to the club Aisling urged him to dance, but he drew the line there. The last time he'd danced had been with Jo, the night they met, and then only because he'd been rip-roaring drunk. But three pints was not enough to persuade him to put his dancing shoes on now, and while Libby encouraged Steve to keep Aisling company she—not being much of dancer herself, she said—opted to stay with him at the bar.

Even a day ago this would have bothered Dan, but since she was clearly getting on so well with Steve he temporarily dropped his guard.

They found a corner, where they propped themselves up against a wall.

They talked some more about the vinyl, and her half-formed plans to maybe buy a decent car with part of the proceeds, and as they did so Dan felt her hip rub against his own. He was pretty much pressed into the corner, and assumed it was the crush behind that was forcing this closeness.

He noticed that she smelled nice. She obviously used the same perfume as Jo did. And what with that and the dim lights and the closeness it was easy to imagine that it was Jo pressed up against him. Especially if he closed his eyes. He did close his eyes, and at that very moment, without any warning, she lunged at him.

And he found himself kissing her back. It went on for quite a long time, so he must have enjoyed it, and it was only when he came up for air and looked into her face that he realised what an awful mistake he had made.

chapter 8

By mid-afternoon I'd sent all the business e-mails through my old e-mail address from work—Jo.H@pisus.co.uk.

The Child Sid, with his usual foresight, had copied all Pisus's relevant data on to his own system and then installed it on the laptop for me. It was probably highly illegal, but I didn't think anyone would bother too much, especially if he succeeded with his plans.

And the more confident he seemed, the more I began to believe in him. As he'd said last night, it would be hard for the company's former clients to start again with someone else. We'd planned their systems, got them up and running, and to begin all over again with a new e-business agency would be inconvenient as well as expensive.

I was even beginning to think that Sid was right about me. I *did* have a good relationship with my personal clients, and so, yes, maybe it really was possible that little old Jo Hurst could actually be an asset to him.

It was good to be doing something useful for a change. It was helping me to see things more positively (including my buttock, which looked a lot better today), and now, having followed Sid's instructions to the letter, I felt that the time had come for a little Sunday afternoon mischief.

I'd already been into Sarah's Hotmail account, found Dan's latest message to her, and was just in the process of writing back.

> *Dear Dan*
> *I'm originally from Truro.*

I wrote that because I happened to know that he had a soft spot for that particular city.

> *I've got a good friend who lives in Leeds, by the way.*

I added that in an effort to create an even bigger connection, and besides, it was true—Sarah did indeed have a very good friend in Leeds, called Joanna Hurst. But I didn't mention any names, of course.

> *We were at school together.*

Then I had to think long and hard about a suitable profession to give to dear Sarah. I considered many possibilities— doctor, lawyer, actress, trainee astronaut. You name it, I considered it. That's the trouble when you can be whatever you want to be—too much choice. I'm not even sure why I opted for an artist in the end. The truth is that I can't draw to save my life, but somehow it just seemed right for Sarah. I told him that it was the proximity of so many good galleries that took Sarah from Cornwall to London three years ago. I would have liked to add that she was a very successful artist. That she was extremely beautiful with sleek golden hair and wore a double D-cup bra, but I didn't want to put him off with all that boasting.

I'd been kind of stunned by his claim to be 'currently single'. I didn't know what to make of it—whether Libby had got it horribly wrong about Aisling after all, whether things had changed since I last spoke to her, or whether Dan was just a barefaced liar and I'd never really known him at all.

I tried calling Libby but there was no reply, and until I could speak to her again I decided that I would keep playing along and see where it led. So I told him that Sarah was single as well.

I went even further. I told him that she had recently broken up with someone she'd lived with for quite a while and that she still thought about him a lot—because I hoped this might open the door for discussions about his own recent break-up...

And an hour later I got a reply.

> *Dear Sarah*
> *An artist. Impressive! What do you paint? Or is painting old hat these days? Maybe you're one of those conceptual types that make statements with old bits of chewing gum and saucepan lids?*
> *Dan*
>
> *PS What do you look like?*

I noticed that the message had been sent only five minutes before I picked it up, so I answered immediately, just in case he was still online.

> *Dear Dan*
> *I'm the old hat kind of artist.*

I said this because I didn't think my imagination would stretch to anything beyond dunking dead animals in formaldehyde, and that had already been done. Nevertheless, I thought it was a bit rich for him to have a pop at experimental art when he listened in awe to *avant-garde* jazz. With this in mind, I added my own little dig.

> *Though I admire those who are prepared to explore the boundaries of what we call art.*

And because that looked just a bit priggish and pompous when I read it back, I decided to lighten the mood of the e-mail.

> *What do I look like? Well, I'm seven feet three inches tall, and I wear size twelve Doc Martens. I have one blue eye and one brown one, but it's hard to see them through my designer target-glass spectacles. Oh, yes, and I've got seventeen facial moles (on the last count).*
> *How about you?*

I hung around and his reply came back within two minutes.

> *Dear Sarah*
> *How do you manage to paint with target-glass spectacles—designer or otherwise?*
> *Dan*

I whipped off a reply straight away.

Dear Dan
Not seeing too well is what makes my work so original.
Sarah

PS You haven't told me what you look like yet.

Three minutes later still.

Dear Sarah
I'm four feet eleven and a half inches, but my polka dot eyes do have twenty-twenty vision, I am happy to say. I don't enjoy the benefits of facial moles, unfortunately, but I make up for this deficiency with my warts (49 at the last count)!
Maybe we should exchange photographs?
Dan

He was clearly getting into the swing of things.

Dear Dan
Sadly I haven't yet found a camera that can do me full jus-tice. Any bad habits you'd like to get off your chest at this stage?
Sarah

One minute, thirty seconds afterwards.

Dear Sarah
I've got several, but I'm keeping them close to my chest at the moment. I don't want to put you off.
So tell me more about this man you broke up with recently.
Dan

Ah, so we were getting serious, were we? Pity. I'd been quite enjoying myself for a while. It was much more fun telling big silly lies than outrageous serious ones. And this was a tricky one to answer. I hadn't really thought it out, and because he was waiting for my reply I found myself sailing dangerously close to the truth.

Sarah: *Not much to tell. We were great together and then it just all fell apart.*

Dan: *Why?*

Sarah: *Good question, Dan, but that's the trouble, I don't know why.*

And now it was crunch time.

Have you ever broken up with anyone important?

Dan: *Oh, yes. Not very long ago either. And before you ask, I don't know why it happened either.*

Nothing to do with a cellulite buttock, I thought—but didn't write, of course. What I did write would be the obvious question.

Sarah: *Whose idea was it to finish things?*

Dan: *Hers. She just disappeared one day. You?*

Sarah: *Mine, I suppose. I was the one who left anyway.*

Dan: *What made you leave?*

Sarah: *He upset me with something he said, and I wanted him to come after me and apologise.*

Dan: *And did he?*

Sarah: *No.*

Dan: *Maybe he didn't know he'd upset you so much.*

Sarah: *He should have known.*

Dan: *So you left him because he wasn't a mind-reader, is that what you're saying?*

Sarah: *I left him because of what he'd said.*

Dan: *What did he say? If you don't mind me asking, that is.*

Sarah: *It's personal.*

Dan: *Fair enough, but you still should have told him.*

Sarah: *I didn't get the chance because the faithless bastard started seeing someone else almost straight away!*

Fuming by now, I'd just clicked the *send* symbol when I heard my doorbell ring. I hesitated. This was getting close to the nitty-gritty and I was very damn keen to see what Dan had to say for himself. But then the bell sounded again, persistently now, and I felt obliged to see who it was.

I left the computer on in my bedroom and went to the intercom at my front door.

'Who is it?' I snapped after I pressed the *speak* button.

'It's Cass,' Cass said. 'Let me in.'

Tempting as it was, I couldn't just send her away. So I

buzzed the main door open, put the flat door on its latch, and ran back to the laptop while Cass made her way up in the lift.

There was still no reply waiting from Dan, and because Cass would be here any moment now, I wrote a brief message explaining that a visitor had just arrived and that I was very sorry but I would have to close down.

'Bugger!' Dan said aloud when he read the message. He'd been in the middle of composing a long note to Sarah explaining that although their situations seemed uncannily similar it was different for him in that he hadn't really looked at another woman since his girlfriend left. He'd been anxious to keep up the exchange. He was beginning to think it just possible that he too might have made a careless remark that had caused Jo to leave. He couldn't think what it might have been, but he thought if he discussed it further with Sarah she might suggest something. Something he'd never even have thought about.

He read through his ramblings again and then deleted the half-written message. What was the point? If it was too late for Sarah now that her boyfriend was with someone else, then it was just as too late for him and Jo now that she was with someone as well.

Besides, he had enough stuff in the present to deal with, without dredging up his past mistakes. And, as if to remind him of this, the phone rang the moment he disconnected his modem.

He snatched at the receiver and took a deep breath.

'How are you getting on?' Libby asked brightly before he could speak.

'OK,' he said as his heart took a dive. 'Steve popped up to

say goodbye half an hour ago and I haven't really got back in the flow yet.'

'I saw them leave,' she said, referring to the fact that Aisling had gone with Steve to the station.

Strange how things work out, Dan thought. He'd never have believed that Steve was Aisling's type any more than he was, but they seemed to have hit it off very well. Aisling had certainly wasted no time in luring Steve back to her flat when they got home from the club, which had unfortunately left Dan and Libby alone.

The trouble was that it hadn't felt all that unfortunate at the time. He'd continued drinking at the club, and by the time they got back to the flat he was as drunk as a skunk. To say that Libby took advantage of him would be an exaggeration. He was as keen as she was at the time, and regret only kicked in when he woke up to the smell of bacon and eggs being cooked in his kitchen. She'd popped her head round the bedroom door and, with a very wide smile, insisted he stay where he was because she would be serving his breakfast in bed. He wasn't used to this sort of treatment, certainly not from Jo. She'd even been out and bought a newspaper and he had a horrible fantasy that she'd turned into a Stepford wife overnight.

And the last thing he'd felt like after a skinful of lager was bacon and eggs.

He'd had to tell her, and to make matters worse she had pretended not to mind. Instead she'd sat on the bed beside him—fully dressed, thank God—and watched him sip tea and flick, bleary-eyed, through a copy of the *Sunday Times*. She'd hoped that they would be spending the day together and he was never so glad that he had the excuse of his book.

'Your line's been engaged for ages,' she said now, with a hint of suspicious accusation in her voice.

'Been doing some research on the Internet,' he lied, and then wondered why he was bothering.

'Well,' she said, sounding slightly appeased by this explanation, 'I've been thinking of cooking a meal for us tonight and wondered if you fancied anything special.'

This was what he'd been dreading all day, ever since he'd managed to persuade her to leave around midday. He glanced at his watch, saw that it was almost five.

'I'm sorry, Lib, but I got off to a slow start today so I'll need to work through. I'll just have to make do with a slice of toast.'

'Does that mean you'd rather not see me tonight?'

Oh, God, he thought, cursing the booze that had got him into this. The stupid thing was that he couldn't even remember ending up in bed with her, but he assumed that something must have happened as she'd still been there in the morning. He wished that he had the guts to say something now, to tell her it had been an awful mistake, but he really didn't want to hurt her feelings. He knew how women could be after sex. He'd just seen *Vanilla Sky* on video, and he didn't want to treat her like Tom Cruise had treated Cameron Diaz. He certainly didn't want to end up like the Cruise character did, and there was something about Libby that made him suspect—wildly, perhaps—that he just might. But then he was still suffering from a very severe hangover, and it was easy to get carried away in that condition. Best to leave it, therefore, till he was feeling better.

'It isn't a case of not wanting to see you,' he fudged. 'I just think it's best if we leave it till tomorrow.'

'Suit yourself,' she said, and put the phone down heavily.

'You seemed a bit sorry for yourself the other day,' Cass said, and she flopped into the chair where Sid had been sitting the night before.

'Did I?' I said, still distracted by the exchange that had taken place with Dan. 'How was the party?' I asked, because

I presumed that was what Cass had come round to talk about.

'Fine, apart from the fact that Phillip Brown was invited and no one told me.'

'Not Flatulence Phil!' He was an old boyfriend of Cass's, the son of her mother's neighbour, and his greatest claim to fame was farting in tune to 'God Save the Queen'. It was a childish talent, but it had been a big hit while we were still at school. 'He didn't do "Happy Birthday", I hope—'

'Thankfully not,' Cass said primly. 'I hope his farting-in-tune days are—if you'll pardon the pun—*behind* him now, and he certainly didn't impress me on any other front.'

'So why was he invited?'

True, Cass hadn't been out with anyone for ages now, but her mother had never seemed the desperate, interfering type, who would try fitting her up with anyone that happened to be available.

'It was my gran. What with me being the eldest, she's pinning all her hopes on me to produce a great-grandchild.'

'Oh, dear,' I said. 'How did you handle it?'

'I lied and told her that I already had a boyfriend.'

Which wasn't like Cass at all—lying, I mean.

'Oh, well,' I said, 'if it got you off the hook—'

'It didn't really, because now of course she wants to meet him.'

'Ah,' I said. 'Tricky.'

'I'm hoping she'll just forget all about it. Anyway—' she shrugged '—are you going to offer me a cup a tea or something?'

I'd taken my detox into a second day and was beginning to feel a bit ill. I had a dull headache, and a cup of tea and a slice of Marmite on toast at that moment seemed the best feast in the world. I got up and went into he kitchen and Cass followed me in. She hitched herself up onto the counter and I worked around her.

'So how's your weekend been?' she asked as I filled the kettle.

I told her a bit about Sid's plans for Pisus, and she wanted to know what he was like.

'He looks like a boy,' I said, 'but he has the mind of a middle-aged man. He seems scarily wise beyond his years.'

I put white sliced bread in the toaster and asked Cass if she'd like some.

She nodded. 'Anything else?' she said probingly, as if she knew I had something else on my mind. I flipped the switch on the toaster and looked at her sheepishly.

'I've been e-mailing someone,' I said cautiously.

'What does that mean?'

'A man,' I said.

'What, through some kind of Internet dating thing?'

'Not exactly,' I said, turning to get the margarine out of the fridge.

'You're going to have to explain,' she said.

It was now or never, and maybe because I was weak with hunger and not thinking straight I went for the 'now' option.

'I've been e-mailing Dan,' I said with my back still to her. 'Only I've been pretending to be someone else.'

'What?'

I turned around slowly and put the tub of margarine down next to her.

'It was just one of those daft ideas that's got a bit out of hand now. He thinks I'm called Sarah Daly and that I'm a very tall, short-sighted artist.'

I'd hoped she might find the last bit funny, but she just stared at me as if I was mad. I'd started now, though, so I told her the rest. Or most of it anyway.

'But what did you hope to achieve by this little deception?' she eventually said—disapprovingly.

By now we'd moved back into the living room and were sipping tea and munching toast.

'I'm not really sure,' I said honestly. 'Not when I started anyway.'

'And now?'

'And now I'm just bloody confused,' I said.

'And you're not the only one,' she said. She chewed her lip for a moment and then frowned at me. 'I hope you're not trying to say that you think you made a mistake about leaving Dan!'

I looked up at her, over my toast. She was wearing her baby-pink fleece and a smart pair of trousers, and there wasn't a single crumb in sight. I brushed my own toast crumbs off my sweater and wondered what to say. I wasn't sure if I did think I'd made a mistake, but even if I did I couldn't admit it after what had happened. She'd hated being dragged into a situation she didn't approve of.

'No,' I said, 'I don't think that.'

She narrowed her eyes. 'Then how come you gave me permission to tell him where you were if he rang?'

'I wanted him to apologise.' Which was certainly true.

'For what?' she said curiously. 'I thought you'd just had enough of him being up his own bottom about his music and always complaining about your new friends. That's what you said anyway.'

'That as well,' I said cautiously, 'but mostly for saying—' I took in a deep breath '—for saying I was like my mother...'

There, it was out, and for a moment she didn't say anything. I was expecting an explosion of minor outrage, or laughter, at least, at the absurdity of such a suggestion.

'And *that's* why you left?' she finally said in exasperation. I nodded.

'Do me a favour, will you?' she said with a sigh.

I looked at her quizzically, hoping for words of wisdom.

'Just don't tell me any more about you and Dan and Sarah Daly, OK?'

'OK,' I said.

chapter 9

After Cass left, I binged on crisps and some ancient sultanas I found in the back of the cupboard—and checked a couple of times to see if there was another message from Dan. There wasn't, and because I needed some time to think I didn't write to him either. I was a bit worried about what Cass had said, how she'd made me feel stupid, and I started to wonder whether it might be best to knock the whole thing on the head before it got even more out of hand.

Indeed, by Monday morning I was really looking forward to starting work at the Italian to get away from it all. I was so keen, in fact, that I decided to go in at nine o'clock, even though I knew the place didn't actually open till ten. It was only when I was almost there that I remembered that the last time I'd seen Marco he still hadn't told Giovanna about me starting work.

Oh, well, it wasn't as if she disliked me, I reasoned, so even if she did overrule her son and explain that there wasn't a job for me after all, she was bound to do it nicely.

There wasn't a bell, so I knocked on the blue wooden surround of the glass door and just hoped that someone was in there. It was beginning to rain, and with no umbrella it would not be too long before my carefully tended titian locks turned into springy orange wire wool.

Thankfully Giovanna was quick off the mark, and the door was opened in seconds.

'Has he told you?' I quickly asked before she could express any surprise.

'Of course 'e 'as, Joanna!' She gave me a welcoming hug. 'And I am-a thrilled to 'ave-a you work-a with me while-a Marco goes off on-a ees-a leetle 'oliday.'

Despite my relief, I couldn't help being aware of the way that Giovanna was talking. I'd noticed that the strength of her accent varied from mild, all the way through to something resembling *stage* Italian. I had no idea what triggered these variations, but there was something distinctly theatrical about today's performance.

And what was all this about a *holiday*? If that was all it was why hadn't Marco told me? He'd made it sound a lot more intriguing than that. I looked around me as if I expected to find him crouching behind one of the tables, then it struck me.

'He hasn't gone already, surely?'

'First theeng this morning a taxi cemma to take 'eem to the airport.'

Now that *was* odd—not to mention thoughtless—dumping me in the deep end like that.

'On his own?' I said, when that seemed a bit odd as well.

'Of-a course,' she said confidently. ''E as nobody in-a ees life at the moment but ees Mamma.' She laughed a bit wildly at this, but sobered quickly. 'But-a all that could-a change...'

she added and gave me one of those looks that meant I would do nicely as far as she was concerned. ''E left a leetle note for you, as a matter of fact.' She went round the counter and produced an envelope. She looked expectantly on as she passed it to me, but after what had transpired between Marco and me last time we'd met caution told me I should open it later. I tucked it into my jacket pocket and told her a fib.

'Some information I asked about, um, travel agents,' I said feebly.

'You do realise I haven't really done this sort of work before,' I told Giovanna quickly, in order to change the subject. 'Only one summer at school, when I worked as a waitress in a tea room.'

'Well, there-a you are then, Joanna.' Giovanna laughed. 'You are fully qualified. I show you around now, OK? And don't-a worry. It'sa easy, I promise.'

As far as food was concerned, she explained crisply—her accent softening now, thank goodness—everything sweet came ready-made from a specialist supplier: it was just a case of keeping the display cabinet nicely topped up throughout the day. So that *was* easy. And as for the sauces—one of the main reasons for the popularity of the Italian—these she made herself fresh every morning in the back kitchen to a genuinely secret recipe. She kept the pasta going as well. My bit was simply to serve it up and take the money, and that didn't sound too bad either.

'You see, Joanna—' Giovanna grinned when I began to relax '—the secret of the Italian's success is *simpleecity*.'

'Apart from the coffee machine,' I said, looking worriedly at the gigantic monster with its seemingly endless gadgets for making cappuccinos, espressos, lattes and a whole lot else besides.

'Geev it a day or two, and you weel be serving cappuccino like a native Italian. Inna the meantime just don't let it sense your fear, OK?' she said, and then laughed like an Italian drain.

I'd worn my only black skirt and a plain white T-shirt, and when she'd finished showing me around Giovanna issued me with a white apron just like the one she wore herself. She nodded approvingly when I put it on, but then her eyes scanned my heeled shoes and came to rest on my head.

'I think-a flat shoes might be better in future, and we're gonna have to do something with that beautiful hair.'

I was pleased that she thought it beautiful, but nervous about what she might have in mind. I pictured myself in one of those peaked white caps with a net and an elastic bit that goes round the back of the neck: the sort people wear in food factories. I wouldn't have minded if it had been a food factory, where no one would see me but people wearing similar peaked caps, but this was a very public place. Celebrities had even been known to patronise the Italian.

She went into the back kitchen and reappeared with an elastic band.

'You will ave to make a-do with that today, but maybe tomorrow you can-a put it up properly.' She touched the back of her own beautifully put-up hair as if to demonstrate what 'properly' meant, but there was no way on earth I could achieve the same effect.

I dragged my hair up and slipped on the band and she smiled at me.

'You know-a Joanna, you and my Marco would make very beautiful *bambinos.*'

I giggled stupidly at this, turned the colour of her famous spaghetti sauce and pretended to try and get to grips with the coffee machine.

The formula itself might have been simple, but the volume of custom made working in the Italian darned hard work. Thankfully we were joined between twelve and two by sixty-eight-year-old Dulcie, who'd been working these hours ever since Giovanna took over the place.

She might have been getting on, but she was lot fitter than I was and she was wearing far more sensible shoes. She was very skinny, but somehow sturdy, and she hardly spoke a word while she whirlwinded her way around the place, clearing tables, washing up and tidying around Giovanna and me. She even found time to help me out with the coffee machine when I dropped my guard briefly in the rush and allowed it to sense my fear.

Giovanna was in good voice throughout, but after several repeats of 'Volaré', I began to wish that she would vary her repertoire now and then. Afterwards, when things quietened down and we all stopped work for a coffee, I asked Dulcie what her secret was.

'Two bananas a day,' she said, straight-faced, 'and regular sex with a man under thirty.'

She and Giovanna waited for my response, but when my mouth seized up they both collapsed in laughter. Which made it sound like a joke—but there was something about the look in Dulcie's twinkling eyes that left me wondering. As did her surprisingly youthful and husky voice, which would have made her a fortune on one of those naughty one-pound-a-minute sex lines.

They both told me what a great job I'd done and I felt ridiculously pleased with myself. I might have been sweaty and very dishevelled, but I felt that I'd actually achieved something for a change.

'Where did Marco go, by the way?' I asked Giovanna as she topped up my cup with decaf. I'd drunk about five cups already so far, and if it had been the real thing I would have been wired by now.

Giovanna threw up her hands. 'Spain!' She practically spat

out the word. 'Crazy boy, ay? I mean-a why the Costa Del Sol when he could 'ave-a gone to beautiful Italian Riviera?'

I considered asking Giovanna about her family then—I guessed that there must be a good reason why she hadn't returned to Milan when she got pregnant with Marco—but I decided I didn't know her quite well enough yet.

After Dulcie left it was mostly about serving biscotti and coffee in between helping Giovanna clear up in the back kitchen. I tried wheedling the secret recipe out of her, but when she said I could only have it if I married Marco I let matters drop.

At five-thirty my feet were so sore that I'd taken my shoes off behind the counter. By now I was over my fear of someone I knew coming in and seeing me in such a state—hair dragged back, unkempt and make-up-less—and, as always happens when you let your guard slip...someone came in who knew me.

'Libby!' I said. 'How nice to see you.' The problem with colouring like mine is that there is no hiding embarrassment, and I can never get away with the little lies that blondes and brunettes take for granted. It was OK if I had a script, so to speak, as when I'd adapted the newspaper article into a cautionary tale for three eager young women. My real problem though, is with off-the-cuff stuff. The tiniest fib can turn me the colour of an overripe tomato, and I was both deeply embarrassed *and* lying as well as I pretended to be pleased to see her.

She looked remarkably smart and attractive, for Libby. That sounds unkind, but she wasn't the sort who usually made much of an effort. So to see her like this, in a well-cut black suit and her hair all shiny—and it looked as if she'd coloured it too; I was pretty sure that it used to be mouse, while now it had a distinctly copper hue—was a surprise.

'You look nice,' I added truthfully, then I remembered what she'd said about her job. 'Been for an interview or something?' As I spoke I was trying to shove my swollen feet back into my shrunken shoes.

She looked surprised. 'No, I've just finished work and thought I'd see how you were getting on.'

I thought I detected the hint of a gloat in her expression. But that could just be envy, I supposed. Because she looked so smart and well groomed while I looked as if I'd spent the day fixing a boiler.

'Well, as you can see,' I said, feigning a devil-may-care demeanour, 'I've come to no real harm from a bit of honest graft.'

She looked at me the way someone looks at people who've got a nasty illness and are trying to make light of it—pityingly.

'Actually, I was wondering if you fancied having a drink when you knock off.'

It was tempting. She looked excited, as if she had some news she wanted to tell me, and although I was still of a mind to drop the whole Dan and Sarah thing, I couldn't help be curious about his claim to be single. Maybe he was now. Maybe Libby had come to tell me that it was all over with Aisling.

'OK,' I said, 'but I don't finish till six.' I looked over at the only customers we had at the moment—a family of four. The kids were currently squirting milkshake at one another through their straws.

Libby looked disappointed. She glanced at her wristwatch.

'Oh, dear,' she said. 'I have to get back soon. I was rather hoping you were finishing now. Maybe you could ask if you could leave early.'

'I don't think so,' I replied, a little shocked by her pushiness. 'This is my first day and Giovanna is clearing up in the back. I really should be helping her.'

'Why don't you ask her?' Libby pressed.

'Ask-a me what?' Giovanna said, appearing now in the kitchen doorway.

'If she could leave early this evening,' Libby said for me, and I cringed with embarrassment.

I shook my head. 'I can't possibly leave with customers still here,' I said.

'They look as though they're about to leave,' Libby said, turning towards the family of four. And, indeed, just at that moment the father, clearly exhausted by a day's serious shopping, began gathering up a large collection of plastic carrier bags.

'Of course it is-a OK, Joanna. We weel be closing soon and I can-a easily finish up on-a my own.'

I still wasn't happy. I still felt that Libby was being just a bit too pushy. But Giovanna seemed adamant. She even fetched my coat and scarf from the kitchen.

'It's-a your first day, Joanna, and-a your feet—' she looked down at them, crammed into my shoes '—they look-a sad and sorry for themselves. You must-a wear only comfortable shoes in-a future.'

Jo hobbled alongside Libby to the nearest pub, which was already bustling with after-work drinkers. They both ordered diet Coke, and because most people seemed to prefer to stand they managed to find a table in a dark corner of the bar.

'I thought you'd like to hear what happened at the weekend,' Libby said as they removed their coats and scarves.

'The weekend?' Jo frowned as she shuffled up on the banquette seating to make room for Libby.

'Yes. With Dan and Aisling.'

'Go on,' she said expectantly.

'We all went out together on Saturday night, me and Steve—you know Steve, don't you?—and Dan and Aisling.'

Joanna nodded, as if she wasn't surprised. 'Then the weekend at Dan's place was cancelled?'

Libby had forgotten about that, but it didn't matter.

'Apparently, yes.'

Jo looked pleased, and Libby looked forward to wiping the smug smile off her face, but she didn't get the chance.

'It's over with them, isn't it?' she said.

Libby looked at her sharply.

'What makes you say that?'

'I know someone who knows Dan,' Joanna said carefully, 'and they told me that he is well, *single*.'

'Single!'

Jo looked puzzled. 'That *was* what you were going to tell me, wasn't it?'

'I was going to tell you that it was over between them, yes...' She hesitated. This had thrown her off balance completely. She'd been about to explain how *she* was with Dan now, but she was worried about this 'someone' who was supposed to know Dan. 'Who is this person you've been speaking to?'

'I can't tell you that,' Joanna said firmly. 'But they do seem to know what they're talking about.'

Libby's mind was racing.

'When did you speak to them?'

'Yesterday,' Jo answered eagerly.

'You're sure it was yesterday and not Saturday?' If it had been Saturday, that would be fine. On Saturday Dan had still been officially single, but not any more. They'd spent the night together since then, and OK, so they didn't have sex— he'd been too drunk for that—but he had kissed her in the club, and he'd kissed her again before he went unconscious.

'Yes,' she confirmed. 'It was definitely yesterday.' She grinned with pleasure and then looked at Libby expectantly again. 'So come on,' she said, 'tell me what happened.'

But Libby didn't feel like talking now. She just wanted to get back to the flat, find out from Dan what was going on. He couldn't expect to spend the night with her and then still claim to be *single*.

'I can't,' said Libby, glancing at her watch. 'I've got to go.'

Joanna looked surprised and disappointed, but Libby couldn't help that.

She stood up, and as Joanna reached for her bag on the floor Libby noticed her scarf on the seating between them. Without thinking why she was doing it, she snatched it up and slipped it under her coat.

'Is Aisling upset?' Joanna persisted as she followed Libby out of the pub.

'She got off with Steve at the club,' Libby found herself saying, 'so I shouldn't think so.'

They were outside the pub now, and Libby had turned and started off down the road, away from Joanna, when she heard her call out.

'Which club were you at?'

She turned back briefly, annoyed at such a stupid and irrelevant question.

'Roller Coaster,' she said, 'though I fail to see what difference that makes.'

It shouldn't make any difference at all, but it did to me. Dan always professed to hate club life—the crush—the wrong sort of music. The only time he'd been in one before was the night I'd met him at Zoot. It was my regular Friday night haunt at the time, and he'd been dragged there kicking and screaming by some band he'd spent the early part of the evening interviewing. And because he was the best thing I'd ever seen in the place, I'd made a beeline for him straight away.

That had definitely been one of our problems. It had been fine for the first year. I'd been happy to stay in with Dan most evenings, listening to music, curling up with him on his green sofa. Then I started my new well-paid job and began insisting that we went out more. I had real money to spend for the first time ever and maybe it just went to my head a bit. He went along with it for a while, but long drinking and gossiping sessions with my new work colleagues just wasn't what he wanted to do.

I told him he was boring and he told me my new friends were a waste of space.

When I finally limped into my flat, kicking my shoes off *en route* to my bedroom, I switched on the laptop and read my mail. There were several responses from my old clients, and they were on the whole pretty favourable. I sent copies on to Sid, and then went into Sarah's Hotmail account.

I wasn't sure what to make of this recent turn of events. I was glad it was over with Dan and Aisling, I supposed, and I was definitely glad that Dan hadn't been lying to Sarah about his single status, but where did that leave me now? I thought about what Sid had said and considered calling Dan, but what would I say after all this time?

And what if he thought I wanted to get back with him?

And did I want to get back with him?

The very fact that I didn't know the answer to this decided me. Right or wrong, it seemed far better to find out what I needed to know through a third party, a third party who seemed to be getting along far better with Dan than I did—near the end anyway.

I'd kept copies of our exchanges and I read them now, and then I began a new message.

> *Dear Dan*
> *Sorry about the interruption. So why didn't you go after your girlfriend when she left?*
> *Sarah*

I sent off the message, went to the kitchen to open a tin of beans, and remembered the note Giovanna had given to me from Marco. I was still wearing my coat, so I slipped my hand in my pocket and took it out. I felt a bit of a tingle as I opened it up. I was remembering the kiss again and, well, it was quite a nice kiss.

It was a single sheet of white Basildon Bond, and I could see at first glance that there wasn't very much written on it.

Bella Joanna, it began and I flushed with pleasure.

> *Can't wait to do it again.*
> *I'll call you.*
> *Marco*

I smiled to myself and folded the paper again and put it back in the envelope. I put it down on the work surface and took off my coat. And as I was doing it I realised I didn't have my favourite scarf.

Libby had headed straight for the nearest taxi rank. She was anxious to get back quickly and confront Dan with this claim of his of being 'single'. However, as she got closer to home it occurred to her that confrontation might be the wrong way to go about things. Besides which, it was early days, and after the experience he'd had with Joanna he might just be playing it cautiously where she was concerned.

With this change of heart, she asked the driver to drop her outside a row of retail outlets not far from the flat and tipped him generously. In the Chinese takeaway she ordered chicken in black been sauce, a prawn chow mein, some rice and a bag of prawn crackers. While it was being cooked, she nipped next door to a branch of Threshers. She went for a good white Bordeaux, aged in oak and already chilled, and added a small box of Belgian chocolates that would do for afters.

When she'd picked up the food, she made her way

home. It had started to rain, but she was in such a good mood now that she didn't care. She didn't bother to go up to her own flat first. There was no point in risking the food getting cold, and she knew from a quick check in the downstairs hall mirror—put there by Aisling, of course— that she looked fine.

She rapped on Dan's door and imagined the delighted surprise on his face when he opened up and saw her there, laden with goodies.

She rapped again, a little harder this time, and when that still didn't produce the desired result she put the bags down on the floor and knocked really hard. She knocked really hard several times, until she heard a voice calling up to her from the hallway below. A high-pitched, silly voice that could only belong to Aisling.

'What's going on? Is there a fire or something?'

Libby took a deep, calming breath and moved slowly to the top of the stairs.

'Just trying to make Dan hear. I think he must have dropped off or something.'

Aisling looked up at her curiously. 'Didn't it occur to you that he might not be in?'

'Of course he's in. He's writing his book and—' She didn't finish what she was going to say—that he should be expecting her...

'But he isn't,' Aisling said coolly. 'He had to go out. There was some band in town that he couldn't miss, apparently. Never heard of them myself, but that doesn't mean much, I suppose.' There was a pause, then, 'Can I smell Chinese?'

Libby nodded. It was important not to show her disappointment. 'I thought Dan would be starving, but since he's out would you like to share it?' It wouldn't do any harm to get chummy with Aisling, she thought.

'Wouldn't say no,' Aisling replied. 'Shall I come to you, or would you like to come down here?'

'I'll come to you.'

'Great,' Aisling chirped happily. 'I'll warm some plates.'

I got up really early the following morning, did the best I could in the putting-up-my-hair department, and with my feet now comfortably ensconced in cushioned trainers I made my way happily enough to work—despite the fact that I hadn't yet had a reply from Dan.

This might have been because Marco had been occupying a lot of my thoughts since reading that note, and every time Giovanna mentioned his name—and she did quite a lot that morning—I'm sure I went red. I know I'd always believed that he wasn't my type, but I'd now got to thinking that just because he wasn't partner/husband potential as far as I was concerned, it didn't mean that we couldn't have great sex.

I kept reminding myself that at the ripe old age of twenty-six I'd only had three sexual partners. Which was practically unheard of these days. Worse was the fact that one of the three hardly even counted. That was Jon Braithwaite, I am ashamed to say—Nic's boyfriend—who seduced me when I was drunk on cheap cider. I can't remember much about it, but it certainly wasn't an experience I chose to repeat. In fact it put me off sex for another four years.

Until I met Bill, that is, on my travels through India. That was good, no doubt about it, but it only lasted three weeks because Bill had to head back to Australia. It wasn't love or anything, but it gave me a taster of how good things could be. And then of course there was Dan. The best by a very long stretch, but with so little experience under my belt how was I to know if it could be even better?

And Marco, it had it be said, was a very sexy man.

In my sensible footwear I got though the busy lunchtime period without so much as a twinge. And it was while I was enjoying a post-rush hour coffee break with Dulcie and Giovanna that my father, of all people, appeared at the counter.

I stared at him for quite a few seconds before I fully accepted that it was my father. 'How did you know I was here?' I finally managed.

'When I couldn't get you at the flat I rang Cassandra,' he answered dolefully.

Cassandra is Cass's real name, the one on her birth certificate, but everyone in the world calls her Cass—except my dad.

Giovanna and Dulcie had stopped talking now, and I remembered my manners and introduced them all. And the moment Giovanna and my dad shook hands across the counter I got a premonition. It was actually a physical thing, a prickle of electricity on the skin of my right forearm. Why that particular spot, I do not know, but it's been like that since I was a kid. It happened the night I met Dan, as a matter of fact, so I know what I'm talking about.

Dulcie felt it too. Maybe not the same kind of forearm

prickle, but I just knew by the way that one of her pencilled eyebrows shot up a fraction that she had sensed something as well. Giovanna just wasn't her usual extrovert self. Instead of making the fuss I'd expected about meeting a parent of mine, she just quietly insisted that I joined my father while he drank the coffee she also insisted he have for free.

'What are you doing here, anyway?' I asked when we were seated.

'I just thought it would be nice to see you, that's all,' he said as he glanced shiftily over my shoulder towards the counter. I jerked my head round just quickly enough to catch Giovanna's glance before she looked guiltily away.

'Do you know Giovanna, by any chance?' I asked my father, who—and I don't know why—just looked a bit different than usual today. I've never thought much about his looks, but it occurred to me then that he was quite a handsome bloke. My mother was right. I certainly hadn't got my looks from Dad's side of the family. His skin seemed almost permanently tanned, and his hair was so dark it was almost black—or had been before middle age crept up on him and started turning it grey at the edges.

'Of course I don't,' he replied. 'I've never been in here before in my life.' Despite his dark skin I watched the redness spread like ink on blotting paper across his face. It wasn't something you expected from a man of his age, but I realised now that he'd always blushed easily and it was seemingly the only characteristic that I'd taken from him. I also realised what was going on. He fancied Giovanna rotten and she fancied him back. I wasn't sure what to do with this knowledge, but I do know it made me think of my father differently after that.

'Mum came up on Friday,' I said. It wasn't a deliberate attempt to take the wind out of his sails of ardour, but it did the trick. He looked quite startled at first, and then he sighed.

'She told me,' he said.

'Did she tell you what she tried dragging me into?' I said, surprised to find myself still angry with her.

He looked vaguely puzzled, but not particularly interested, so I decided to drop the subject. There didn't seem much point in telling him anyway. We both knew that his wife was a law unto herself.

'I need to tell you something,' he said.

Oh, dear, I didn't like the sound of that.

'What?'

'Your mother and I have been living apart for over a fortnight.'

I thought about laughing, but it didn't seem very appropriate because I knew that he wasn't joking. The really funny thing was that although I was surprised it wasn't for the obvious reasons. What perplexed me most was why it had taken so long. She might be my mother, but if I were a man I'd have been on my bike years ago.

'I take it it's *you* that's left *her*?' I said, feeling oddly proud of him.

'Sort of,' he said, and I decided not to spoil things by pressing the matter further just at the moment.

'Where are you staying?'

'In a guest house.'

'That must be expensive,' I said. 'Not to mention lonely.'

He lowered his eyelids and I reached for his hand over the table. He allowed me to squeeze it briefly before withdrawing it.

'Why don't you come and stay with me?' I said, without really thinking.

'I couldn't,' he said. 'Your mother wouldn't like it. She'd think you were taking sides.'

'Hah! My mother didn't even have the decency to tell me

what's happened. And besides, she should be pleased you'll be saving some money.'

He grinned sadly. 'Well, there is that, I suppose.'

'And it's handier for work,' I said, feeling strangely mature and grown up.

He nodded, and looked me full in the face for the first time. 'To be honest, I hoped you'd say that, but I promise it won't be for long. And I'll stay out of your way if you have people over.'

'Dad,' I said seriously, 'I'm as lonely as you are at the moment. You'll be doing me a favour. And so long as you don't mind sleeping on the sofa bed and chipping in a bit for the bills, I think it's going to work out fine.'

He admitted he already had his stuff with him in the car, and I gave him my key so he could drop it at the flat. He'd taken the day off work and he promised to have something ready for me to eat when I got home. I didn't like the sound of that too much, as my father is a famously terrible cook, but I didn't say anything.

After he left, Giovanna was very quiet for some time. And when Dulcie winked at me in a conspiratorial fashion as she left I felt a bit affronted. I wanted to explain that my father was a married man. OK, he might be living apart from his wife presently, but that didn't mean he was fair game. I might think my mother deserved to be left, but only to be taught a lesson, and part of the reason for having Dad stay with me was to keep an eye on him. He was vulnerable at the moment, anyone could see that, and fond as I was of Giovanna I didn't want her damaging the prospect of an eventual reconciliation between my parents.

It was four o'clock before she brought up the subject, which was pretty good going, I thought. I could tell she was

…ions about my father, and I'd been ready

…your *papa* to call in and see you like-a

…earranged cups that didn't need rear-

'Hmm,' I said casually, noting her pale moustache for the first time. I wondered if I should tell her what was going on, but I didn't want to admit that there was any trouble between my parents so I decided it was best to say as little as possible. 'He's going be staying with me for a day or two,' I added, just in case I let it slip at a latter stage. But apart from that I remained tight-lipped. She tried again a couple of times, fishing for information about my dad, but I ducked and dived until she finally gave up.

Libby was very annoyed with Dan. She'd had to spend hours listening to Aisling prattling on about all the people she knew, and even when she finally managed to get away he still wasn't back. She'd left a note pinned to his door, asking him to ring when he got in, but he hadn't. And she knew that he had come back because the note was gone when she went to work in the morning.

When she'd managed to get a word in edgewise with Aisling, and told her she'd spent the night with Dan, Aisling's response had rankled with her.

'But he was rather drunk,' she said, in that innocent way she had that didn't fool Libby one little bit.

But at least her one-sided conversation with Aisling had assured her that she was no longer interested in Dan herself. Which was something, Libby supposed. She'd been worried that Dan would eventually give in to her full-on attentions, but it seemed now that Aisling had given up on him. In her usual silly and naïve way, she'd frankly admitted that she'd fancied Dan rotten—but not any more, apparently. It was surprising to Libby that she seemed to be so taken with Steve. With all those flash friends of hers he seemed a very dull choice. But there was no accounting for tastes, she reminded herself.

She'd thought about ringing Dan from work. She'd thought about little else, as a matter of fact. So much that it had been very hard to concentrate on work. So, when Nicola Dick appeared at her desk in the late afternoon she felt a bit uncomfortable. She and the other recruitment consultants had been issued with a list and instructions to try and create some new business. It was a cold-calling exercise that Libby did not feel very enthusiastic about at the best of times. And today, with so much else on her mind, it was the very last thing she felt like doing. So she hadn't.

'Had a good day?' Nicola enquired as she parked her bony bottom on the edge of Libby's desk. She folded her arms and looked intently at Libby as she waited for a reply. She was wearing a very expensive grey suit, and at the V of the neckline a crucifix glinted under a ceiling spotlight.

'I've got a few leads,' she lied.

'You've done something to your hair,' Nicola observed, surprisingly changing the subject. Whether she liked what Libby had done to her hair she didn't say.

Libby shrugged. Nicola's own hair was short and spiky blonde and suited what Libby regarded as her rodent-like features. She was feeling edgy, but then she suddenly had an idea. Something she hoped would distract Nicola from digging too deeply into what she'd been up to for most of the day.

'I understand that you know Joanna Hurst,' Libby said. It was probably the first thing she had ever said to Nicola that wasn't directly connected with work and Nicola looked very surprised.

'Yes,' she answered cautiously, and then nodded and smiled as if she understood. 'Has she been on to you for a job?'

Libby shook her head. 'No...' She coughed uneasily. 'It's just that she mentioned you—said that you were an old school-friend.'

Nicola raised one of her finely plucked eyebrows. 'I wouldn't go that far,' she said. 'We were at school together, but I wouldn't call her a *friend*.'

It looked for a moment as if that was the end of the matter as far as she was concerned, then Nicola spoke again.

'I understand that she's jobless as well as boyfriendless now,' she said with smug pleasure. 'Pity about the delightful Dan,' Nicola went on with a smile that quickly faded. 'Not surprising, though, really. He's well out of her league.'

It was clear to Libby that Nicola disliked Joanna even more than she disliked her, and it was possible that she could use this situation to her advantage. If she could just create some kind of bond of animosity with her boss against Jo it might take the pressure off her. And there had been quite a lot of pressure of late, including rumours of sackings for those not pulling their weight.

'I agree,' said Libby chummily. 'I live in the flat upstairs from Dan. That's how I know Joanna. But I can't say that I ever liked her much.'

Nicola seemed pleased about this.

'I can't think what he ever saw in her.'

'Me neither,' Libby agreed, pulling a face and shaking her head for added effect. 'The worst bit is that she keeps phoning me up to ask about him. It's quite pathetic, really.'

'I didn't know she still cared,' Nicola said with an interested smirk.

'She's still very cut up. I keep telling her that it's time to move on, but she can't stop quizzing me about who he's seeing and what he's doing.'

'How sad,' Nicola sighed happily. 'She hasn't got much going for her really, has she?'

'Well at least she has a sort of job,' Libby said without thinking.

'Oh?'

Libby nodded. 'She works in the Italian—you know, that café on Carlton Lane.'

Nicola pondered this for a moment. 'Still quite a comedown, though,' she said.

Libby shared a falsely pitying smile with Nicola and hoped very much that she would go away now. But she had miscalculated.

'Well,' Nicola said, changing the subject abruptly, 'I've spoken to everyone else, and I'm satisfied with what most of them have achieved today. Can you tell me about these new leads of yours?'

But Libby couldn't, of course. Normally she would have been able to bluff her way out of tight spot, but her mind at that moment went blank.

'I'm sorry,' she said, backtracking now, 'but I don't think I had a very good list to work from.'

'Your list was no different from anyone else's,' Nicola answered coolly. She stood now, and with her arms still folded peered down at Libby. 'Then I'm afraid that you'll have to leave,' she added with a heavy but insincere sigh.

Despite everything, Libby was genuinely shocked.

'You're sacking me?'

'Shall we say a month's notice? We can't afford to carry dead weight, and you have been under-performing for quite some time now. Today, in effect, was your last chance.'

'You can't do that,' Libby answered hotly.

'Oh, yes, I can. And that's another thing,' she said. 'Your attitude. It sometimes borders on rudeness. I'm afraid I will have to mention that in your reference.'

There was silence suddenly in the office that Libby shared with four other consultants. Everyone had stopped talking on the phone, stopped tapping on their computer keyboards.

'And yours,' Libby responded, icily now, 'borders on the ridiculous. Do you know how stupid you look with that thing round your neck? Pretending to be such a good Christian when everyone knows what a bitch you really are!' She glanced around the office as if hoping for back-up, but no one looked up from their desks.

Nicola's small eyes were as wide as they'd go now, with indignation.

'How dare you?' she screeched. Then, because she must have realised how crazed she appeared, she lowered her voice. 'There can be no comfortable working relationship between us now that you have made your feelings about me so clear,' she said. 'I must therefore ask you to clear your desk immediately.'

'Suits me fine,' Libby said with a shrug. She stood up and glared back at Nicola so hard that her boss actually flinched and stepped back. 'But expect to hear from my solicitor very soon.'

With that she gathered up her bag, gave Nicola one final withering look, and with as much dignity as she could muster strode purposefully out of the office.

'She left a couple of months ago and I've been feeding you bullshit ever since.'

Dan was on the phone to his mother again, and Jo had come up in the conversation as usual. For some reason he had decided that the time had come to tell her the truth.

'I guessed that something was up,' she said. 'But I'm not sure why you felt you had to do that. Feed me bullshit, I mean.'

'I was hoping that she'd come back, I suppose.'

There was a short silence at the other end of the line. 'Did you try and get her back?'

'It was her decision, Mum.'

'Honestly, Dan. I thought I'd done a better job on you, I really did.'

'Are you saying I should have done the Stone Age thing and dragged her back to my cave?'

'More or less, yes. A woman needs to feel that she's wanted passionately.'

Dan wasn't sure that he liked the sound of that very much. For some reason he didn't care to think of his mother as a passionate woman. It conjured up all sorts of things he preferred not to contemplate.

'And don't be such a prude,' she said, apparently reading his mind. 'I might be your mother but I'm a woman as well. And anyway,' she went on quickly, 'what went wrong? What did you do to make her leave in the first place?'

'Thanks for the vote of confidence,' he said. 'What makes you think it was all my fault?'

'I expect it was both your faults,' she replied with a sigh, 'but something must have happened to make her actually leave.'

Dan turned and looked out of his bedroom window. On the other side of the street was a row of Victorian houses just like the one he was in, but beyond them, out of sight from the window, was Finchling Park, a place where he and Jo had often been for a stroll on summer evenings. He thought again about what Sarah had said of her former boyfriend. *He upset me with something he said.* But, although Dan had been racking his brains ever since, he couldn't think of anything he had said that could possibly have upset Jo so much.

'It isn't as simple as that,' he finally said. 'I don't think there was one particular incident that made her leave. And anyway, she's seeing someone else now.'

There was a short silence, then, 'And what about you? Have you been seeing anyone else?'

Dan hesitated. He picked up a pencil and started rolling it around in his free hand.

'Well, there is someone who lives in one of the other flats, but...'

'But what?'

He regretted it immediately. He had been going to give her the full rundown on his problems with Libby, but since his mother already seemed to have a low enough opinion of him he left it at that.

'But nothing,' he said.

My heart sank when I got home and saw the state of my formally pristine kitchen. My father was oblivious to the mess he'd made, creating what was without any doubt the most disgusting mess that had ever been set before me. He called it chilli con carne, but it could just as easily have been a dish of reheated, two-day-old vomit.

He made me sit down the moment I entered the kitchen, and was so pleased with his efforts that I hid my dismay as he spooned the revolting concoction onto two plates. Until I tried forking a red kidney bean, that is.

'Er, Dad?' I said as he beamed at me over the table. 'Did you get the beans from a packet, by any chance?'

Still wearing a flower-patterned oven mitt on each of his hands, he nodded happily. 'They're organic,' he said. 'A bit more expensive, but much better for us.'

'Well, I'm sorry, Dad, but you're supposed to soak dried kidney beans overnight before you use them for cooking.'

'I thought they were a bit hard,' he said, determinedly cheerful, 'but then I remembered you liked things a bit crunchy.'

If only he hadn't been serious—

'Vegetables, maybe,' I said with a sigh, 'but these beans are so hard it could cost a fortune in dental repair work.' And that wasn't even the worst of the problem. 'And I'm sorry, but they can be dangerous if they're not cooked properly.'

He looked completely bewildered as he removed his oven mitts. 'Are you telling me that this meal is inedible?'

'I'm afraid so.' I was tempted to tell him he should have read the packet, but I didn't want to rub his nose in it. 'And I really am sorry,' I added instead, 'because it looks so good and you've obviously gone to such a lot of trouble.' I glanced round at the bombsite that was my kitchen and wondered how long it was going to take me to clear the place up.

He looked despondently at the mess on his plate. 'What if we pick the beans out?' he suggested, without much enthusiasm.

I shook my head firmly. 'If there is a problem with the beans it might have affected the rest,' I said, unsure of my facts but not willing to take a risk even to please him.

He stared a bit longer at his efforts and then looked up at me with a wry grin. 'Can't say I fancied it anyway. It does look a bit like sick.'

'Minus the carrots,' I said, and we managed a weak laugh together.

'How about I do the cooking in future?' I said as we washed up together. 'And you just chip in for the food.'

'Fine by me,' he said, plainly relieved. 'And thanks for not biting my head off. If that had been your mother she'd have gone crazy.'

I'd have gone crazy myself if it had been Dan, I thought, remembering how often I'd trashed his culinary efforts. And he was a far better cook than my father ever could be.

'Which reminds me,' I said. 'I think I should call her this evening and tell her what's happening. If she finds out from someone else she'll just think we're being sneaky.'

We ate the last of my old standby, Marmite with toast, and when Dad took up my suggestion to have a long soak in the bath I rang my mother—but she wasn't in. I noticed she'd already changed the answer-phone message. It was no longer 'Mary and Andrew' who couldn't take the call at the moment, but just 'Mary', and she sounded so pleased with her new single status that it made my stomach churn up a bit. Nevertheless, I was pretty relieved that I wasn't required to speak to her directly.

I kept my message brief. 'Just ringing to let you know that Dad's staying with me for a bit. We thought it made sense till you sort things out.'

I made Dad's bed up on the sofa and took myself off to bed at about eleven o'clock. I was very tired, but I knew I wouldn't be able to get to sleep till I checked to see if Dan had got round to replying to my last message.

He had.

Dear Sarah
Why didn't I go after Jo when she left?

I felt queasy when I saw my name there. It was OK when it was Dan's anonymous girlfriend we were talking about, but now it was beginning to feel very strange. The message went on.

Funny, but someone else asked me that same question today,
and I guess the answer is that old demon called pride.
So what do you really look like, Sarah Daly?
Dan

PS Do you ever visit this friend of yours in Leeds?

I had some thinking to do about the first part of the
e-mail, but I felt quite excited by the PS—especially now that
I knew he was free. Was it a hint that he'd like to meet Sarah?
And, if so, was I completely crazy in wishing for a moment
that I really *were* Sarah Daly? Some artist in London who
might just be about to embark on a brand-new relationship
with a gorgeous man, without any of the luggage that Dan
and Jo had acquired? Probably. But the thought really did
only last for a moment.

I decided to keep my reply brief and light-hearted in the
end. It had all got a bit heavy of late, and I wanted to restore
some flirty sparkle.

Dear Dan
It's hard to describe yourself honestly, so the best I can say
is that I'm averagely gorgeous!
Sarah

And then, just to prove that some of my mental health was
restored...

PS No current plans to visit Leeds.

chapter 11

Libby had spent part of the morning with an Armani-clad lawyer whose office was above a discount shoe shop in one of the seedier parts of Leeds. Specialising in unfair dismissal and personal injury claims, the aptly named Nigel Leach was not at the most reputable end of the legal profession, but his confidence made up for his shortfalls. He seemed to think there would be no problem at all in obtaining an acceptable settlement from her former employers and agreed to act on a no win, no fee basis. In other words she had nothing whatever to lose.

'They usually fall at the first fence,' Nigel Leach assured Libby glibly, 'so long as we're not too greedy, that is.'

Despite the rundown state of his office, it was clear from his suit that he was relatively successful—though Libby judged this to be based more on volume of business rather than the level of compensation he managed to obtain for individual clients. But the fact was that Libby didn't really care how much she got. This was a matter of principle. The Nicola Dicks of this world couldn't go around getting rid of people just because it suited them, using any old excuse that happened to take their fancy. And the point was, while dealing with a compensation claim might be a commonplace inconvenience for some people, Libby had good reason to suspect that it would affect Nicola more than most.

'Quick results are more important to me,' she told him coolly. 'I've got a feeling the company might be in trouble, so the sooner we get moving the better.'

'We invariably win because employers usually want to avoid bad publicity,' he said with a satisfied nod, 'and the shakier the business the more likely this is the case.'

Nigel Leach was not unattractive, as it happened—not as far as Libby was concerned anyway. He was tall, sturdy, and handsome in an obvious don't-I-know-it, let's-pile-on-the-hair-gel sort of way, but she quite liked that. He wasn't in Dan's league, of course, but then she wasn't very happy with him at the moment.

She'd gone round to see him last night after work, and he wouldn't let her in his flat.

'Sorry, Lib,' he said, looking harassed as he stood there in the frame of his doorway. 'I've got to keep working, I'm afraid.'

She'd wanted to tell him about losing her job, but she held it back and mentioned a more pressing matter instead.

'I've had a call from Baz,' she told him quickly. 'He's had an offer for one of the rarer albums, but it's a lot less than the asking price. Do you think I should take it or hold out longer?'

Dan shook his head firmly. 'You're going to have to make that decision yourself, I'm afraid. I don't want it on my conscience if you're disappointed.'

She'd felt hurt by that, and he must have seen it because then his manner softened a little.

'Why don't you come round for a drink tomorrow night?' he said. 'I think that we need to talk.'

Which had quite cheered her up at the time, but since she'd had a chance to think about it she'd decided those words had an ominous ring.

Nigel Leach shook her hand warmly and promised to be in touch very soon.

When she got back to the flat there was another telephone message waiting from Baz—more news, he said, about her collection. He asked her to call him back, and when she did he informed her that he might have found a buyer for most of the records.

'Only he seems quite keen to meet the seller,' he said. 'He's the cautious type, and he wants to be sure that everything is above board, so to speak.'

But there was nobody more cautious than Libby, and she didn't like the sound of this one little bit.

'I thought I'd made myself clear about that,' she told him. 'And anyway, isn't it a bit *irregular?*' A bit fishy, she meant, but she could hardly say that.

'Not when there isn't any proof of ownership. It's up to you, of course, but I don't think you'll get a better offer.'

'What's this would-be buyer's name?' she asked carefully.

She could hear the sound of papers being shuffled, pictured Baz's disordered desk.

'Waites,' he came back. 'Michael Waites. He's from Manchester, apparently.'

It sounded OK, but she still wasn't sure.

'I'll need to think about it and ring you back.'

She'd just made herself a pot of freshly brewed strong coffee when she heard a knock on her door.

As was often the case, it looked as if Aisling was off to some fancy dress party. She was wearing a netted green satin skirt with a violent pink cardigan, and this on a Wednesday, midday in November. The hair extensions were currently gathered into a Fifties ponytail, with some of the false hair wrapped round the elastic.

'I saw you come in a while ago and I wondered if everything was OK?' she said. 'You're not ill or anything, are you?'

It was quite hard not to like Aisling, even if she did look and sound ridiculous, and seeing her now had triggered off the beginning of an idea in Libby's head.

'Come in,' she said.

As she poured an extra mug of coffee for Aisling, she told her that she had been made redundant.

'Which means the quicker I sell that vinyl now, the better.'

Aisling knew all about Libby's collection after the other night, and she nodded her head sympathetically. They took the mugs back to the plainly decorated sitting room and sat side by side on Libby's stripe-patterned sofa.

'In fact you could be a great help to me, if you wouldn't mind.'

Aisling looked at her with wide-eyed surprise. 'I'd love to help if I can.'

Libby smiled warmly at her. 'Well,' she began, 'it's like this...'

On Sid's instructions, I made a few follow-up calls to my old clients on my mobile during a half-hour break that Giovanna insisted I take when I told her about Sid's plans for Pisus. She was very excited for us and left me alone to make the calls from the back room. It seemed a bit odd, ringing important clients from the kitchen of an Italian café, but the responses I got were quite encouraging. Five out of the seven on my list had agreed to meetings with Sid over the next couple of days, and the others said that they would get back to me later.

One of the clients had been particularly pleased to hear

from me. Tim Bailey, who owned a chain of camera shops, had always made it clear that he liked me. He'd known I was living with someone, though, and had never come on really strong, but he'd clearly given me to understand that there was an opening in his affections if my circumstances ever altered.

'So,' he said, when he took my call, 'any other changes I should know about?'

I could hear the smile in his voice and I knew that he meant changes of a *personal* nature. I was tempted to tell him about Dan and me, but I thought it was best to stick to business.

'Only good ones,' I said. 'I honestly believe that with Sid in charge the management of your website can only improve.'

He chuckled at that. 'Are you going to be there at the meeting?' he said.

'I'm afraid not. I've got prior engagements for the rest of the week,' I said as I stirred pasta sauce with my free hand.

'Well, hopefully see you very soon,' he said. 'Oh, and good luck. I admire your enterprise.'

'Thanks,' I said, and I felt a little flutter of pleasure at being taken so seriously as a fledgling businesswoman.

Sid seemed quite pleased with me as well, when I called to tell him the news.

'We'll need someone else to help get things off the ground,' he said. 'A good all-rounder who's not afraid of hard work. Know anyone like that?'

I thought of all the people I'd worked with at Pisus, but none of them fitted that description. They were either very afraid of hard work or they had very specific job descriptions.

'I do know someone like that,' I said, suddenly inspired, 'the only problem is that she isn't much of a risk-taker.' And joining Sid and me in trying to revive a company that had already gone bust seemed a heck of a risk for someone who cared about job security as much as Cass did.

'Try her anyway,' Sid instructed, very much in boss mode, 'and if she really is any good I'll definitely make it worth her while.'

And then later, just when I thought I'd got used to the idea of people seeing me serving behind the counter of the Italian, Nicola Dick made an appearance and I was back to square one—self-conscious and insecure.

'I heard you were working in here,' she said, down her nose, 'but I just had to see it for myself.'

I was glad Giovanna had just popped out to Boots for a while. I don't think she'd have taken too kindly to someone sneering at her café the way Nicola was so obviously doing.

'Imagine,' she went on smugly before I could get a word in, 'a descendant of the aristocracy reduced to serving up spaghetti and cappuccinos.'

Oh, no, I thought, cringing inside. That foolishly misguided mother of mine had gone right ahead and told everyone that ridiculous story about the Fothershaws. But the important thing, I told myself, was not to make things worse by taking the bait...

'Did you want something?' I said, in a dignified if frosty manner.

She ordered a double espresso and I'm ashamed to say that I was seriously tempted to spit in it. Fortunately for her I controlled the temptation, but unfortunately for me there were no other customers waiting to be served, so she did not feel obliged to move to a table.

'I was talking to a friend of yours recently,' she said, and I wondered what was coming now. 'And she tells me that you're still pining after Dan.'

She could only mean Libby, and either Nic was putting an unpleasant spin on an innocent comment made by her, or Libby wasn't the genuine sort of person I'd taken her for.

'I wouldn't call Libby a friend exactly,' I said, smiling

tightly. 'And I've no intention of discussing my feelings for anyone with you.'

Nicola looked a bit thwarted, uncertain now how to respond.

'I understand that congratulations are in order,' I went on pleasantly, moving my eyes to the rather modest engagement ring on her left hand.

She began to smile, pleased that I'd provided the opening for some serious one-upmanship. Only I didn't give her the chance. 'And I also hear that you've found God,' I said, allowing my eyes to linger on the ostentatious gold crucifix in the V of her neckline. 'Do you feel that it's made you a better person? Do you forgive me now for stealing your boyfriend when I was seventeen?'

The static given off by her anger was like an aura, and if it hadn't been for the arrival of two fairly good-looking businessmen at the counter who knows where it might have led? As it was, she gave me a superior look, eyed the businessmen speculatively, and departed the café without even having touched her spit-free double espresso.

I was really annoyed with my dad when he came to the café again. He said that he'd thought it might be nice if we walked back to the flat together, maybe get some shopping on the way home. I might have accepted it at face value if he'd been able to keep his eyes off Giovanna as he was talking.

She wasn't any better either. Like some blushing teenager, she was practically tongue-tied in his company. And I didn't think anything was capable of tying up Giovanna's tongue.

Then he really went for it as we were taking our leave. 'I've got an idea,' he said, bold as brass. 'Since Marco's away at the moment, and Giovanna is all on her own...'

Yes, he invited her round to the flat for a meal on Friday night.

And she, very coyly, accepted.

I was furious with him, especially since I'd already arranged to meet Cass on Friday night. I wanted to talk about the job and I'd decided to ask Sid along as well. She'd never trust my word that Pisus was about to rise from the ashes, but I had an idea that Sid might be more successful. I'd called her quickly on my mobile while Giovanna was still shopping at Boots. And that was another odd thing, come to think of it. She'd come back laden with smelly things—bubble bath and perfume—and some make-up as well. She'd said it was time she treated herself, but after that weird exchange with my dad the first time they met I was a little bit suspicious even then.

Now I was more than a little bit.

I gave Dad a rollicking as we walked home in the darkness. I reminded him that he was still a married man, but he was completely dismissive.

'I think you're overreacting, Jo,' he said, eerily calm. 'I just thought it would be nice to get to know your employer. She seems a very nice lady.'

Oh, yes, she was a very nice lady all right. And gorgeous as well, for her age, despite her moustache.

'And how was I to know that you'd made plans for Friday night?'

'Because that's what people who are twenty-six and single do, Dad. And what about Mum?' I persisted. 'What would she think of you "getting to know" my employer?'

He turned to me now and his expression under the street-lights was serious.

'I know I told you that it was me who'd left, but the truth is your mother threw me out.'

That shut me up for a bit.

'You know what she's like, though.' I eventually started up again. 'She has a sharp tongue, but she loves you. I'm sure.' But was I? I'd seen the way she treated my dad, humiliating him in front of friends, making fun of his Yorkshire accent.

She could be a real cow at times, and deep down I didn't blame him for trying to find a bit of happiness. But I couldn't be seen to be encouraging him, now, could I? And if Mum ever found out I'd allowed him to entertain an attractive woman in my flat she'd never forgive me.

We'd just reached the late-night deli on The Calls, and I stopped him before we went inside.

'Look, Dad...' I said. I told him that it wasn't on. Firmly. I said that if he wanted to have dinner with Giovanna then he'd have to take her out somewhere and I didn't want to know anything about it.

'Thanks, Jo,' he said simply when I'd finished my lecture.

'And besides,' I added with a hint of a grin, 'you don't want to put her off on the first date by serving up one of your specials, now, do you?'

There was a message on the answer-phone when I got in. It was from my mother and it was very brief. 'Check your Hotmail immediately,' she instructed bluntly.

I looked over at Dad, who was hovering in the kitchen door with the deli carrier bag. He looked worried.

'She'll have to wait,' I said. It was a very small act of defiance against my mother's demands.

Dad had bought a nice bottle of red wine that he opened straight away in silence. We drank it quickly as we ate game pie and salad, also in silence, and the time eventually came when I could put off the evil moment no longer.

Dan waited until the end of his work day till he dealt with his e-mails. There was one from his favourite wacko, Jedski, drawing his attention to the fact that three members of Crypt Factory were born under the same astrological sign of Scorpio.

Can that really just be coincidence Dan my man? he wanted to know. *Or are there mysterious forces at work here…?*

He was always supplying 'interesting facts' that supported

his theory of there being something almost supernatural about the band.

Very possibly, Dan wrote back with his tongue in his cheek. *You should set up a website and share your thoughts with a wider audience.*

He dealt with a few other communications and then wrote a reply to Sarah's latest message.

> *Dear Sarah*
> *I'm trying to imagine 'averagely gorgeous' and I can't quite get a handle on it.*
> *I've got to make a trip to London tomorrow and I wondered if we could possibly meet, so I can judge for myself...*
> *Dan*

He'd had a call from his editor during the day. Vantage-Point had a single coming out very soon and there was apparently a buzz going round about it making number one in the charts. This was good news for the book, and the publishers wanted further discussions with its author. He'd tried explaining that with such a tight deadline it didn't make sense to take a day out, but his editor had been adamant. And since she'd offered to pay all his travel expenses he'd reluctantly agreed in the end. But then he'd thought about Sarah Daly and his reluctance had lessened. It would probably be a bit short notice for her, but it still seemed worth a try.

And, come to think of it, a day away from the flat might not be such a bad thing. He had Libby to deal with shortly, and he wasn't looking forward to it one little bit. But he was fed up with trying to avoid her—going out when he should be writing, making endless excuses. And being honest with her had to be better than spending the rest of his life ducking and diving.

He felt very uneasy, though, when he heard her knock on his door, just after seven-thirty.

She looked nice in her red sweater and tight jeans, but wary. As if she had a good idea about what was to come. He had a bottle of cheap red wine from way back, and he opened it now when she followed him into the kitchen.

'I've been fired from my job,' she said gloomily, and he almost faltered in his resolve.

'I'm sorry to hear that,' he said as he pulled the cork. 'Do you want to talk about it?'

'Not really,' she said, as she sat down heavily at the table. 'I'm more interested in what you've got to say at the moment.'

He poured the wine up to the brim of both glasses and passed one to Libby. He sat down opposite her and looked at her directly.

'I'm sorry about the other night,' he said. 'I'm afraid it was a mistake.'

'A mistake?' she repeated as her eyes flashed angrily.

'Only in that I'm not ready for a new relationship yet,' he said, revising the speech he had planned on the hoof. He'd intended to be completely frank, to tell her she wasn't his type any more than Aisling was, but he didn't think that would go down too well. She'd probably tell him he should have thought about that before he spent the night with her, and that was the truth. He should have. 'I suppose I haven't really got Jo out of my system yet, and you did kind of remind me of her the other night.'

'So it's my fault?' she said acidly.

'Of course not. It's not anyone's *fault*. It's more about timing, I suppose.' Which wasn't strictly true, but he was keener than ever now to soften the blow.

'So if I hung around for a couple of months things might be different then, is that what you're saying?'

He wasn't sure if she was being sarcastic or not, but he still couldn't bring himself to tell her the truth: that he didn't fancy her one little bit. Not when he was sober, at any rate.

He took a long swallow of wine. It left a metallic taste in his mouth.

'Maybe,' he said. 'But at the moment I'd prefer it if we could just be friends.'

She got up.

'Well, there's not much else to say, really, is there?'

'I suppose not.' He felt pathetically inadequate at that particular moment.

He got up as well, and followed her to the door.

'Did you decide what to do about the offer you had for that album?' he said, trying to lighten things between them.

'I've had another offer since then—but you're right. I have to make my own decisions, and I have.' She sounded cold, and he hated leaving things like this.

'I have to go to London tomorrow,' he said, 'but maybe we could do something together on Friday night.'

'As friends?' she said sourly.

He nodded, and as he looked at her he could have sworn he saw a glint in her eye.

'What time will you be back tomorrow?'

'Not sure,' he said, still hoping that he would hear from Sarah. 'Late, I expect.'

'Well, have a good time,' she said, and with that she turned and ran up the stairs to her flat.

I went into my Hotmail account and opened the dreaded e-mail from my mother.

Dad was hovering close by, but I told him I'd better read it in private. When he went to the bathroom I steeled myself to read what she had to say for herself. I was expecting the worst, and as usual she didn't disappoint me.

She began in her favourite style—attack.

> *Your father left me to fend for myself and you choose to take his side! The only chance you have of forgiveness is to turn him out straight away.*

It moved quickly into self-pity.

> *After all I've done for you as well. How could you do this to me, Joanna? I only wanted to teach him a lesson. He was supposed to come back after a day or two with his tail between his legs. He'd been getting so belligerent, you see, arguing with me all the time. I don't know what came over him but he just wasn't being himself. So I had to teach him a lesson. You can see that, can't you?*

Then came the real reason she was so upset.

> *He must come home immediately. I can't be held responsible for my actions if he doesn't. I shall be an absolute laughing stock if anyone gets wind of this. Barbara Dick already has scent. She was round here today nosing about, asking awkward questions.*

Then a little added titbit that had nothing to do with her current plight but pleased me enormously.

> *I knew she was after something because she hardly ever gives anything away, and she must have been trying to trade information because she told me that Nicola's company is in trouble. I didn't tell her a thing, though. And if you do right by me now I won't have to.*

Finally, an attempt to put all the responsibility of her future happiness on to me.

You have to send him back, Joanna. I'm relying on you to save our marriage.

If my life had depended on it I would not have turned my father out of the flat and back into my mother's clutches after that. He could stay for ever as far as I was concerned, and if he fell madly in love with Giovanna—well, then, she only had herself to blame.

I never did get round to checking Sarah's messages that night. Dad and I talked for a very long time about my mother, and I didn't feel remotely guilty about taking his side. Someone had to, and if even half of what he told me was true, his life with her had been very much worse than I'd ever imagined. And I'd imagined it was pretty bad anyway.

'But why did she actually throw you out?' I asked. 'She said something about you being argumentative.' Which didn't sound much like my father.

'It was the Dicks,' he said surprisingly. 'We'd been seeing a lot of them for some reason recently—dinner at their place and ours. I'd never liked either of them very much, and I just got fed up with being unfavourably compared to Brian Dick all the time. She even wanted me to take elocution lessons so I could learn to speak "nicely", like Brian.' He shrugged. 'So I told your mother I didn't want them around any more and she was furious. She gave me a few of her famous home truths, which included the fact that I was boring and common.'

'Huh!' I exclaimed in hot, indignant defence of my dad. 'Next to Brian Dick you're the most interesting man on earth.' Which was a bit of a back-handed compliment, but luckily my dad didn't seem to notice.

'And because I was adamant for once in my life, because I refused to go to the Dicks' next time they asked us, your mother decided I needed to be taught a lesson.'

'So she threw you out,' I said, appalled.

He grinned at me and shook his head. 'Little does she know what a big favour she did me.'

'Does that mean you have no intentions of going back?'

'I don't know, Jo,' he said grimly. 'I really don't.'

This was not what I wanted to hear now. I wanted my dad to be strong and stand up against my mother, but it wasn't for me to say. 'And what about Giovanna?'

He looked surprised. 'I think you might be jumping the gun a bit there,' he said. 'I haven't even spoken to her yet about us having a meal on our own. She might turn me down flat.'

But I think by the look we exchanged that we both knew she wouldn't do that.

'Let's just see how things go,' he said.

I felt uneasy when I eventually went to bed. I was just getting used to the fact that my mother and father were splitting up, and now I had this uncomfortable feeling that if she played her cards right she might get him back. And I know it was none of my business, but what was the point if they didn't love one another? And I was certain they hadn't for a very long time.

Then I had a really horrible thought. I remembered comparing Dan unfavourably to my flash new friends—people who mattered so little now that I hadn't spoken to any one of them since Pisus folded. And I'd even accused him of being boring—the same accusation my mother had thrown at my dad.

So did this mean that Dan might be right after all? About me being like my mother.

They say the truth hurts, and that comment had stung me like hell at the time. It frightened the life out of me now.

chapter 12

I didn't sleep too well that night, and I got up very early the following morning. It was still dark outside and I crept around the flat as I made some tea, so as not to wake Dad. He was sleeping soundly on the sofabed, and as I passed him on the way back to my room I moved the curtain a little and looked out of the French window over the river. I found myself wondering what had ever made me think that this was the place I wanted to be. In the weeks I'd been there I don't think I'd ever got any actual pleasure from looking out over that murky stretch of water.

If I'm honest, I think the main reason I took the place was because it was so expensive. Because it was in the coolest part of the city and living there meant I'd *arrived*. Which was more or less the same reason that my mother had insisted on moving to Piper Hill. Because Piper Hill was the place to be *seen* to live—because Piper Hill was where the likes of the Dicks lived.

I took my tea to the bedroom and turned on my computer. When I read Dan's message to Sarah I was relieved I hadn't read it last night. At least now I could honestly say that Sarah didn't receive the message in time. As well as everything else, I'd been giving some thought to what he'd said about *pride* stopping him phoning me, and I'd decided that was bullshit now. The truth was that he was didn't phone me because he was too busy with Aisling, and now it was over with her he was after Sarah.

I wrote back with a certain glee.

> *Sorry, but only just picked up your message (a.m. Thursday) so too late to set anything up, I'm afraid. Hope whatever brings you to the smoke goes well.*
> *Sarah*

I wasn't sure where I was going with this any more, but it still seemed important to keep it on track. Besides, I was curious about the book he was writing.

I wrote therefore:

> *What are you working on at the moment?*

I had to make another cup of tea before I could bring myself to aptly *Hot*mail my mother. I was so mad with her that my hands were actually shaking over the keyboard. Why couldn't she just call, like other mothers? Why did we have to communicate through electronic mail, for God's sake? I knew perfectly well that she'd deliberately left the message while I was at work so that she wouldn't have to speak to me. If she'd wanted to do that she would have called my mobile. But there was one good thing about it, I supposed. At least I could be more honest about my feelings by e-mail. And I felt like being particularly honest with her that morning.

The sun was up now, and I could hear my dad moving about. I called out to tell him that he could use the shower first, and he grunted some sort of affirmative reply.

Dear Mum, I started, and that was about as friendly as it went.

> *How dare you tell me what I should and shouldn't do regarding my father? Now we can go two ways from here on in. You can carry on being demanding and difficult, or you can phone Dad or write him a letter and try and sort things out. THIS IS NOT MY PROBLEM and I refuse to be your go-between.*
> *Joanna*

I sent it quickly before I lost my nerve, then I lost it anyway. The moment the 'Message Sent' sign appeared on my screen I felt like a gibbering wreck.

'That got here quickly,' I said when Giovanna produced a postcard from Marco. I'd felt a bit uncomfortable with her till then, but it sort of broke the ice between us.

It was a typical scene of a Spanish beach, and the words he'd written on the back weren't particularly inspiring either. The usual 'having a nice time' scenario, and how much better the weather was there than in Leeds. He did mention me briefly. Just a quick, 'say hi to Joanna for me', but it was enough to bring a warm glow to my cheeks.

'But it won't be great,' I said of the weather, to distract her attention from my blushes. 'I mean, it is November. And I know you think he should have gone to Italy,' I continued, going on a bit now, 'but he'd have been better off in the Canaries or Florida if it was sunshine he wanted.'

Giovanna frowned at my garrulousness and put the card in her apron pocket.

'He seems 'appy and that is-a what matters.'

She grinned then, and gave me one of her sudden enveloping hugs, and it struck me that she was the very opposite of my cold, self-centred mother.

'You look-a tired Joanna,' she said when she let me go. 'You don't-a sleep too good?'

'Things on my mind,' I said, but I managed a smile.

She held her head quizzically on one side.

'And you don't mind-a your papa asking me to your place for dinner?'

I wondered then if I should tell her that he'd only just left my mother. But that would be to presume she thought there was something romantic about the invitation, so I decided it best if I left the explaining to him.

'I don't mind in the least,' I said, truthfully now, 'but I think the plans might have changed.' I told her that I was going out and that Dad was going to ask her out for a meal in a restaurant.

She looked just a bit embarrassed by this, but definitely not displeased.

Lunchtime was busier than usual, and Dulcie was agog to hear about my father. Between serving and clearing scores of bowls of pasta, I managed to tell her what was going on.

'Do you know, that beautiful woman hasn't been out with a man in years?' she confided in me when Giovanna was in the kitchen. 'It's just been Marco and the café. And it's not as if she hasn't had her chances.'

I didn't doubt that she'd had her chances for a moment.

'Is it because of Marco's father?'

'Could be. He did hurt her very badly.'

'Maybe nobody else has ever lived up to him,' I said slushily.

Dulcie's eyes flashed at this, though. 'What? To a lily-livered swine who left her when she was pregnant?' She was obviously not so sentimentally inclined as I was.

'But she's done very well for herself,' I said, glancing about the café, not even sure as I said it what relevance it was supposed to have.

'Of course she's done well for herself, she works hard, but do you think that makes up for losing her family? Things might be different now, but Giovanna was a good Catholic girl and her family would never have accepted an illegitimate child thirty years ago.' The anger died suddenly and she shook her head sadly. 'What kind of man pretends to be free when he's married to someone else?'

Oh, God, I thought. A man like my father, maybe?

But it was different with my dad, surely, I reasoned. He wasn't some sort of…philanderer. He wouldn't mess Giovanna about and then go back to my mother. Would he?

Then I thought of my mother and how determined she could be when she wanted something. And at the moment she wanted my father back. Not for the right reasons, of course, but what did that matter? It was all about saving face with her. And while it was one thing throwing her husband out of the family home for a while in order to teach him a lesson, it was quite a different story if he chose not to return. And Dad hadn't exactly ruled out the possibility of going back.

I might love my mother, but at that moment I didn't like her one little bit. I was even despairing of my father, who might be a much nicer person than she was but he could be such a drip at times. Just for a moment part of me thought that they deserved one another, but then, out of the blue, it occurred to me that maybe they both deserved better. I didn't think for a moment that she loved him any more than he loved her, and if they got back together they might never get the chance to find something better.

It was my duty, therefore, to keep them apart.

Dulcie hardly got a word out of me for the rest of that busy lunchtime period as I thought long and hard about this, and when Giovanna started off on 'Volaré' I was glad for once, because it meant I didn't need to talk to her either. I was thinking how I was going to deal with my mother, what approach I could take. Nothing presented itself very clearly, but I knew I would have to do it face to face. And when my dad turned up at the café that evening again, and Giovanna blushingly agreed to a meal à deux the following night, I realised that there was no time to waste.

'You go back to the flat on your own,' I told him as we left the Italian. 'I'm going to meet Sid to discuss a few things.' I didn't like lying to him, but I preferred it to explaining why I was going to see my mother.

'See you tomorrow, then,' Libby said as she stepped out on to the pavement in the centre of Leeds.

'I'm looking forward to it,' Aisling said with a smile. They'd gone over the plan on the way into town, and Aisling seemed quite excited about it all. Of course she wasn't aware of the full facts, but that was her fault for being so gullible and failing to ask the right questions.

Libby closed the car door and waved as Aisling forced her way back into the rush hour traffic. She stood there until it was out of sight and then turned and headed quickly for the nearby taxi rank. She'd had no option but to accept the lift when she'd turned down Aisling's invitation to attend a grand opening event on the grounds of a prior engagement. It might have looked strange, and as it turned out the lift provided her with a very neat alibi.

It would be touch and go with timing, of course, but it was still only six o'clock. She could be in and out again by seven and, fingers crossed, that should be all the time that she needed.

I just made the crowded six-thirty shuttle train. I wasn't hopeful of getting a seat, but when I spotted a single space halfway down the carriage I made a triumphant dive at it. Only to find I was sitting right next to Nicola Dick.

I couldn't believe my bad luck. Of all the spaces in all the trains...

She obviously felt the same way, by the look she gave me, and after our recent exchange she didn't even put on a show of friendliness.

'There must be somewhere else you could sit,' she hissed.

'Well, there isn't,' I said, 'and I've been on my feet all day, so if anyone's going to move it'll have to be you.'

She gave me a withering up and down look, and then re-arranged her legs to exclude me from her personal space—something I'd read in an article about body language. Then she drew the newspaper she had been reading closer to her face in order to complete the process. Which suited me just fine. For a while anyway, until the train got going and I remembered what my mother had put in her e-mail about Nicola's recruitment firm.

'I understand things aren't going too well for you at the moment,' I said pleasantly.

As she slowly lowered the newspaper an expression that was both puzzled and irritated revealed itself. 'Are you talking to me?'

'I'm not yet in the habit of talking to myself,' I replied, keeping my voice steady and even.

'Things are going perfectly well for me in every aspect of my life,' she said coolly, but I could see she was troubled. I could see her mind working overtime, wondering what I could possibly know.

'There's no shame in admitting that your firm's in trouble,' I said sympathetically. 'We live in troubled times, after all. And it's just possible that I may be able to help you out.' There had been no discussions with Sid about this as yet, but the way things were going it wouldn't be long before we would need to take on some additional technical staff. He'd called me earlier and told me that two of Pisus's former clients were definitely back on board—including Tim Bailey—and that he had high hopes of getting all of them by the end of the week. And he wouldn't be able to handle seven projects all on his own.

She was obviously speechless, so I decided to enlighten her further. Cautiously, in a vague sort of way, because I didn't want to end up with egg on my face if it all fell apart. I didn't mention any names, either. The last thing I wanted was Nicola contacting Sid behind my back and cutting me out of the picture. It might be Sid's money and brains that were behind the venture, but this was my moment and I was determined to enjoy it.

'So you see, Nicola,' I said rounding up, 'much as I appreciate you suggesting to my mother that I contact you about a possible job...' I left the sentence hanging in the air. To rub her nose in it any further would be overkill. It had given me a great deal of pleasure watching the changing emotions on her face. The scornful disbelief, the uncertainty, and, finally, the big-time squirm, the awful realisation that she could not afford to turn business away. Not even mine.

'And I promise to bear your firm in mind if everything goes according to plan,' I concluded in my best businesslike manner. 'So long as you put in a favourable bid for supplying the staff that we'll need.'

'I'd be only too delighted to talk again when you have something more concrete to discuss,' she said importantly. She folded the newspaper carefully when we moved off after the latest stop, and twitched her small nose. It was hot in the train with so many bodies, and I guessed she was becoming increasingly aware of the aroma of spaghetti sauce that clung to the clothes I hadn't had time to change. Which dented my confidence a bit, and made me more vulnerable to the sly look that appeared on her face. Somehow I just knew it was payback time.

'I'm not in the habit of listening to rumours, Joanna, and correct me if I am wrong—'

Yes, of course. She'd heard about my father moving out and now it was her turn to gloat. I agreed that he had indeed moved out, but I didn't answer any of her probing questions. I said that I didn't know anything, and that was why I was going home.

We were silent after that, but just as we were arriving at the terminus it occurred to me how odd it was that she was on her way home too. That we'd both chosen this particular evening to visit our parents—or *parent* in my particular case.

'There's nothing wrong at your place, I hope,' I asked in an unguarded moment of genuine concern. As far as I knew it was no more like Nicola to go home in the middle of the week than it was for me, and, much as I disliked the Dicks, I wouldn't wish any real harm on any of them. We were making our way to the exit now, swept along by dozens of commuters all keener than I was to reach their homes.

She turned and gave one of her superior looks.

'Of course there's nothing wrong at *my* home,' she said, as if the very suggestion was absurd.

Dan put down his book and glanced at his watch. It was just after seven, and as usual the train was running late. He'd hoped to be back in Leeds by now, but it looked as if it would be another half an hour at least. The day, as far as he was concerned, had been a complete waste of time. It had been nothing more than a charm offensive on his publisher's part, now that there was a very good chance of the book doing really well. There was even talk now about the single staying at the number one spot till Christmas, which was a bit premature as far as Dan was concerned—especially since it hadn't even been released yet. On the back of the hype, his publishers had decided to up the initial print run of the book from twenty to fifty thousand, which was very encouraging as far as potential earnings went, but they could easily have told him that on the phone.

He'd had a good lunch in a trendy restaurant, but he'd found himself thinking about Sarah a lot. He'd been disappointed not to hear from her. It would have been a great opportunity to meet up with her, though he wasn't quite sure what his motives were. He told himself that he just liked the sound of her, that they seemed to have a lot in common and that it really would have been good to talk face to face with someone who'd been through a similar experience as himself. That was what he told himself anyway, but now and again he couldn't help wondering if there might just be something more to it than that.

He sighed and turned back to his book. It was a recently published biography of Bob Marley. Not bad, but he couldn't help thinking that he could do better.

As our parents' homes were both on Piper Hill, it would have been natural for us to walk home together part of the way if circumstances had been different. But that would have been very awkward for both of us, and thankfully Nicola solved the problem by heading straight for the taxi rank on the High Street, leaving me free to walk home alone.

Staley is one of those places described by estate agents as 'extremely sought after'. There are three main types who live there. The locals—people like Cass's parents, the Fosters—ordinary working people who were usually born and bred there. Then there are the seriously wealthy, who may have been born and bred there but probably didn't attend the local schools. Finally, there are those who aspire to rub shoulders with the seriously wealthy—my mother and Barbara Dick being two good examples of this particular category.

It was originally the location that made the town so popular with the Victorians, whose stout architecture dominates the town. Just half an hour from the centres of both Leeds and Bradford, Staley High Street is within champion spitting-distance of a stretch of beautiful high moorland that looms over the town and gives it an almost Swiss mountain appeal.

Large terraced houses, many of which have been turned into flats, make up the lower reaches of Piper Hill, then eventually give way to more modern homes. These were built in the last twenty years or so, to accommodate the town's ever-growing appeal for the group of individuals to which my mother and Barbara Dick belong. These houses vary in size quite a lot. The Dicks', for example, is larger than ours, but, as my mother never fails to point out, the fact that ours is practically on the edge of the moor makes it more desirable—i.e. valuable. And the fact that it is on the edge of the moor—i.e. a hell of a hike up the hill—no doubt explained why I was at near passing out point by the time my sadly out of condition body staggered through the front gate at about twenty past seven that evening.

The place was in darkness and I was annoyed. I knew I should have telephoned first, but somehow, even now, I expected someone to be at home whenever I happened to show. But I knew that I could get in. I still had my old key, so even if I had to hang around for a while at least I could do it in comfort. And with some time to myself I might even be able to work out what I wanted to say.

The house was dark and silent, and I felt a bit spooked till

I found the switch and turned on the hall light. I had absolutely no reason to feel remotely fearful in a house I was so familiar with, but a definite chill came over me briefly, which I managed to laugh away only when I'd assured myself that all was well. Once I'd slipped off my trainers out of habit, this involved calling upstairs and turning on lights in all of the ground-floor rooms.

Despite its familiarity, I couldn't say that I liked the house very much—this insipid, unimaginative shrine to revolting knick-knacks and chintzy sofas that no one but guests dare sit upon for fear of squashing the cushions and upsetting my mother. It was never a place to feel really comfortable in.

By the time I got to the kitchen I was feeling better, and the warmth from the Aga completed my recovery. I'd thought my mother had completely flipped when she'd insisted on having the thing installed. It was something I'd always associated with farmhouses and vicarages. But the minute Barbara Dick announced that she was having one it was a matter of honour for my mother to go one better. She'd achieved this with a red four-oven model, as opposed to Barbara's cream meagre two-door version. It had meant ripping the new kitchen apart in order to accommodate the monster, but she had been determined. It threw out so much heat that the relatively small kitchen was practically unbearable in summer, but now, on a cold November night, with me in definite need of some comforting cheer, it came into its own.

The really ridiculous thing was that my mother didn't even cook very much. She preferred Marks and Spencer ready-made meals, and I was certain her crudely obvious one-upmanship, her rip-off designer suits and her pitiful attempts at a BBC accent served only to make her the laughing stock of the neighbourhood.

I lifted the lid off one of the plates and rubbed my hands together over it until I felt the circulation returned to my extremities and a residue of unease finally left me. Then I went to the phone that was fixed to the wall and called up my dad. It had occurred to me that I shouldn't have lied to him, that it all might backfire on me if my interference came out at a later stage, so I decided to tell him where I was.

'I'm at home,' I said when he answered.

'What are you doing there?' He sounded distinctly un-comfortable.

'I'm not going to tell her about Giovanna, if that's what you're worried about.'

'I take it your mother's not in earshot at the moment,' he said anxiously.

'Of course not. She's not here, as a matter of fact. Any idea where she might be?'

'None at all. She's usually home on Thursday evenings.'

I hadn't intended doing it now, but it seemed as good a time as any to voice my concerns about Giovanna. I began by telling him how she'd once been badly let down by a married man.

'And I know it sounds a bit old-fashioned, but she is Ita-lian and she is of a different generation. And the point is that she doesn't know *you're* still married.'

'I am separated, though,' he said defensively.

'For two weeks! I'm not even sure that counts. I'm sorry, Dad, but you're going to have to be up front with her. It's only fair. It was OK when she was coming to my place as a guest with you there as well, but taking her out for a meal on her own makes everything different.'

'I don't know what you think my intentions are, Jo,' he said with a smile in his voice, 'but I do consider myself to be an honourable man.'

I knew what he was getting at, and I was glad he wasn't there to see me blush.

'I'm sure you are, Dad, but that isn't the point. What is, is that I'm pretty sure she would never have agreed to go out with you if she knew the situation.'

There was a slight pause as I listened to the cogs in his brain turn over.

'So you want me to ring and tell her. Is that what you're saying?'

'Yes, it is. She might think you're trying to deceive her otherwise. Which wouldn't be a very good start.'

'OK,' he said. 'But I'll have to do it tomorrow—unless you have her home number.'

'No, I don't.' But I wasn't going to let him off that easily. And, because I didn't want her taking any awkward calls when I was around tomorrow, it was best that he got it over and done with tonight. 'But I'm sure you'll find it in the book.'

I finished the call and, feeling a little overpowered now by the heat from the Aga, I closed the plate lid and decided to take a look around, to see if I could find any clues as to where my mother might be. For all I knew she could be out for the whole of the evening, in which case I'd be wasting my time hanging around.

There was nothing obvious downstairs, so I turned off most of the lights and headed up the stairs on my way to her bedroom. On the way there I stopped off at what had been my room until I moved to Leeds. I switched on the light and felt immediately depressed by its cream and pink blandness. My mother hadn't wasted any time in removing all trace of my former presence and turning it into a dull and uninspiring spare bedroom-cum study.

She'd set a desk up in there for her computer, which she used to send her Hotmails to me and my brother Matthew. I don't think it had any other purpose until she started on the Family History search, and after recent events my guess was that would fall by the wayside soon. I thought about Barbara Dick, whom she'd been trying to outdo as usual, and I shook my head in despair at their so-called friendship. No wonder Dad had put his foot down about seeing so much of the Dicks. It must have been a nightmare listening to the two of them trying to better one another all night long, in between criticisms about his Yorkshire accent.

I moved on to my brother's room, that was more or less as he had left it three years ago. It was still crammed with his boyish bits and pieces, a mute testimony to the fact that Matthew had always been our mother's favourite child.

I was beginning to feel quite sorry for myself, so I switched off the light and went on to my parents' bedroom, where I received a major shock. Every other part of the house had been in its usual spick-and-span order. But here, in the very heart of my mother's powerhouse, disorder reigned. And it reigned magnificently. There were expensive paper shopping bags everywhere, all over the floor and bed. Wardrobe doors were gaping and drawers were erupting, revealing my mother's vulgar taste in fashion and underwear. Some things were even strewn on the floor. A black bra, for example, and a pink chiffon thing I'd never seen before. I crossed the room to pick it up and discovered that it was *almost* a dress, the like of which I'd never seen my mother wear in her life. It was the sort of thing I might have chosen myself for a night at a club if I was feeling particularly sassy—far, far too young for my mother.

It occurred to me that she had been collecting for a jumble sale, from her rich would-be friends, but then my eyes fell on the bags again. Harvey Nichols, Karen Millen, Ted Baker for Women—top end of the high street, not her usual naff, gold-braided stuff that she erroneously believed was *designer*. These were the sort of shops I like to go to when I can afford it, that rarely give change from a hundred quid per item. I scanned the room quickly again and realised there had to be a thousand pounds' worth of carrier bags there.

I slumped down on the reproduction brass Victorian bed

and sighed. I had a bad feeling about all this. It occurred to me that the only time a woman spends this kind of money at the shops is when she's fed up or when she wants to look good for a new man in her life. I really hoped that it was the 'fed up' option, but by the look of the black bra that was still on the floor I had my doubts. However fed up my mother had been in the past, she'd always stuck firmly to M & S undies. I sighed and picked up the bra, but even before I read the fancy label I knew that it was from somewhere exotic.

So it had to be a man. And, as she'd plainly spent ages trying on so many different things, it must be a man she was extremely keen to impress.

I felt a momentary panic and looked at my watch. It was ten past eight now—plenty of time to have had an early dinner and be heading back. For a night of…I wouldn't let myself formulate the thought, but then I looked at the bra in my hands again and dropped it as quickly as if it had suddenly burst into flames. I glanced distractedly about the room again, and although it didn't seem likely that she would bring a man back to this mess, there was always the sofa—

Oh, God! I had to get out of there. And quickly.

I dropped the pink chiffon back where I'd found it, kicked the bra to its more or less original position, and legged it. I didn't even tie my trainer laces, but I still wouldn't be surprised if I broke records that night, from my house to the station. Thankfully I only had five minutes to wait till the next train for Leeds left the station, and this time I practically had a whole carriage to myself. It was only when we were well out of the station that my heart-rate began to return to normal, and it was soon after that when my mobile started to ring.

My first thought was that it must be my mother, who'd just seen me tearing down Piper Hill when she was on her way home, and I prepared a lie. She'd never forgive me if she knew I'd uncovered her smutty little secret, so I would tell her I'd found the house empty and, having forgotten my key, I'd turned straight round and headed back for Leeds.

However, a quick glance at the display screen revealed that it wasn't my mother at all. I didn't know who it was at first, because the caller's number was not logged in my mobile's memory, and I was tempted to switch it off. I couldn't cope with anything else untoward, and the bad feeling that had started in my mother's room hung around me still like a bad smell.

I resisted temptation, though, on the sensible grounds that it might just be important.

'It's Nicola,' Nicola said before I could speak, and the first thing I thought was, How did she get my number?

'I just rang your flat to leave a message and your father answered.'

A silence followed that I didn't think it was my job to fill.

'He gave me this number.'

'And?' I said.

'And I need to talk to you. Can I meet you at the station? We could travel back to Leeds together.'

'Can't do that, I'm afraid. I'm already on the train.'

She thought about that for a moment, but chose not to share her conclusions.

'Then it will have to be tomorrow.'

Which annoyed me. How dared she think I could drop everything just because she wanted to talk?

'I've got work tomorrow, and I'm going out in the evening. If what you've got to say is so important why don't you just tell me now?'

'I can't,' she said shortly. 'It's far too complicated. How about we meet before work. Say eight-thirty outside the Italian?'

I felt myself frowning. It was beginning to sink in how odd this call was.

'Can you give me a clue what this is about?'

'Sorry, can't do,' she said dangerously. 'All I *can* say at this point is that it's as much in your interests as it is in mine. So be there.'

And then the phone went dead, and it was as if I'd just woken up from a dream in which lots of cloaks and daggers had been involved.

The door of Dan's flat stood ajar, and at first he thought that he must have left it open when he'd rushed out that morning. It was dark on the landing, and it wasn't until he pushed the door open wider and switched on his hall light that he saw the damage to the door. He rushed straight on into the living room and looked round it quickly. To his great relief, everything seemed to be fine.

He went into the bedroom and then the kitchen; all appeared well. Then he went back to his bedroom and opened his wardrobe. He moved his clothes aside and let out a heartfelt, 'Phew!' His precious guitar was still where he'd hidden it before he left that morning. He couldn't really afford insurance, and because the guitar was precious to him he always hid it when he left the flat for more than a couple of hours. He took it out of the wardrobe now, and carried it into the living room where he placed it lovingly back on its stand.

By now he'd come to the conclusion that he'd had a very lucky break. Someone had clearly broken into the flat but had been disturbed. It occurred to him that he should check with Aisling and Libby. To see if they were all right and ask them whether they'd heard anything.

He went up to Libby's flat first. Her door seemed fine, and when he got no reply he went down to Aisling's. Her door looked secure as well, which was a relief. He wasn't surprised to find her out, she usually was, but it was while he was standing in the lower hallway that he wondered how the would-be burglar had got through the main door, which showed no signs of forced entry.

It was then that he remembered the key that they kept outside for emergency lock-outs.

He opened the door, stepped out into the darkness and walked along the side of the building. They kept it lodged in the spout of a downpipe that led into a drain, and he reached down now and felt for it. It was gone.

This was very strange indeed, as only those who lived in the house knew about it and it seemed unlikely to Dan that an opportunist thief would have stumbled upon it. But, since there seemed to be no other possible explanation, he had to assume that this had happened.

He went back to his flat, and it was just as he was heading towards the kitchen to make some tea that he spotted the scarf lying over the arm of the sofa.

chapter 13

I arrived ten minutes early and was surprised to find Nicola already there. I didn't have a key for the Italian, and as there was nowhere open nearby as yet it meant that we had to huddle for warmth in a jeweller's shop entrance on the other side of the precinct. Nicola was wrapped in a floor-length overcoat that must have cost a bomb, but I, rather foolishly, had only a jacket over my skirt, and although I was wearing thick black tights, my legs were still freezing. If global warming was a reality, then somehow the city of Leeds had managed to escape its effects.

'So what's all the fuss about?' I began, trying to keep my teeth from chattering.

Nicola gathered her scarf around her chin. 'It's about our parents,' she grimly replied.

'All of them?' I asked her blankly.

'Effectively, yes, but essentially just my father and your mother.'

And that was it. She didn't need to say any more. I just knew.

'Oh, God,' I said.

'So this hasn't come as a complete surprise, then?'

I shook my head. 'It's all beginning to make perfect sense, I'm afraid,'

'There's nothing *perfect* about it,' Nicola said indignantly. 'And it's got to stop. My mother's threatening to kill herself if it carries on.'

I knew how histrionic Barbara Dick could be, but I didn't say this.

'I don't expect she means it,' I answered lamely instead.

The precinct had been practically empty when we'd arrived two minutes before, but like magic now scores of people were already milling around us. Tables and chairs were being erected outside coffee houses—though I couldn't imagine anyone being daft enough to use them today—and some of the jeweller's shop staff had started to queue outside the doorway we were occupying. With a silent nod of agreement we moved away, and together, a disconsolate pair, we wandered up and down the precinct discussing our errant parents.

'The thing with our mothers is that they are just so competitive,' I said with a sigh. 'And, ashamed as I am to say it, I wouldn't be surprised if that's what this is all about. Getting her hands on your mother's husband has got to be the ultimate coup.'

Nicola nodded agreement. 'I know, but it's not going to bring my father back. He's told her he's in love with your mother.'

'No!' I stopped and stared wide-eyed at Nicola. I couldn't

believe it. It was one thing having a fling, but... 'And how does *she* feel?'

'That's what I was hoping you could tell me.'

I shook my head and we moved off again. Oddly, I didn't feel the cold any more—which must have meant I was in a state of shock, I think.

'I haven't a clue what's in my mother's head at the moment. All I do know is that two days ago she was demanding that my father went home, so it must only just have started.'

'As a full-blown affair, maybe, but they've been flirting with one another for months, according to my mother.'

I thought about this for a moment. 'I'm not sure if my dad realised that, but he did say they'd been seeing a lot of your parents and I do know he wasn't very happy about it.'

'Is that why he left?'

I just nodded. There didn't seem any point in telling her the whole story.

'I didn't know anything till I got home. I take it you weren't expected last night?' She glanced at me sideways, then suddenly let out a little gasp. 'Oh, my God, you didn't find them together, did you?'

'Of course not,' I said, shuddering at the thought. 'This is the first I've heard about it. The house was empty when I got home.' I considered telling her about my suspicions, about the state of Mum's bedroom, but I didn't think it would throw any new light on the situation so I kept quiet.

'She was with my father. He was very up-front about it to my mother,' Nicola added wryly. 'He told her he was going to suggest moving in with your mother.'

'But he can't! My dad's only been gone for a couple of weeks,' I said, as if that sealed the matter.

'Well, there's one way to stop that happening,' Nicola said slyly.

'How?'

'You must speak to your father. Tell him he must go home at once, before it's too late.'

I remembered how I'd felt yesterday, how I'd believed my parents could be happier without one another, and despite all these uncomfortable revelations it struck me now that nothing had changed.

'Have you considered the possibility that we should just leave them to it?'

Nicola stopped in her tracks and a young man in a hurry walked straight into her back. She gave him a withering look and turned her attention back on me.

'That's easy for you to say,' she hissed. 'You haven't got a fiancé whose parents believe in marriage for life. They're due to meet my parents next weekend, and Lord knows what they'll make of all this if they find out about it.'

'If they're decent people they'll feel sorry for you, I'd have thought,' I said a bit pompously.

'I don't want them feeling sorry for me,' Nicola snapped. 'And besides, they're not decent people. They're religious bloody maniacs!'

We looked at each other for about ten seconds—me trying to keep a straight face, her trying to keep up the act. I'm not sure who it was that laughed first, but I do know that it became a bit raucous. Not the sort of laughter you normally hear at that time of the morning in a busy Leeds precinct.

It was getting close to nine when we finally pulled ourselves together. Too late for any more talking. So we said our goodbyes and promised to keep one another informed of any further developments.

Dan had sent a reply to Sarah's e-mail the night before and gone to bed early. He'd tried reading his book, but had found his concentration kept wandering. He was worried about that scarf. He couldn't be sure, but it looked like Jo's. She'd had one very like it, anyway, a genuine Burberry that his mother had given to her the previous Christmas. And he'd certainly have noticed long before now if she'd left it behind when she moved out.

The first thing he did when he got up was to call a locksmith. It wasn't just his flat door that would need a new lock, he'd realised during the night. The front door lock would need to be replaced as well, because if someone had a key to it they could easily come back. The locksmith promised to be there within the hour, so while he waited for them to arrive he went downstairs to Aisling's flat and knocked on her door.

She was still in her pink bathrobe, but when he told her what had happened she insisted on going up to the flat to see the evidence for herself.

'Wow!' she said as she examined the splintered wood on the door. 'Wait till my parents hear about this!' She grinned at Dan. 'On second thoughts, maybe I'd better keep quiet. Or they'll insist I move out immediately.'

He told her about the missing key and her eyes rounded with excitement. She looked like one of the Famous Five, on the verge of a big adventure.

She followed him into the flat and looked around.

'Seems you've been really lucky,' she said. 'They could have had a field-day with all those CDs.'

He nodded in agreement. He'd already scanned his CD collection, and been reassured by no obvious gaps, and his expensive hi-fi system was still mercifully intact.

'They must have been disturbed,' Aisling said, voicing Dan's original theory.

Unless it wasn't a burglar, he thought now, but didn't say. Unless it was Jo, who'd come back to the flat for a reason that wasn't clear to him yet and then just left her scarf by accident. She certainly knew about the front door key, and since she'd left her flat key behind she wouldn't have had any other way of getting in without breaking the door. But, although he'd gone over this scenario many times in his head, it still didn't feel right. It didn't seem like something that Jo would do, and what possible reason could she have had for breaking into the flat?

He went into the kitchen and filled his kettle.

'I don't suppose I can tempt you with anything,' he called out to Aisling, remembering her previous comments about his coffee.

'No, thanks.' She followed him in and stood in the doorway, watching him as he rinsed one of several unwashed mugs. 'Have you spoken to Libby about it?' she asked.

'Not yet.'

'Well, she was out too, so I don't suppose she'll be able to help.'

Dan dried one of the cups on a grubby teatowel.

'She said that the two of you have decided to stay friends "for the time being",' Aisling said speculatively.

Dan groaned. 'I was trying to be gentle.'

'Chicken,' she said.

'How does she seem?' he asked.

Aisling shrugged. 'Not bad for someone who's been rejected after a one-night stand. But that's probably because she thinks she's still in with a chance.'

'It wasn't like that,' Dan said as he got the jar of coffee out of the cupboard. He looked over at Aisling. 'To be honest I'm not even sure anything happened. I can't remember much after we got back to the flat. I was pretty far gone, I'm afraid.'

'We all were,' she said reassuringly.

'But I presume you knew what you were doing when you invited Steve in?'

'Oh, yes,' she said, grinning. 'And I expect you'll be horribly jealous, but it's too late now. You had your chance and you blew it.'

'I'll just have to get over it,' he said, playing the game. Then he frowned. 'But you'd think I'd remember it if we actually, well, you know...'

'Had sex?'

He nodded his head.

'Well, maybe you didn't. Maybe you fell asleep before it got that far.'

That was what he was beginning to think, but it wasn't what Libby had implied. He poured water over the coffee granules.

'She didn't tell you that we had, then?'

Aisling thought about this. 'She didn't go into any details. It was just an impression I got. I'm going out with her soon, though,' she said. 'I'll ask her if you like.'

'No, thanks,' he said with feeling. 'Best leave it as it is, I think.' He looked over at Aisling again and shook his head. 'Don't you ever do any work?'

'Just because I don't have a typical nine to five job, it doesn't mean I don't work hard. I was out till gone midnight last night.' She told him briefly about a new bar that she'd been to the night before. She'd been in charge of the opening night PR and made it sound very exhausting.

They went back to the living room together and Dan put his mug down on the coffee table.

'So, what are you up to with Libby?' he asked as he wandered over to the CD collection and browsed the 'D' section.

'I'm doing her a favour, as a matter of fact.'

'Oh, yes?' he said as he took out Miles Davis's classic 1959 five-star album *Kind of Blue*.

'Uh-huh. I'm going to pose as her and meet a would-be buyer for some of her vinyl.'

Dan, who was heading towards the hi-fi, looked round at her sharply.

'You're what?'

'Well, you know she doesn't want any of her father's friends finding out that she's selling his collection? And because this man wants to meet the seller, I'm going to pretend that it's me.'

'Isn't that a bit odd?' he said.

Aisling shrugged. 'Maybe, but I'm looking forward to it. I've always fancied myself as an actress.'

Dan was still frowning as he opened the CD case. Then he frowned harder and shut it again. It couldn't possibly be.

He opened it again and shook his head. It was.

'What's up?' Aisling said. She moved towards him and looked down at the case. The CD was inside, but it was broken into tiny pieces, as if it had been smashed with a very hard object.

'Wow,' she said as he handed the case to her and went back to the shelves.

He took another one out at random, and with a sigh of relief found it intact. Then he took another, just in case, and it was smashed too.

'Shit!' he said.

He took several more off the shelves, and most were OK, but some definitely weren't. It could take all day to go through them all, but he was fairly sure that there would be others.

'Jeez,' Aisling said as she inspected the damage. 'Looks like you weren't so lucky after all.' She looked at him doubtfully. 'I take it you are insured?'

He shook his head. 'Unfortunately not.'

I was dying to tell someone about what was happening with my parents, but there was only Giovanna and I could hardly tell her. Besides, I knew by now that she'd spoken to my father last night. To my great surprise, she'd agreed to go out with him anyway. He must have more charm than I'd ever have guessed.

It was still a bit tricky, though, working with her. She

knew that I knew that she was going out with another married man, and the fact that this one was my father naturally made it awkward for her. It made it awkward for both of us, and I thought I should say something really, but I didn't know what. I tried a few openings out for size in my head but they all sounded wrong. The best I could come up with was, Don't worry, Giovanna, I won't tell anyone if you don't. And somehow I didn't think that would go down too well.

Besides, although she was particularly quiet that morning, keeping her head down in the back kitchen, I kept getting the feeling that she wanted to say something to me, and I decided in the end that would be best. Let her do the talking if she felt like it.

Dulcie was very excited that lunchtime. She kept asking questions. She wanted to know everything—where Giovanna and my father were going for their meal, what she intended to wear, what time they were meeting—and poor Giovanna flushed and mumbled and altogether looked thoroughly miserable.

It was when Dulcie left that she finally opened up.

'I can-a stand it no more, Joanna,' she said unhappily, and as she did so I noticed that her moustache was gone. 'What must-a you think of me?'

I was thinking that there must have been some Immac amongst that big Boots shop of hers, but I didn't suppose that was what she meant.

'I mean-a going out for a meal with your-a papa when he is still-a married to your-a mother.'

I was serving two cappuccinos at the time, and I waited until I'd taken payment from two young women who looked disappointed about being moved on. They were plainly intrigued by Giovanna's outburst.

'I don't think badly of you, if that's what you mean,' I told her quietly and calmly, quite relieved that it was out in the open at last. 'I was a bit annoyed with my father at first, but now that he's explained the situation I'm fine about it.'

'And your-a mamma?' she went on anxiously. 'How will she feel if-a she finds out?'

'She's not in a position to offer an opinion,' I said with a shrug. And because she looked so doubtful, because she looked so unhappy, I told her everything. It took about half an hour in between serving coffees and biscotti, but I felt a lot better for it afterwards.

'And so you think she is in-a love with this man?' she asked gently of my mother, when I'd finished pouring my heart out.

'I really don't know.' I shrugged. 'But I can't see my parents getting back together after this. She's just gone too far, I'm afraid. And besides, I don't think they should get back together. I haven't seen my dad this pleased about life in years.'

She smiled fondly at me as she passed me a weak milky coffee.

'You are-a a lovely girl, Joanna, a beautiful girl. And your-a mother—she did a good job on you, so don't be too angry with her.'

I wanted to say that she didn't know what a bitch I could be, which I definitely had my mother to thank for, but enough was enough for one day.

'I don't know about that,' I did say, 'but I do know that my dad's very much looking forward to tonight, and I don't want you feeling guilty in any way.'

'I don't-a. Not now.' She gave me one of her terrific hugs and then we knuckled down to clearing up. Giovanna had decided to close the place an hour early that evening, to give her the chance to go to the hairdresser, and I wasn't complaining. I wanted to get back to have a long soak in the bath before Dad got back and hogged the bathroom.

★ ★ ★

Libby had been in the dress shop for about twenty minutes. It was in the Victoria Quarter and had the best view over the bagel stand which Aisling had suggested as her rendezvous point with the would-be buyer. But the would-be buyer was late, and Libby was beginning to get anxious.

In fact, as she moved hangers along clothes rails in a pretence of interest in what the shop had to offer, she seriously considered calling the whole thing off. Until a few minutes ago she'd managed to convince herself that it couldn't possibly be Paul who was behind it all, that he wasn't capable of such an elaborate deception. But now, in a complete turnabout in her thinking, she was sure that it was.

But it wasn't him that was worrying her now; it was Aisling. She had been primed with a story that would convince most people that she was genuine, but how would she cope if Paul pressured her? How would she react if he told her the truth? Libby could have kicked herself for not thinking about this in advance, and the more that she thought about it now the more she began to panic. She looked out at Aisling, sitting there on the bench next to the bagel stand, and tried to imagine what she would think if Paul spilled the beans—especially after their conversation on the drive into town.

They'd been talking about Dan, and speculating on the damage to his CDs.

'It seemed so...spiteful,' Aisling said. 'Like the sort of revenge a woman takes when she's been hurt by a man.'

'Do you think it could have been Jo?' Libby said.

Aisling frowned at this. 'I never thought of that. But why would she do that after all this time?'

'Who knows?' Libby said, and then left it at that. She didn't say any more because she wanted Aisling to think that the idea had been hers when she next spoke to Dan. It was clear that he hadn't mentioned the scarf as yet—which she thought was strange—but he might if someone voiced any suspicions. And if Dan believed that Jo was responsible, then he wouldn't be hung up on her any longer. He'd hate her for what he thought she had done, and then, at long last, he would be ready to move on to someone else. Someone very like her—

But the whole careful plan might fall apart if Aisling learnt what she had done.

It was then that she saw him. He was watching Aisling from the other side of the bagel stand, and his expression was puzzled and uncertain. He was dressed casually in jeans and a brown leather jacket, and just for a moment Libby's stomach gave a little lurch of regret. She'd been crazy about him once, but he'd let her down badly and regret quickly gave way to self-preservation.

She saw that his expression had changed, as if he'd suddenly realised what was going on. He ran his hand through his fair hair and then made a move towards Aisling. At which point Libby bolted from the shop and intercepted him before he got there.

He looked confused for a moment when he saw her, and then he shook his head.

'So it was you,' he said.

Libby turned and glanced at Aisling. She hadn't seen them, and was at that moment frowning as she looked for something in her bag. Without any further thought Libby took hold of Paul's arm and led him quickly away from Aisling.

chapter 14

Dad, strangely enough, was at that moment attempting his own particular rendition of 'Careless Whisper' as he got ready in the bathroom. He'd already been through several Gilbert and Sullivan tunes that I recognised from my childhood, and he was giving the George Michael classic the same light operatic treatment. He was making it sound upbeat and cheerful, and if I hadn't known better I'd never have guessed that its themes were betrayal and regret.

He'd been fretting about what to wear. He didn't have all that many clothes with him at the flat—just work things mostly, that he'd crammed alongside my stuff in the inadequate wardrobe in my bedroom. There had even been talk about driving home to get some additional clothes, but I'd managed to persuade him he wouldn't have time, that his best work suit would be just fine. I didn't want him turning up unannounced and finding Brian Dick there, warming his guilty feet by the gas coal-effect fire.

I hadn't heard any more from Nicola, and I didn't want to. Not tonight, anyway. Not while my father was making ready for his big date. I didn't want to spoil it for him, and if she phoned up while he was here it might be awkward. If I got the chance I intended ringing my mother once I'd packed Dad off on his date. I wasn't particularly looking forward to it, but I was determined to get some answers to my questions. If Brian Dick was moving into the family home then I wanted to know about it.

I was more or less ready myself for the off, but I wasn't much looking forward to the evening. I'd already had Cass on the phone, complaining about the venue I'd chosen to meet up with her and Sid.

I was being a bit selfish, really. I didn't fancy trailing across the city so I'd picked the Blue Tube, a new bar that had recently opened not far from my flat. It was handy for me, but a long way for Cass to come. I hadn't told her that Sid was going to be there either. I didn't want her thinking I was trying to play cupid or anything, which is what she always used to accuse me of when I brought a spare man along in the past. As if I'd do that now, when I didn't even have a man myself!

I no longer had any high hopes of Sid persuading her to join us. Cass, I'm afraid, was just too stuck in her ways, and to be honest I wasn't too bothered whether she came or she didn't. So I gave her short shrift and told her it was the Blue Tube or nowhere, which surprisingly shut her up.

At that moment, as I listened to Dad murdering another good song from a previous era, I was trying to think how to respond to Dan's latest message to Sarah.

Dear Sarah

The trip to London went OK, but sorry we didn't get to meet up. I've been thinking about what you said about the break-up with your boyfriend. And I'm wondering if you are sure that it's really over with him? Maybe if you phoned and talked to him—told him how you felt.

By the way, in reply to your question about what I am currently doing work-wise, I'm putting together a largely cut and paste biog on the boy band VantagePoint. Ever heard of them? I feared that you might have!!! Not particularly edifying, but it pays the rent.

Dan

It didn't sound like a come-on to Sarah at all, but almost like an invitation for me to call him. And I was very tempted. Especially since he'd clearly come down off his high horse and was writing for profit these days as well as his *Art!* That had been another big bone of contention between us. I used to moan at him when he would turn down well-paid commercial offers in favour of doing a freebie for a low circulation jazz magazine. He wanted to get a name as a serious writer, and I could understand that, but I couldn't see why he wasn't prepared to compromise. And it looked as if that was exactly what he was doing now.

But what would be the point of calling? He'd asked Sarah if she was really sure that it was over with her boyfriend—by which I presumed that he meant was there any chance of her and the boyfriend getting back together? And if I applied the same question to Dan and myself I couldn't come up with an answer.

Maybe there was a chance, if we were as honest with one another as Dan and Sarah were, but would we be? Perhaps it's easier to be honest with strangers, and besides, should I be even considering trying to get back with Dan when I kept thinking about other men? Marco, with his come-and-get-it sex appeal, and Tim, with his flattering happy-to-wait-in-the-wings allure.

It was all this stuff going on in my head that had taken the edge off an evening I'd been looking forward to up until now. I'd been really keen to find out what was happening with Pisus. Sid had some important news—*good* news, he said—and I should have been thrilled about everything—exciting new job prospects, a possible share in the business—but what with my flipping parents, and now this new development with Dan—

I'd got only as far as *Dear Dan,* in my reply when I heard my dad call out to me. He sounded anxious, so I shut down the computer and went out to see him. He looked good for a man of his age, I supposed—apart from his tie, which I insisted he change.

He'd gone for the smart but sombre look, plain navy blue to match his suit, but I thought Giovanna would prefer something brighter. He didn't have that big a choice, they were all pretty plain, but I opted for the red silk—a tie I'd bought him two Christmases ago and as far as I knew had never been worn.

'Don't you think it's a bit showy for me?' he said as he frowned at himself in the mirror.

'Hardly, Dad,' I said with a roll of my eyes.

'Don't get me wrong,' he said, suddenly concerned that I was offended. 'I love it. I'm just repeating what your mother said. She's always refused to let me wear it.' There was a silence and then an, 'Oh, dear.' He turned to me and sighed. 'Now I've offended you anyway.'

'No, you haven't,' I said, straightening the tie. 'I know what my mother's taste is in ties,' I told him wryly, 'which is the very opposite of her taste in clothes for herself. You look great,' I said, standing back. 'You'll knock Giovanna dead.'

'You look pretty OK yourself, if you don't mind me saying.'

I was wearing a flowery strappy number that didn't suit my mood in the least.

'Are you sure it's only Cass and Sid you're meeting?' he said with a lift of his eyebrow.

I'd told him a bit about Sid and Pisus, but not too much because I didn't want him getting his hopes up for me.

'Very sure. Now,' I said, glancing at my watch, 'you'd better go or you'll be late.'

And off he went like a nervous lamb. I felt like a mother sending her teenage son off on his first date.

By this time I was well and truly ready for my mother.

Amazingly, she picked up on the second ring—which afterwards made me suspect that she'd been sitting by the phone waiting for someone else to ring.

'Mother!' I said.

'Oh,' she replied gloomily. 'It's you.'

I doubted very much that Matthew would have got a response like that, but this wasn't about sibling rivalry. 'You didn't answer my e-mail.' I said.

'Why should I? You were very rude and unkind.'

Oh, God, I thought, she's in one of her sorry-for-herself moods. The worst kind. The sort that was deliberately and calculatedly designed to make whomever she was talking to feel guilty. But, hey, she was talking to the wrong person just at that moment.

'I've had a good teacher, then, haven't I?'

There was a shocked pause. Followed by a croak. Followed by full-blown noisy crying. Or something that sounded like crying. It went on for about twenty pence worth of call, and then it calmed down to the odd shaky sob.

'Oh, Joanna,' she managed, between sobs. 'You really don't know what it's like.'

'No,' I said harshly, 'you're right. I don't know what it's like to have a really good husband *and* a bit on the side.'

A banshee-like wail then emitted from my earpiece. This went on for some time, during which I held the receiver well away from my head, until it eventually subsided to a strangled groan.

Then I heard several choked words that might have been spoken in Swahili for all the sense they made. It took a while before my scrambling facility kicked into action, but eventually, after about ten seconds of so, the coded message finally deciphered itself.

My forty-nine-year-old mother had just told me that she was pregnant.

'You do realise that you could have gone to prison for what you did,' Paul said with a sigh.

Libby was sitting with him in his car, under a streetlight on a road just round the corner from her flat. They'd been together for hours now, and still he seemed reluctant to let her go. It was as if he'd been trying to impress on her the seriousness of what she'd done. But if that was his plan then he was wasting his time as far as Libby was concerned.

'What do you want?' she said irritably. 'A medal, or something, for not turning me in?'

'An explanation would do,' he said.

She'd been thinking about what she was going to tell Aisling. Why the would-be buyer had failed to show; why Libby had disappeared without giving a reason. Which seemed a lot more important than providing explanations to Paul.

'Look,' she said, 'it's getting late. You've got your property back, so what's the problem?'

'Not without a fight,' he said cynically.

It was true she had not given up the vinyl with very good grace. It had only been when Paul threatened to tell Baz everything that she'd agreed to give the damn records back. He'd brought documentation along to prove that the collection belonged to him, and she'd been afraid that Baz would tell Dan if she didn't co-operate. The vinyl was now stacked in the boot of Paul's car, and the knowledge that thousands of pounds had slipped through her fingers made her feel deeply resentful.

'I hope you don't expect an apology,' she said. 'What you did today was just as bad as anything I've ever done. That was very devious of you, pretending to be someone else.'

He shook his head in disbelief.

'Your brand of logic astounds me,' he said. 'And it's not an apology I want, but a reason for why you stole those records.'

'Isn't it obvious?' she asked.

'Not to me, no.'

'Because you dumped me,' she said.

'And do you know why I did that?'

'Does it matter why you did it?'

'It should matter,' he said with a sigh. 'I *dumped* you, as you put it, because you went around telling everyone that we were getting married and that wasn't even on the cards.'

'It was as far as I was concerned,' she said, even though she wasn't quite sure what she'd ever seen in him now. He was all right to look at, she supposed, but he was such a drip. OK, so maybe he had tracked her down, which was pretty smart after all this time, but if he had anything about him he wouldn't just *talk* about turning her over to the police, he'd do it.

'But we were only together for a few weeks,' he said with a sigh.

Libby shrugged. She was getting really bored with this now.

He looked at her without speaking for some time. She

couldn't really see his face because the streetlight was not very bright.

'Are you seeing anyone now?' he eventually asked.

'That's my business,' she answered stiffly.

He shook his head. 'Well, I hope if you are that he doesn't upset you—for his own sake.'

'You make me sound like a crazy,' she said. 'And there's nothing crazy about getting even.'

'I don't think you're crazy,' he said, and then he reached over her and opened her door.

'Is that it?' She sounded surprised.

'Absolutely,' he said as he turned on the engine.

She hesitated.

'How come?' she said. Although she'd been desperate to get away she was curious to know what had made the difference.

'Well, if you must know, the reason I didn't inform the police is because I actually did believe that you were disturbed.'

She frowned at him heavily, uncertain how to take this.

'And you don't any more?'

'No,' he said, looking at her as he waited for her to get out of his car. 'I think you're bad now, rather than mad, and I very much hope that you get your comeuppance.'

'I didn't realise you two knew one another,' I yelled over the collective drone of the three hundred or so drink-fuelled young people I'd had to negotiate my way through to the bar of the Blue Tube. Above that particular sound I could just about make out some bluesy music that was presumably all part of the *blue* theme of the place. There were a lot of *tubes* involved as well—chrome tubes which had been moulded into seats and tables. It was as if the designer had taken the name rather too literally—either that or they were just having a laugh.

When I'd recovered sufficiently from my shock, I'd decided

to phone them both to cancel our meeting. But that kind of shock takes a lot to recover from, and by the time I got round to making the call it was far too late. It was already well past the arranged meeting time, and I knew that Cass would kill me if I failed to show.

My mother had put the phone down on me when I'd let out an involuntary little cry of disgust, and for what must have been a good half-hour or so I'd sat looking blankly at the sitting room wall. When I began to come round a bit from my stupor I thought about phoning Matthew. But, although she hadn't said that I shouldn't, I knew it would be the last thing she'd want me to do. And I owed her that much, I supposed.

As it was I arrived twenty minutes late, which under normal circumstances would already be a hanging offence as far as Cass was concerned, so I was grateful to find her looking so chilled. The really big surprise, though, was Sid. He was smiling and chatting happily away as if he smiled and chatted happily away all the time.

I looked from one to the other and then focused my attention on Cass. She was looking particularly good, I thought, in a black sleeveless dress with a silver cardigan draped loosely over her shoulders—quite daring for her. Only her hair let her down a bit. It was so annoyingly neat I was tempted to ruffle it for her, but then it occurred to me that there was something quite sexy about her naughty-librarian-out-on-the-pull look.

She looked up at me, surprised. They both did. Then they looked back at each other and frowned in puzzlement.

'We don't know each other,' Sid yelled back at me. 'We've only just met.'

'But this is Cass,' I said. 'The friend that I wanted you to meet. And this is Sid,' I added quickly to Cass, 'who's hopefully going to be my new boss.' Because she was beginning to look suspicious, I cut to the chase. 'Sid's looking for someone with your sort of experience to join us, so I suggested he came along as well.'

I smiled widely at them both and they looked at each other again, shyly now. Then, when Sid turned to the bar to get me a drink, I apologised to Cass.

'I thought if I told you that you wouldn't want to come,' I mouthed.

'He seems very nice,' she mouthed back, with a definite twinkle in her eye.

'He is,' I said, 'and I think he's going to do really well. It could be a great chance for us all,' I added, even as my mind drifted back to my mother's bombshell. I was dying to tell someone about it, but this was neither the time nor the place.

Just then Sid passed me a glass of white wine, and as I took my first sip I was already wondering how soon I could leave.

'I realise you probably won't be interested,' I said to Cass, yelling again now so that Sid could hear what I was saying, 'but I thought it might be worth a try.'

'I was thinking about moving on somewhere quieter,' Sid bellowed back, but he was looking at Cass.

'Good idea,' Cass bawled, and then they both looked at me. I shrugged.

'I just need to go to the loo first,' I said, knocking back the contents of my glass in one. 'I'll meet you outside.'

I pushed my way through the pulsating throng and eventually made my way into the cloakroom. I was resigned now to spending the evening with Cass and Sid, but that didn't mean I was happy about it. I still had a lot of brooding to do and I'd far sooner have got on with it straight away.

There were about five or six other women in there, in different stages of their ablutions, and I was just washing my hands when I noticed that I was standing right next to Aisling Carter. She noticed me at about the same time and we looked at each other through the mirror over the sink for a moment before she spoke.

'It *is* you,' she said, clearly as embarrassed as I was but just as intent on not showing it.

'How's it going?' I asked as I flipped off the tap. She was the last person I wanted to see but I had my dignity to maintain.

'Great,' she said, full of what sounded flike alse cheer to me—but it was hard to be certain with Aisling. 'I'm here with Steve and couple of friends.'

She was just about wearing a fluffy red thing that could loosely be described as a dress, I supposed, but looked to me rather more like stretched snood. And I don't know why but her dress was suddenly not the only red thing in the ladies' toilets. My eyes were filled with it briefly as all the resentment I felt about Aisling turned to hot anger.

'So what happened to Dan?' I said. I could feel my dignity falling apart, but I couldn't stop myself now. 'Did he finish with you or did you just fancy a change?'

Everyone in the cloakroom had stopped what they were doing now, and were looking at me. Well, I had raised my voice quite a lot.

Aisling looked at me too, in what seemed like genuine puzzlement.

'How could Dan finish with me when I've never been out with him?' she said, clearly a lot less conscious than I was of people staring at us.

I was beginning to feel a little less certain of my ground, and I couldn't speak for a moment. Her tap was still running, and because I hate waste I was tempted to reach over and turn it off.

'I don't know who you've been talking to,' she went on, 'but I'm telling the truth.' She finally turned off the tap and shook hands. 'I'll admit I was keen on him for a while, but he made it clear from the start that I wasn't his type.' She looked me up and down then, curiously, as if trying to come to terms with the fact that I clearly *had* been his type. She moved over to the dryer then, and it droned into action as she rubbed her hands beneath the heat.

The spectators started moving off, bored now that the tension seemed to have gone out of our exchange. My own hands were practically dry now, and I rubbed the residue lightly on my dress.

'They told me that it was serious,' I said, bewildered still. 'Then they said it was over suddenly.'

'Well, who knows what that was about?' she said, as if the matter was done with. She scowled at her reflection in the mirror and began fiddling with one of the hair extensions that looked in danger of coming adrift from her own hair. Suddenly she turned on me and looked me straight in the eye.

'Where were you last night?' she asked abruptly.

'Last night?' I repeated. 'Why?'

'Someone broke into Dan's flat and smashed up some CDs. Libby thought that it might have been you.'

'Me?' I said, shocked. 'Why the hell would I do that?'

She shrugged. 'Revenge, I suppose. It would make sense if you thought Dan was seeing me.'

My mind was racing. I couldn't believe what I was being accused of.

'But I went to my mother's place last night. I caught the train there straight after work.' I thought of Nicola on the train and felt relieved. 'And I can prove it too.'

Aisling shrugged her bony shoulders. 'I didn't think it was you anyway. Not really your style, I shouldn't have thought.'

'But Libby thinks it was me?'

'So she says.'

I couldn't take this all in. How could Libby possibly say such a terrible thing about me? Then I remembered what Nic had said about Libby—how she'd been talking about me—and Sid's hints that my informant might not be reliable. And I felt such a fool.

Aisling was looking in the mirror again, applying red lipstick to match her dress.

'Was it Libby who lied about me and Dan?' she wanted to know.

Since I didn't think Libby deserved my discretion, I nodded—yes.

'I guessed as much,' she said. She looked thoughtful for a moment. 'She probably did it to keep you and Dan apart. If you thought he was seeing me, chances were that you wouldn't make contact.'

She smiled at me wryly through the mirror, aware that she'd hit the nail right on the head.

'Well, you didn't exactly make a secret of your feelings for Dan while I was still with him,' I said.

'Guilty as charged. But you were perfectly safe. And, yes, OK, so I may have overstepped the mark—but things were already going sour between you when I moved in. You were out a lot, and I thought Dan deserved more attention than you seemed prepared to give him.'

I wanted to argue the toss about that, but there didn't seem any point. Besides, I was more interested in Libby at the moment.

'But that doesn't explain *why* she wanted to keep me and Dan apart.'

Aisling pressed her lips together and put the lipstick back in her bag.

'Because she wanted him for herself, of course.'

My heart sank.

'Are you saying that Dan and Libby are together now?'

'No. They've decided to stay friends. At least Dan has decided, after he spent the night with her.'

I was stunned.

'Dan slept with Libby? When?'

'Last Saturday.'

And Libby had been in to see me on Monday. She'd seemed excited, and then she'd gone a bit strange and had to rush off.

Aisling turned away from the mirror again and looked at me.

'Between you and me, though, nothing happened. I suspect it's just wishful thinking on Libby's part.'

This was all very hard to take in. Libby's lies, Dan's CDs…

'I hope Dan doesn't think it was me that broke into his flat.'

'I doubt it,' Aisling said breezily as she snapped her fluffy red bag shut. 'Now, are you ready?'

Feeling dazed now, I nodded, and she linked my arm like an old friend, and together we walked out of the cloakroom as if nothing of importance had happened.

The roar of the crowd felt as if it had been switched up a notch or two in our absence, and I was very glad to be leaving the place. I tapped Aisling's bare shoulder and indicated with sign language that I was going. She shook her head, though, and hung onto my arm.

'I just want you to meet someone before you go,' she mouthed, and because her grip was so firm I found myself being dragged along after her.

Luckily we were heading in the right direction, towards the exit, and just by the door she stopped and drew me into a small group of people that included Steve. We gave each other a what-a-surprise-great-to-see-you sort of hug, in the way people do who are a little embarrassed—though I wasn't sure what we had to be embarrassed about. I didn't catch the name of the young women Aisling introduced me to, but that may have been because I was feeling a little distracted by this time. I'd started to notice that people were staring, that there was a very distinct aura about this little gathering that seemed to have the attention of those crushed all around us. I didn't have time to wonder why, because Aisling was already introducing me to the last member of the group, at which point everything was explained...

'And this,' Aisling said, in a tone that savoured a great deal of pride, 'is Jamie.'

I didn't know what surprised me most. The fact that Aisling really did know Jamie Astin, the latest pop sensation, or that I managed to appear as if nothing unusual was happening when he took hold of me with a sweeping motion, arched my back as if we were doing the tango, and then planted a kiss on my throat.

When I say I acted as if nothing unusual had happened, I mean that I didn't giggle stupidly, or go all coy, or ask him for his autograph. I just nodded when he returned me to an upright position, told him how nice—yes, *nice!*—it was to meet him, and apologised for having to dash straight off. I said that someone was waiting for me outside, and that they weren't going to thank me for leaving them hanging around in sub-zero temperatures, and he smiled that gorgeous smile of his that I'd seen on many a record shop poster.

I think I even managed to retain a sense of normality when I met up with Sid and Cass, and although I was desperate to tell them what had just happened—not with Jamie Astin, but about my conversation with Aisling Carter—the strong sense that I was interrupting something shut me up. I'd been expecting a serious ticking off from Cass for keeping them waiting so long, but she couldn't have been more pleasant.

'We've been thinking,' she said, and I knew somehow that the 'we' really meant 'I'. 'If we're going to talk properly about this proposition we should go back to my flat, where it's quiet.'

'But—' I started, and then stopped again quickly. I was about to object, point out that this didn't make any sense. That my place was just around the corner while hers was way across town—not far from Sid's, come to think of it. And then

I saw the glint in Cass's eye, and the awkward shuffle of Sid's feet, and I got it. And, despite the fact that I was greatly relieved, I was a little miffed as well, if the truth were known. This hadn't been all about offering Cass a job. We were meant to be discussing Pisus as well, and my role in the company, which was a lot more important than Cass's *possible* role. But it was clear now that my presence was not required. I was obsolete. Redundant. My best friend was dismissing me and my soon-to-be boss was backing her up.

'You said you had something important to tell me,' I said a bit stiffly to Sid. 'I take it that everything's going to plan?'

'Couldn't be better,' he said, and yes, he was actually smiling again, which annoyed me intensely. 'We've got seven certainties back on board now.'

'So when do we start?' I said, because I needed to get this straight. I needed to be certain he wasn't thinking of cutting me out now and replacing me with ultra-efficient Cass. I was getting quite rattled, as a matter of fact.

'Nine o'clock on Monday?' he said, and my spirits lifted a little. He was beginning to sound his old gloomy self and I was a lot more comfortable with that. 'I'm meeting the agent with the key to the old offices then,' he went on, 'and the quicker we get moving the better.'

Cass was sensibly wrapped in a thick overcoat, and although I was getting close to the teeth chattering stage by now, stood there as I was in my flimsy dress in temperatures that would have tested a South Pole explorer, there was still something I needed to know. By now I was beginning to accept that I was suffering from mild paranoia—that it was quite possible Cass fancied the pants off Sid and just wanted to get him alone in order to ravish him. I couldn't see it myself, but then Cass always did have very strange tastes in men.

'And have you given any further thought to that other little thing we talked about?'

I couldn't spell out what I meant because I didn't want Cass thinking that she too might be entitled to a share of the business, so unless Sid wanted a gooseberry along for the evening his comprehension skills had better be in good working order. I was feeling a little bit ruthless, if the truth be known, which wasn't like me at all.

'Is five per cent OK with you?' he said, and even in the darkness I could see that he was blanching a little.

I hadn't even considered an actual figure but five per cent of what could possibly turn out to be a successful business sounded good to me. Especially as I had nothing to lose, so I nodded accordingly.

'We'll firm things up on Monday,' he added, and as my spirits were at soaring point now I did what was expected of me. I made my excuses.

'I hope neither of you minds very much, but I've got work tomorrow,' I said, and then *they* did what was expected of *them*. They accepted my excuses with an almost embarrassing amount of feigned regret.

Libby went straight to Dan's flat when she got back. He was expecting her, after all. He'd suggested himself that they got together on Friday night. As *friends*.

She hadn't spoken to him in a couple of days—not since he'd discovered his break-in.

He looked tired when he opened the door.

'Aisling told me what happened and I wondered what the damage was,' she said.

He let her in, and she followed him through to the living room. There were dozens of CD cases piled on the coffee table, and she sighed in sympathy.

'That's terrible,' she said. 'How many have been broken?'

'A hundred or so,' he said wearily as he slumped into the armchair.

She looked around the room for a sign of the scarf, but she couldn't see it.

'Any idea who might have done it?' she said.

He shook his head.

'No clues?'

He shook it again.

This was getting annoying. The scarf was gone from the arm of the sofa, where she'd left it, and the very fact that he wasn't mentioning it meant that he knew exactly whom it belonged to.

'Well, I have,' she said, as she sat on the sofa. She had hoped that Aisling would have said something by now, but she couldn't wait any longer. 'And I'm afraid that it might have been my fault.'

He looked puzzled, but he still didn't speak.

'I spoke to Joanna on Monday evening, and I'm sorry but I mentioned that we—' she shrugged '—that we'd spent the night together.'

His eyes opened wide in what looked like horror.

'Why the hell did you do that?'

'Because it was true, of course,' she said reasonably. 'And I didn't want her finding out from someone else.' She sighed. 'I thought I was doing the right thing.'

'And you think she did this—' he held his hand out in the direction of the smashed CDs '—because of that?'

'It's possible,' she said.

He sat up straight in his seat.

'But why would she do it when she's happy with someone else?'

Damn, Libby thought. She'd forgotten she'd told him that.

'I don't know,' she said. 'It's only a suggestion, and maybe I'm wrong, but it does seem quite a coincidence.'

He looked thoughtful as he turned this over in his mind, then he sighed.

'I dunno,' he said. 'It just feels wrong. I know Jo pretty well, and I don't think it's something she'd do.'

Libby could see he needed more convincing—but not just now, she thought.

'Have you eaten yet?' she said, changing the subject.

He looked dazed. 'I've been too busy.'

'Well, why don't you have a shower, relax a bit, and I'll cook you something.'

'I can't ask you to do that,' he said, but she could tell by his tone that he wouldn't take much persuasion.

'No trouble,' she said with a smile, 'and no strings either.'

He looked uncertain for a moment, then shrugged.

'Well, I was thinking of having a bath,' he said, 'and I wouldn't say no to beans on toast.'

She stood up and did her motherly thing.

'Off you go, then,' she said, flapping her hands. 'I'll just pop up to my flat and get what we need, and if I leave the latch on your door I can let myself in again.'

It was just as she walked back into the flat ten minutes later that the telephone started ringing. Dan had put a CD on before he'd got into the bath, and since he obviously couldn't hear it ring Libby answered it herself.

I jumped straight under a hot shower when I got back, and after wrapping myself in a couple of bath towels I made some tea and thought about my conversation with Aisling Carter. By now I'd consigned my mother's situation to the back of my mind. I couldn't cope with too many things going on at once—and besides, when all was said and done, at the end of the day, in the final analysis, the problem was hers, not mine. I knew in my heart that it didn't really work that way, especially with my particular mother, but I managed to convince myself that it was so for the time being.

So what conclusion had this new information led me to?

I asked myself reasonably as I tucked my feet under my bottom on the sofa and sipped my tea.

From what I had learnt, it would appear that Libby was a scheming bitch who had simply wanted her evil way with Dan. And I, like a fool, had trusted her. Not that it had done her very much good, as it turned out. But then it hadn't done me much good either, come to think of it. Because I'd believed everything she'd said I'd ended up half crazed with jealousy. This in turn had led to the invention of Sarah, whom Dan seemed to be getting quite fond of. And, just to add to the mess, it was just possible that Dan believed I had broken into his flat in a fit of revenge.

Aisling might well have said that he didn't think that, but if Libby thought it then she might just convince him I had. She certainly seemed to have it in for me, and I knew better than most just how convincing she could be when she wanted.

The sensible thing would be just to phone him. Explain I'd met Aisling, tell him what she'd told me, and that I was completely innocent. After all, he *should* know that Libby was being so deceitful, I reasoned.

So I did it quickly, before I had time to change my mind. I picked up the phone and dialled Dan's number, which I still had stored in my memory.

It rang four times before the connection was made.

'Hello?' a familiar female voice said, and I think I gasped just before I slammed the receiver back in its cradle.

Libby had answered Dan's telephone.

I went straight to bed after that, and lay awake for a very long time until I heard my father come in. He was humming quietly to himself as he got ready for bed, and it occurred to me that he too would soon be in for a great big shock.

I waited till I could hear him snoring, then I got out of bed again and turned on my computer. I knew what I needed

to know, and after hours of deliberation I'd come to the conclusion that there was only one way of getting the answer.

Dear Dan
I've been thinking about what you said about my ex, and
I was wondering if you are really so sure that it's over with
yours.
Sarah

It was nearly 1:00 a.m., and Dan was just cleaning his teeth in readiness for bed when he heard a heavy knock on his door. Libby had left ages ago, soon after ten, and then he'd started making a list of the CDs that would need to be replaced when he could afford it. Luckily, quite a few of those broken didn't matter very much to him, but there were some—about thirty or so—that he couldn't really imagine living without.

He was glad to say that it was beginning to look as if Libby would not be a problem after all. And, although he'd been really pissed off with her at first—for talking to Jo, for telling her what had happened between them—he could see now that he only had himself to blame for that. They'd talked about things over beans on toast, about Jo in particular, and Libby had made a very good point.

'Is there anything that really bothered her while you were still together?' she'd asked him, frowning.

'Everything seemed to bother her near the end,' he answered ruefully. He wouldn't normally talk about his relationship with Jo to anyone else but his mother, maybe, but Libby was involved, in a way. And she was a very good listener. 'But especially the music, I suppose. She said that I thought more about it than I did about her.'

Libby nodded her head sagely. 'Then I'm sorry, Dan, but what better way to get back at you than through your music?' She shrugged. 'It's what some women do, I'm afraid. They hit out where they think it will hurt the most.'

She hadn't said anything else; she hadn't needed to. She was obviously convinced that it must have been Jo, and she didn't even know about the scarf. She'd left soon after that and, glad as he was that she really did appear happy just to be friends, he hoped very much that it wasn't her back at the door. It seemed unlikely, at this time of night, but he couldn't think who else it could be.

He was still holding his toothbrush when he opened the door.

'What the hell are you two doing here?' he said, frowning at Aisling and Steve.

'Nice welcome!' said Aisling.

She nudged past him, and Steve grinned at Dan as they followed her into the living room.

'I've come to inspect the damage,' Steve said. He gave a long, low whistle as he looked at the piles of broken CDs still there on the coffee table. 'Good job you'll be earning soon from that book of yours, because I'll lay odds that you're not insured.'

Dan shrugged, and when Aisling flopped on the sofa he rolled his eyes.

'Who are you supposed to be?' he said wryly. 'Mother Christmas?'

'No need to be rude,' she said breezily. 'This is a very expensive designer number, if you must know.' She frowned at his crumpled T-shirt and jeans. 'And at least I don't look as if I've slept in my clothes.'

'Got anything to drink?' Steve wanted to know.

'I doubt it,' Dan said. 'Looks like you've had plenty already,' he said to Aisling, when Steve headed towards the kitchen to look for himself.

'That's not very polite,' she said haughtily, then she patted the seat next to her.

'Go and get rid of that disgusting toothbrush, and then sit down here and talk to me.'

Dan did as he was told, and when he returned from the bathroom he found Steve pouring a yellow substance into three glasses. It was some cheap Spanish liqueur in a knobbly bottle that someone—he couldn't remember who—had brought back from holiday years ago and had been hanging around ever since.

'Not for me, thanks,' he said. 'And don't blame me if it makes you ill.'

'It was all I could find,' Steve said. 'I expect you've hidden the decent stuff.'

Dan sat down next to Aisling, as he'd been instructed.

'So,' Dan said. 'What have you been up to tonight?'

'We went to a new bar,' Aisling said as she took a half-filled glass from Steve. 'And guess who was there?' Her eyes were glinting mischievously.

Dan took a stab. 'Arnold Schwarzenegger?'

Aisling shook her head, as if the suggestion had at least been half-sensible. But she obviously didn't want to hear any more wild guesses.

'Your ex!' she said, fixing her eyes firmly on Dan.

'She looked great,' said Steve. 'Although she didn't hang around too long.'

'You're talking about Jo, I take it,' Dan said, and as he said it he could feel his pulse quicken.

'I introduced her to Jamie Astin, and he asked me later for her number. He seemed quite taken with her,' Aisling added in a bewildered manner.

'Jamie Astin?' Dan said, frowning.

'Don't pretend you haven't heard of him,' Aisling said scornfully. 'He had a number one hit three months ago.'

'Of course I know who he is,' Dan said. 'I just didn't know you were acquainted with him.'

'I'm acquainted with lots of people, sweetie, though I'm not sure you entirely believe that.'

'Was she with anyone?' he found himself asking.

'Jo?'

He nodded.

'Didn't see anyone,' Steve said. He took a sip of the yellow liqueur and shuddered. 'That's disgusting,' he said. 'It's tastes like something you'd put in an engine.'

'But she did rush off,' Aisling said, picking up where Steve left off. 'She said there was someone waiting outside—and it must have been important, with Jamie around!'

Dan sighed, picturing Jo with some mysterious man. He thought for a moment, and although he hadn't intended saying anything now that she'd been brought into the conversation it seemed the natural thing to do.

'Libby said she thinks it might have been Jo who did all this.' He tilted his head towards the stacks of broken CDs.

'Ah,' Aisling said with nod. 'I wondered when she'd get round to that.' She glanced at Steve, and he nodded too.

Dan looked at both of them curiously. 'Am I missing something?' he said.

Aisling smelled the liquid in her glass and shuddered as well. She handed the glass to Dan, who found a place for it on the table.

'I've been telling Steve about our conversation,' she said. 'And he thought I should tell you.'

'Your conversation with whom?'

'With Jo, of course. I met her in the cloakroom and we talked for ages.'

Dan slumped back on the sofa and listened to the brief gist of their exchange.

He let out a long sigh when she'd finished talking.

'So let's get his straight,' he said. 'You're saying that Libby told her a pack of lies about me and you?'

Aisling looked over at Steve apologetically.

'Well, I did fancy him for a while—but that all changed when I met you, darling.' She put her fingers to her lips and blew him a kiss, and then she turned back to Dan.

'My guess is that she did it because she wanted to make damn sure that Jo didn't call you.'

'Because she didn't want you getting back together again,' Steve put in.

'So that she could have her wicked way with you herself,' Aisling said with a grin.

Dan shook his head. 'I can't believe it. It's just so...*weird.*'

'Not necessarily.' Aisling shrugged. 'All's fair in love and war, and all that baloney. Though I think she went a bit far when she tried to blame the break-in on Jo.'

'So you don't think she did that?' Dan said thoughtfully.

She shook her head. 'She said she didn't, and I believe her.'

'You told her about it?'

'Of course.'

Dan rubbed his forehead. He thought for a moment, and then got up and went to his bedroom. When he returned he had Jo's Burberry scarf in his hand.

'Then how do you think this got here?' he said.

Steve and Aisling looked at one another again and frowned.

'Are you saying it's Jo's?' asked Steve.

'I'm almost certain it is, and I found in here that night I got back to the flat.'

'A bit careless of her to leave it behind,' Aisling said.

'I know, but how else could it have got here?'

Aisling chewed her lip for a moment. 'Maybe someone planted it here to make it look like Jo. Maybe Libby did it?'

'This is a bit of a turnaround,' Dan said, looking puzzled. 'I thought you and Libby were the best of buddies these days.'

'That was before I knew she'd told lies about me,' she answered indignantly. 'And before she left me hanging around in the middle of Leeds for hours on end. She was supposed to meet up with me when I'd spoken to her would-be buyer, but he didn't show and she disappeared.'

Dan thought about this, then shook his head with a sigh.

'She might have inconvenienced you,' he said wryly, 'and, OK, she's clearly a liar, but that doesn't automatically mean she did all this damage. And as for planting Jo's scarf—well, I'm sorry, but that does sound just a little bit too far-fetched.'

'Maybe,' Steve said, frowning again, 'but Libby has caused a lot of trouble. If she hadn't interfered maybe you and Jo would have got back together.'

'Maybe we weren't meant to get back together.'

He looked at Aisling, hopeful that she might put up some further argument in Jo's defence, but she didn't. She didn't say anything else on the subject at all.

Having given up on the Spanish liqueur, they left the flat soon afterwards, and Dan, although it was nearly two o'clock when he went to his bedroom, turned on his computer. There was a message from Sarah waiting for him and he responded to it immediately.

Dear Sarah
Until recently I wasn't sure it was really over. But I am now.
You still haven't answered my question, though…
Dan

★ ★ ★

God, I was furious when I read that e-mail after crawling out of bed at seven a.m. Because, although poor Sarah would have been mystified by that response, I knew exactly what it meant.

As soon as Libby answered the phone I guessed what had happened. I could picture the sneaky, scheming...vandal—who had almost certainly broken into his flat herself, for whatever crazy reason, who may or may not have had sex with Dan but had obviously not given up on becoming more than just *friends* with him—telling him anything she liked about me, and the sucker believing every word.

God, men could be stupid.

I thought about ringing him again, of giving him hell, but I was afraid that he wouldn't listen. Libby had clearly done a very good job on him, and I was the baddy now, the wicked, vindictive ex, and anything I had to say was not to be trusted.

I sat there for ages, looking at that brief message, and I knew it should be Libby that I was angry with. And I was—but I was angrier still with Dan. For thinking so badly of me, for allowing himself to be conned by such a conniving cow. I thought and I thought, and then, at about eight o'clock, when I heard my dad moving about in the living room, I wrote a reply from Sarah.

> *Dear Dan*
> *I'm sorry to hear that.*
> *I presume the unanswered question you refer to is whether or not I think that it's completely over with my ex. Well, yes, it definitely is. I recently found out what a low opinion he has of me and I've decided the time has come to move on.*
> *I'm starting with a trip up to Leeds, and I'd like to meet*

up with you if you're free this evening…? Time's a bit tight,
and I have to leave here pretty soon, but I'll be at a club called
Zoot, say around ten o'clock? I'll hang about the bar area for
a while, in case you can make it, and I'll be wearing red so
that I stand out dangerously…

Here's hoping, then.
Sarah

'Ha!' I said aloud as I sent it. I felt warm all over with
wicked pleasure as I imagined him reading the message. I felt
sure that he'd go—that he wouldn't be able to resist it. My
only regret was that I wouldn't be there to witness him being
stood up.

Which is when I had my next bright idea.

It was still pretty early for making calls, but it couldn't be
helped. I went into my list of business contacts on the laptop, and took a note of a number.

I rang it quickly, before I lost my nerve.

'Tim!' I said brightly. 'I hope you don't mind me ringing
your mobile at the crack of dawn, but I was just wondering
if…'

I didn't have to wonder for long. He couldn't have been
more pleased to hear from me, apparently. And when I suggested a night at Zoot, he suggested dinner first. It was that easy.

'You look cheerful,' my father said when I left the bedroom. I was dressed now, and I'd made an effort with my
make-up to reflect my sparkling new mood.

'I am,' I said. 'And what about you?' I knew the answer to
my question already. He looked positively radiant, if it's possible for men to look that way. He was sitting on the unmade
sofabed in his striped pyjamas. Unlike me, he didn't have a
job to go to today.

'She's a wonderful woman,' he said.

I poured tea from the pot he had made and noted that it was Earl Grey, not the usual stuff—a sure sign that Dad was celebrating life.

I stood by the window and let him prattle on for a while about the great evening they'd had. I wasn't really listening that hard, but when he mentioned his plans to take Giovanna to see *The Pirates of Penzance* in two weeks' time I suddenly remembered my Gilbert and Sullivan-loving mother. Bugger! How could I possibly have forgotten her latest bombshell?

'Dad,' I said, interrupting his flow. 'There's something you ought to know.'

I told him that his estranged wife was pregnant. And, not content with pulling the mat from underneath his happiness, I also told him that Brian Dick was in love with her and in all probability would soon be taking his place in the family home.

And, because by the time I'd said all this it was half past eight, I couldn't even hang around to see how he was going to deal with the news once the state of shock that I'd left him in finally wore off.

Dan didn't know what to do. He'd been very keen to meet up with Sarah a few days ago, but he wasn't nearly so certain about it now.

He had enough stuff going on in his life, what with Libby's lies and Jo's spiteful acts of revenge. Did he really want to complicate it further?

He'd just picked up her latest e-mail, and had been pleasantly surprised by it at first. But now he was feeling confused. He hadn't slept very well, and although he'd started early on the book he was finding it hard to concentrate. He was working on some fatuous anecdote about one of the band members who'd once been in trouble with his headmaster for passing a rude poem around the school. It was about the worst dirt he could dig up on the lad, and he wondered—as he had many times before—what had happened to rock 'n' roll.

Between that and Sarah's surprise invitation, his mind kept going back to the conversation he'd had with Aisling and Steve last night. Something about it was bothering him. And he knew it was useless. Until he spoke to Aisling again he wouldn't get anything done.

He got up from his desk and for want of something better to do switched on the radio. Someone was doing a re-worked cover version of 'Careless Whisper', and with a jolt Dan suddenly realised that it was VantagePoint. How had he overlooked that? His publishers must have mentioned it to him, but he'd been so distracted of late that it hadn't sunk home. It seemed especially strange, since it was one of his mother's favourite songs—and a point of reference in one of those early e-mail exchanges with Sarah.

And that did it. It made up his mind there and then to go to Zoot and meet the woman who for some reason reminded him so much of Jo.

'I'm glad you could make it,' Nigel Leach said in a manner that would seem smarmy to most women but which Libby found quite flattering.

His hand lingered slightly too long as he shook hers, while his eyes scanned her face admiringly.

He'd called her at nine that morning and asked if he could see her as soon as possible. She'd been surprised to find that his office was open on a Saturday, but it had sounded so urgent that she'd agreed to go there immediately.

'I've got good news for you,' he said as she took the seat in front of his desk. This time he didn't go around to his own chair, but sat on the edge of the desk, so close to her that their legs were almost touching.

'I've been in negotiations with your former employers,' he continued importantly, 'and they have agreed to a settlement.'

'So soon?' she said, very surprised.

'I imagine they want the matter dealt with as quickly as possible in order to avoid any adverse publicity.' He looked very pleased with himself.

'How much?' Libby said, cutting to the chase.

He reached behind him and picked up a sheet of paper, then passed it to her. It was blank but for a figure written in blue ballpoint pen.

'Ten grand?'

He nodded.

'I hope you're pleased.'

Darn right she was. She looked up at him and smiled. What a difference a day makes, she thought happily. Only yesterday she had lost a small fortune, but today things were definitely looking up. And in more ways than one, perhaps...

'I didn't expect that much,' she said, batting her eyelids.

'We do our best,' he said smugly. 'Of course there's the little matter of my commission, but that still leaves you with a healthy sum.'

'Indeed,' agreed Libby, already wondering how she would spend the money. She would have to keep some aside for overheads, until she found a new job, but that still left a fair bit to play with.

'How long before I get the money?' she wanted to know.

'A month or so.'

'Excellent,' she said, and handed the sheet of paper back to him.

He coughed. 'I don't usually do this,' he said, 'but I was wondering if you'd care to join me for a celebratory meal. This evening, perhaps?'

Libby was delighted that she hadn't been imagining his interest in her, but although she was tempted there was still the matter of Dan to consider. She was making headway in the *good-friends* department, and she'd been planning to go round to see him tonight.

'Would you mind if I rang you later?' she said, hedging her bets. 'I just need to see if I can get out of a prior arrangement,' she added, because it wouldn't do any harm to make it sound as if she was a woman in demand.

'I'll look forward to it,' he said, apparently taking it for granted that she would readily drop someone else for him.

I was tempted to tell Giovanna what was happening that morning. She just seemed so *happy*—happier even than my father had been. Until I'd spoilt everything, that is, and told him about Mum. But I couldn't do it to her—a) because it wasn't my business, and b) well, because I just didn't want to spoil everything for her as well. She was going to find out soon enough. She might just as well have a single day of thinking that life was wonderful.

But it was hard to be normal with her, so, rather than get into conversations that might lead to lies, I invented a very sore throat that hurt so much it was hard to speak. And because she is such a nice woman she had a word with Dulcie, who agreed to stay on after lunch so that I could go home and rest.

And just to make things worse, just to add to my guilty conscience, she whacked six fifty-pound notes into my hand when I was leaving. I'd kept her informed about Pisus and she knew I would be starting there on Monday, that I didn't need the job any longer, but I didn't expect *that*. I hadn't a clue how much she'd intended paying me, but three hundred quid was a lot more than I'd ever have guessed.

I wondered if it was some kind of reward for bringing my father into her life, and if so then I might just be taking money under false pretences. For all I knew he was back with my mother by now, having turned nasty on Brian Dick and demanded his rights as homeowner and husband. True, this wasn't an image I could easily conjure up in my mind, but I'd given him a lot to be riled about.

I got in at three-thirty and found the flat tidy but deserted. I did a quick check in my wardrobe, and when I found my dad's clothes were still hanging there I took it as a good sign. Trouble was, I so badly wanted things to be OK that I'd have taken a decapitated horse's head in my bed as a good sign at that very moment. But it was enough for the time being, and, because I hadn't slept too well the previous night, and because I knew I'd be late tonight, I climbed into my bed and went out like a light the moment my head hit the pillow.

I woke some time later to the sound of the telephone ringing, and my heart beat fast as I clutched the receiver.

'Hello,' I said in a frightened child-whisper as I waited for my mother to explode.

'It's me,' Dad said, and I was glad of the lesser of two possible evils. But I still held my breath till he spoke.

'It's sorted,' he said cheerily, and I wondered if he was drunk.

'What's sorted?' I asked him cautiously.

'Your mother's not pregnant and Brian Dick isn't moving in.'

I was coming to gradually, but this still wasn't making much sense. I decided to take one thing at a time.

'What do you mean she's not pregnant?' I said, sitting up in the bed.

'She was jumping the gun as usual—making assumptions. She had a test a few days ago and the results arrived this morning.' I could detect a hint of a chuckle in his voice. 'It turns out that she's menopausal.'

Oh, God, I thought. That was probably a bigger blow to my mother than pregnancy. But it was a very great relief to me.

'And the Dick?' I said disrespectfully of my mother's lover.

'And the Dick,' Dad repeated, 'has changed his mind. Barbara got tough and told him she'd take him to the cleaners, so he's gone home with his tail between his legs.'

It took a moment for that mixture of metaphors to sink into my brain, and then it occurred to me that it was Nicola's toughness behind all this and not her mother's. But I didn't say anything. I was more interested in knowing where this left my parents' marriage.

'And you, Dad? What are *you* going to do?'

'That's the main purpose of this call,' he said, cheerful as ever. 'I just wanted you to know that I won't be back at the flat tonight.'

Oh, dear, I thought. Poor Giovanna. She was so looking forward to seeing my father that evening, and I was annoyed with him now for not seeming to care. 'Have you called Giovanna yet?' I asked him stiffly.

'Yes. I told her I was going to be a bit late and that I'd explain everything when I saw her.'

Now I really was confused.

'I don't understand,' I said. 'What about Mum?'

'Your mother? I'm not sure what she's doing. Drowning her sorrows, I wouldn't wonder.'

I lifted the duvet and put my feet over the edge of the bed. I hadn't even got around to undressing before I'd fallen asleep, and my pasta-sauce-smelling clothes were deeply crumpled.

'I'm not sure what you mean,' I said, then I had a bad thought. 'You're not thinking of two-timing Giovanna, are you?' Which seemed a strange thing to say about the *other* woman.

'Oh, I see what you mean now. I haven't explained myself very well, have I?'

There was a slight pause, and while I waited for him to go on I moved to the window and shut the night out of my room.

'I have no intention of going back home,' he said. 'It's over with me and your mother and I've just made that abundantly clear. She wasn't very happy about it, of course, but she could hardly make demands on me after what's happened.'

Which was perfectly true. But I was still a bit stunned by my father's self-assurance. He'd always been so under my mother's thumb in the past—it was hard to take in that he was the one in control now. Had Giovanna done this for him after one single date?

This was going to take some getting my head around, but in the meantime something else needed an explanation.

'What did you mean about not coming back to the flat tonight?'

'I'm, erm, well—you know...staying with Giovanna.'

'Oh,' I said uncomfortably, 'I see.' I was a little shocked, as a matter of fact. He'd only been out with Giovanna once and—I dismissed the thought before my imagination ran away with me. One promiscuous parent was quite enough to deal with in any given week. Besides, I was beginning to feel annoyed with him. It was all very well, him being firm with my mother for once in his life, but it would be me who'd have to pick up the pieces. Then something else struck me.

'Does Mum know about Giovanna?'

'Not as such,' he said sheepishly.

'Don't you think you should tell her?' But even as I said it I wasn't so sure about that. Once she found out who he was seeing it would be me, no doubt, who got the blame for introducing them to one another.

'Not just yet,' he said. 'It's quite a nice feeling, having the moral high ground for once in my life, and knowing your mother she'd only twist it all round and blame Giovanna for breaking up the marriage.'

Which no doubt was true, but I was still uneasy. If she found out from someone else it could blow up in our faces.

'It's a pity we couldn't get her out of the way for a while,' I said, thinking more of myself than him. I was dreading her ringing me up, demanding that I went to the house to listen to her pouring out all her sorrows.

I lay back down on the bed and looked up at the ceiling— and the idea suddenly came to me.

'You'd better go,' I said to my dad. 'You don't want to keep Giovanna waiting too long.'

'OK,' he said. 'See you erm…tomorrow, then.'

'Look, Dad,' I said, rolling my eyes. 'If I'm going to get used to all this it might be best if you stopped sounding quite so embarrassed about it. Because that makes me embarrassed as well.'

'OK,' he said, trying out unabashed boldness for size. 'See you tomorrow, then.'

I got up, put the receiver back on its cradle and fetched my bag from the sitting room. I took out my address book and found my brother's home number. I reckoned it must be about ten in the morning in California, and with a bit of luck I might just catch him in.

For once I wasn't concerned about the cost of the call. If I could just persuade Matthew to invite our mother to stay with him for a while, it would be worth every penny…

Dan was on his way down to Aisling's flat. He'd tried her earlier, but she and Steve were either out or involved in a marathon sexathon that had made them deaf to his knock at the door.

He'd spoken to Libby since then. She'd been round to ask

what he was doing tonight and he'd taken the opportunity to give her a piece of his mind. Or that had been the idea anyway.

The reality, however, had been somewhat different.

'How do you know that it's me who's been lying?' she said coolly when he told her what he'd learnt last night. That, for whatever reason, she had clearly told Jo that Aisling and he had been an item.

He didn't let her into the flat. He just stood at the door, with folded arms, as if barring the entrance.

'Because Aisling has no reason to lie about it,' he said.

'I wasn't thinking of Aisling.'

He had to hand it to her; she was a very cool customer. He'd expected her to crumble when he accused her of lying, but she seemed determined to brazen it out.

'Are you trying to say that *Jo* made it all up? Well, I'm sorry, Libby,' he told her firmly, 'but that really doesn't make any sense.'

'But why would I tell her something like that?' she said. She shook her head in a bewildered fashion, and then suddenly her face twisted into a sneer. 'Oh, I get it,' she said. 'You think I did it so that I could have you all to myself, don't you?'

She was either an excellent bluffer or she was telling the truth, and for a moment Dan couldn't decide which. When she put it like that it did sound unlikely, not to mention egotistical. He decided not to pursue that particular line for the moment. Instead he mentioned something else that had begun to bother him.

'You suggested that Jo probably broke into my flat because she knew that we'd spent a night together—'

Libby tilted her head defiantly, ready for anything he could throw at her.

'So if she really was crazed with jealous anger—' it sounded so ridiculous when he said it that he wondered how he could ever have believed it for a single second '—why didn't she do it when she thought that I was with Aisling?'

Libby thought about this for a moment, then a familiar glint appeared in her eye.

'But don't you see that *proves* I'm telling the truth?' she said, shaking her head as if she was dealing with an idiot. 'If I'd really told her such a stupid, pointless lie, she probably *would* have done something sooner.'

He found himself rubbing his left temple at this point. He hadn't thought of that.

He sighed. 'I dunno, Libby, I really don't. But something very odd is going on here.'

'It certainly is,' she said sarcastically. 'But if you prefer to take the word of a nutty ex-girlfriend, that's up to you.'

And with that she had turned and flounced on up the stairs to her flat.

'What's up?' Aisling wanted to know now. 'You look like shit.'

'Cheers, Ash,' he said as he followed her into her pink and white living room that looked like a set piece from *Barbie, the Movie*.

Steve was not in evidence, and Aisling explained with a wink that he was 'recovering' in the bath. She was wearing her bathrobe, and presumably was meant to join him there, but Dan needed to talk too much to feel any guilt.

'I spoke to Libby earlier,' he said as he flopped on the sofa he'd helped move around several times in the past, 'and I'm more confused than ever now.'

Aisling sat down next to him, and when he'd given her the meat of their conversation she shook her head.

'Jo wasn't lying,' she said adamantly. 'I admit I don't know her that well, but I do know when someone is mad with me and she was as mad as hell. To start with anyway.' She batted her eyelids. 'Until I worked my charm on her.'

Dan scratched his head.

'And she would only be angry if she really believed that we'd been together? Is that what you're saying?'

'Precisely. But she was *normal* mad, not *crazy* mad—just like I would have been if the situation had been reversed.' She held out her hands as if her point was proved. 'So Libby *must* have told her.'

'Just like she told her that we'd slept together.'

Aisling looked perplexed now.

'Who'd slept together?'

Dan sighed. 'Libby and me.'

Aisling frowned and shook her head. 'No,' she said. 'I told her that, and you should have seen her face! I felt so bad that I said I didn't think anything had actually happened.'

'This is starting to do my head in,' Dan said. 'Are you saying that Jo *didn't* know about Libby before last night?'

'Definitely not. Why?'

'Because Libby said that *she'd* told her and that was the reason she must have broken into the flat. I said that it bothered me—why hadn't she done it before?—but Libby just twisted it round and used it as proof of her innocence.'

'And talking of *proof*,' Aisling said, suddenly very animated now. 'I forgot to tell you last night, but Jo said that she was at her parents' place on the night of the break-in and that *she* could prove it. Cheer up,' she added, when Dan didn't speak for a while. 'At least you never got around to actually accusing Jo—which is something, I suppose.'

'I suppose,' said Dan, but, although he didn't know why, he still had a very bad feeling about it all.

chapter 16

I was lucky in more than one way. I just caught Matt on his way to the gym, and because he was late, anxious to be on his way, I think I also caught him off his guard.

I didn't go into too many details. That is I didn't tell Matt about Brian Dick, or Giovanna. I just said that our parents were having difficulties in their marriage and a break would do them both the world of good.

It was obvious he wasn't very keen on having our mother to stay with him. He put up several quite legitimate objections—that she'd be on her own all day when he worked, for example—and a few lamer ones as well, but in the end I pulled out my trump card and hit him with a dollop of guilt.

'She's in a bad way at the moment. She feels unloved and, let's face it, you haven't made very much effort with her since you left. It would make her year to get an invitation from you.'

The gym was evidently calling, and he made a reluctant grunt and finally agreed.

'I'll call her when I get back,' he said gloomily, 'but if she's a pain I'll hold you responsible.'

'What's new?' I said. 'I get the blame for everything anyway.'

He laughed, and told me to cheer up, and I thought that I probably would the minute my mother was well and truly California-bound.

Meanwhile I had another couple of calls to make.

I tried Cass first. I was curious to know how things had gone with Sid, and whether I could expect her to be joining us at Pisus. I was a little miffed that neither one of them had bothered to call me, but I was very determined not to show it.

She did answer the phone, but she sounded funny—as if, well, as if someone was in the room with her and it was making it difficult for her to speak. So I did what we'd always done in the past on such occasions. I asked her questions that required only yes and no replies.

'Have you got someone with you?'

'Yes.'

'Is it Sid?'

'Yes.'

'Are things going well between you?'

'Yes.'

'Are you going to take up his offer of work?'

'No.'

I wanted to ask why, but I couldn't think of the right questions to ask, so I left that one.

'Will you ring me and tell me why at a later stage?'

'Yes.'

Then she giggled a bit, a very un-Cass-like sound, and I felt myself blush.

'Are you in bed at the moment?'

'Yes.'

'Do you know that he's only twenty-one?'

'Yes.'

'Better leave you to it, then,' I said with a sigh.

'Yes,' she said, and giggled again.

Then I had a horrible thought.

'Please don't tell Sid about Sarah Daly. He'll think I'm mad and sack me before I even start.'

'You're not still doing that, are you?' She sounded serious now.

'No,' I lied.

'Then I won't.'

'Cheers, Cass.'

It was getting on for six when I replaced the receiver, and I'd agreed to meet Tim at seven-thirty. We were going to start off at a restaurant handy for me to walk to in my high heels, and then hopefully we'd take a taxi on to Zoot.

I made a cup of teabag tea and took it back with me to the phone.

I thought it was probably a good time to ring Nicola now. She'd said that her fiancé's parents were supposed to be meeting hers over the weekend, and now that Brian was back in the fold I assumed it was going ahead. She hadn't said when, exactly, but even if it was tonight I didn't imagine they'd arrive as early as six o'clock.

I rang her mobile and she picked up on the second ring.

'It's Jo,' I told her quickly. 'Is it OK to speak?'

'Perfectly,' she said in a dubious tone that made me worried straight away.

'My father rang and told me what happened. How are things now at home?'

'Lousy,' she said. 'I've just come from there and it's been like treading on eggshells. They're trying to pretend that nothing's happened.'

'I don't know your fiancé's name—' I began. I'd been about to ask if he was with her, but she interrupted me.

'*Ex*-fiancé! And his name doesn't matter much now.'

I was shocked. 'I'm sorry—'

'Nothing to be sorry about. It's all for the best.'

Now, when anyone says that things are for the best, they are, in my experience, usually trying to kid themselves. I thought about asking if she'd like to come over and talk, but then I remembered my date with Tim.

'Do you fancy getting together tomorrow? For lunch, maybe?'

There was a short silence while she thought about this.

'OK,' she said. 'Know anywhere that does a proper roast lunch? I feel like a pigout.'

I smiled, glad that we had something in common.

'There's a pub near my place that does great Yorkshire pudding.'

'You're on,' she said.

I gave her the address of the pub and we agreed to meet at twelve-thirty.

When I put the phone down I decided to check my e-mails before I got ready. I didn't know whether to be pleased or not when there wasn't a message waiting from Dan. I reasoned that he would have responded by now with his excuses if didn't plan on going to Zoot, which was good in that Sarah would get her chance to stand him up. But I couldn't help wishing that he *had* made his excuses. That he wasn't showing quite so much interest in another woman, even a woman of my own invention.

But I was over all that, I reminded myself firmly. Dan was a fink—whatever a fink was, but somehow it seemed to fit.

Dan had listened to and, more importantly, *believed* bad things about me. And Sarah, dear Sarah, was to be my avenger. So there was absolutely no sense being jealous of her.

There was, however, a message from my mother. I thought about leaving it till later, but dreadful temptation got the better of me and I clicked it open.

> *Dear Joanna*
> *Thankfully one of my children still cares about me. I just wanted you to know that I fly out on Monday to spend a month with Matthew.*

Poor Matt, I thought gleefully. I doubted he'd been banking on her staying that long!

> *We won't have a chance to talk before then, but I do hope you will use this time to do the right thing for once, and persuade your father to return to the marital home. I am prepared to put all our past difficulties behind us, and if he has any sense he will do the same.*

There was a kind of threat in that last line, I thought. An If not, then I'll take him to the cleaners, sort of threat. She'd clearly seen how it had worked on Brian Dick and was expecting the same sort of success with my father.

'Well,' I said out loud to my absent mother, 'we'll just have to see about that, won't we?'

By the end of the meal Libby had fallen *out* of love with Dan and *in* love with Nigel.

Just like with Paul, who'd turned out to be such a disappointment, she could hardly imagine what she'd seen in Dan now. Dan, with his grubby little flat, his obsession with music, and his ridiculous hang-up about a silly ex-girlfriend.

With Nigel, however, she'd already discovered that he had almost everything that she'd ever wanted from a man. Nice car, a fat wallet, good-enough looks. And at that very moment she was on her way to his place in the nice car to check out the final part of the package. And if the flat measured up, well, then it was goodbye for ever to hard-up, hard-work Dan.

And Nigel clearly liked what he saw in her as well. He had hardly been able to keep his hands off her since they'd left the restaurant, and while some women might have found that off putting, Libby was delighted. She'd made quite an effort with her appearance—new hair colour, new skimpy dress—and it was nice to be appreciated. She didn't often have that effect on men, and it was doing wonders for her slightly dented ego.

For which she held Dan entirely responsible. He'd treated her shabbily. Leading her on and then dropping her when he felt like it. Accusing her of being a liar! And, OK, so she might have told the odd fib or two, but all in his best interests. And maybe she had smashed a few of his precious CDs, but he had thousands more, and it had been in a very good cause. But if he couldn't see that—well, then he deserved what he got.

'We're here, sweet thing,' Nigel said now as he took one hand off the steering wheel and rubbed her thigh.

She looked up at the swish block of purpose-built flats that happened to be in a very desirable part of the city and smiled as she mentally ticked off the final good reason for being newly in love.

The food had been great, the restaurant fab, and Tim himself—well, he was he exactly the sort of man every girl's mother and especially mine would like her to bring home.

Good-looking, rich, courteous, attentive... So why had I spent most of the meal suppressing a yawn?

I wouldn't say he was boring—exactly. He had lots to say for himself about...cameras, and lenses, and shops that sold cameras and lenses. And he didn't even talk about himself all the time. He wanted to know all about me and my life, and he sat there rapt as I treated him to the odd amusing tidbit.

But I think it was the look on his face that got to me. That expression of his as he listened to me, as if I was a wondrous thing to behold. I don't know why, but I found it quite annoying. I could see him building a pedestal for me in his mind, and I'm not very good with heights.

'You look amazing,' he'd said, for example, when I stumbled into the restaurant. I'd tripped over the step on the way in and Dan would have laughed till his sides split. But Tim? No, Tim thought that I looked *amazing*.

I think we were only fifteen minutes into the meal when I realised why this apparently extremely eligible man was still single in his mid-thirties. I'd fantasised that it was because he'd been waiting for someone just like me, but now I was beginning to see that he was waiting for *anyone*. Anyone who wanted to be adored—and if they liked cameras and camera accessories, then so much the better.

And, despite the fact that the whole point of the date was to go to Zoot, he wasn't even dressed for a club. I was wearing my halfway-house vintage dress that looked elegant enough for a fancy restaurant but still sassy enough to dance in. Tim, on the other hand, was wearing a suit that would have looked good in a boardroom but not in one of the city's hottest venues. He was going to look a prat, and if I hadn't been so keen to get there on time I'd have suggested he went home and changed. I even considered cutting short the date, going to the club on my own—but it was important that if Dan saw me I had someone reasonably presentable at my side.

I was worried about the doormen, though, when we got there. They can be very choosy about whom they let in, and I thought they might object to Tim on the grounds that he might spoil the club's funky image. But we made it OK, and we were safely inside by ten minutes to ten.

Tim was in very high spirits, unfortunately. And because he believed the reason that we were there was to dance, dance was what he insisted on doing. Straight away, before we even got a drink. And he was as bad as I thought he would be— arms flying, not to the sound of the music at all, but to some wild beat that existed only in his own head.

It was one of those moments when you feel like telling everyone around you that although it might look as if you're with this embarrassing individual, you aren't really. You're just keeping an eye on them for someone else.

I suffered it as long as I could, and then signed to him that I needed a drink.

He was obviously enjoying himself so much that he was disappointed, but first and foremost he remembered he was an *attentive escort.*

'Phew,' he said as he caught up with me, 'that was fantastic. I'd forgotten how good it was to let yourself really go like that.'

I didn't think I'd ever forget what it was like when Tim let himself really go, personally, but I managed a smile.

I was already scanning the bar area for Dan as we approached it. It was pretty crowded, but I sensed that I'd spot him immediately if he was there, and my senses told me he wasn't. I glanced at my wristwatch: it was ten-fifteen, and I don't know why but I felt slightly relieved. OK, so I'd decided that I wasn't jealous of Sarah, that she was doing this for me, but I couldn't quite shake off the feeling that she was muscling in. That she had her own agenda. And, yes, I know that sounds nuts, but that's how it was, I'm sorry to say.

And then I didn't have time to analyse the strange workings of my mind any more, because I saw him. He was just moving through the crush to get to the bar, some distance from me, and the first thing I thought was that he needed a haircut. Then I was afraid that he might see me, so I ducked behind Tim.

He'd just got our drinks—white wine for me, mineral water for himself—and he seemed keen to hit the dance floor again. He started heading that way, but I grabbed him.

'You can't take glasses on the floor,' I reminded him, with a mixture of sign language and shouting over the racket going on around us. 'Besides, I haven't got your energy,' I flattered him. 'I could do with a break.'

'Perhaps we could drive out to the country tomorrow,' he shouted back, and I pretended not to hear.

I was moving my head to the music and I hoped he'd shut up while I kept up my surveillance on Dan. He'd ordered a pint of beer and had parked himself with his back to the bar so he could see what was going on around him. Despite the hair, he looked great, in simple white T-shirt and Levi's. I noticed that he paid special attention to anyone wearing red, and the only good thing I could make of it all was the certain lack of enthusiasm in his expression. That might be because he hated clubs, but—and maybe I was imagining it—I thought there was more to it than that.

'So tell me about your parents?' Tim shouted at me, and I shook my head. I certainly wasn't going down that particular road.

'Another time,' I said, though I already knew there wouldn't be another time.

Dan glanced at his wristwatch. He wasn't looking around so much now, and just at that moment he turned back to the bar and stared into his glass.

I don't know what got into me, but once it did, I couldn't resist it.

'Oh,' I said to Tim in sudden surprise, 'there's someone I know over there.'

I took hold of his free hand and dragged him after me.

'Hello, Dan,' I said, all bubbly and bright as I tapped him on the shoulder.

He turned quickly and the slight smile on his face turned to shock when he found me standing there instead of Sarah. We hadn't spoken since I'd left without a word, so he was entitled to be shocked I suppose, especially since he thought I was crazy enough to break into his flat and smash his beloved CDs.

And I think that's why I did it. If I'd been guilty, the last thing I would have been doing now would be drawing attention to myself. And I wanted him to think about that.

'This is Tim,' I said, gripping his hand more firmly than ever.

They nodded at one another, and, keeping up the show of bonhomie, I asked Dan if he was on his own.

'Looks like it,' he said, and as he spoke he seemed to search my face—looking for signs of madness, maybe. It had an effect on me. It made me feel bad. I should have been gloating, but quite suddenly I'd had enough of this little charade. And Tim, poor Tim—I'd had enough of him too.

'Well, we're just off,' I said to Dan.

'Are we?' asked Tim, surprised.

'I'm tired,' I lied.

'Nice meeting you,' Tim said, and ever the gentleman he reached out his hand to Dan.

They shook hands, and with a quick nod at Dan I whisked Tim away.

I think he thought I wanted to be on my own with him, that I was going to invite him into the flat, but I soon persuaded him otherwise.

'Thanks for everything,' I told him as we pulled up outside the building, 'but I've got some things I need to sort out.' Which was pretty close to the truth.

'What about tomorrow?' he said, unperturbed. 'How about that drive in the country.'

'I'm seeing a friend for lunch,' I said, which was also true. 'But I'll be in touch,' I added, which wasn't. Or at least not in the way he was clearly hoping.

Dan left the club at eleven o'clock. He'd have left a lot earlier, but after seeing Jo he'd needed another drink, and then another. He hadn't thought much about Sarah at all. There hadn't been room in his head for her as well. He wasn't even pissed off with her for not turning up. Because if he hadn't gone there to meet her he would never have seen Jo. Who'd looked so good in that dress he'd always liked so much, and who quite obviously hadn't broken into his flat—scarf or no bloody scarf.

Why would she, when she was clearly so happy with that twerp in the suit? He'd been beginning to think that Libby might have lied about that as well, and the fact that she hadn't was what he'd found really disappointing, not the failure of Sarah to show.

He took a taxi home, and when he opened the main door of the house he thought about calling on Aisling and Steve. They were playing loud music, lots of drum and bass, and although he'd had his fill of that at the club he would gladly have put up with more for the sake of some company.

He was at the very point of knocking at the door when he suddenly came out of his stupor. This was crazy, he told himself. What he needed now was what he always needed when things were bothering him: some *decent* music. And if there was any of that Spanish liqueur left over—well, maybe some of that too.

★ ★ ★

I'm plainly not very good at revenge—either that or it isn't
nearly so sweet as people say that it is. Because I didn't feel
very good at all about pulling that fast one on Dan. In fact,
now that I'd seen him, all I could think about was how much
I'd missed him, and what a fool I was for running out on him.
Oh, yes, I'd had my reasons, but they seemed pretty flimsy
now in the scheme of things.

And, OK, he'd been quick to condemn me for something
that I hadn't done—would never dream of doing—but I already knew how convincing Libby could be. And maybe I'd
have thought the worst of him if it had been the other way
round.

But it was too late now to undo anything. I had to accept
that it really was over—though I didn't want him thinking
badly of Sarah as well. I made up my mind to write an apology from her for not showing up. As soon as I'd sent a message to Tim.

I know it was cowardly of me, sending an e-mail instead
of calling, but I thought I could do it better that way. I therefore wrote from my business address:

> *Dear Tim*
> *I had a great evening with you tonight, but I'm worried that
> if I continue seeing you in a personal sense it might affect our
> business relationship.*

Pretty good so far, but I needed a clincher. Something to
soften the blow. I was worried that our business relationship
might already be affected, and I didn't want him pulling out
of Pisus because of me. Sid would never forgive me.

> *Besides which, when I got back tonight I realised that I'm
> not ready to get involved with someone else just yet.*

I know it's an old chestnut, that particular line, but on this occasion it just happened to be the truth.

I sent it, and then made some tea. And when I came back I wrote a quick message to Dan.

> *Dear Dan*
> *Sorry I didn't make it. I met up with my ex on my way to the station, and guess what? You were right. It wasn't over with him at all...*
> *I'm sure that you'll understand.*
> *Sarah*

I hadn't planned it in advance, but it was a sort of good-bye from her, I suppose. I was exhausted with all the deception, and I wanted no more of it. If he wrote back then I wouldn't reply. That was it, I decided there and then. The end.

I was so intent on getting it off, so distracted by everything going on in my head, that it didn't occur to me that I'd written it from my business address.

From Jo. Hurst@*Pisus* dot fricking com.

That wouldn't sink in for another eighteen or so blessedly ignorant hours.

It was just after midday on Sunday and I was beginning to wonder where Dad was. I was dying to tell him that Mum was going to stay with Matt, that we were both in the clear for a month, and when the telephone rang I guessed that it must be him. I was wrong, though.

'It's Marco,' said Marco, before I could speak.

'Oh,' I said, flustered. As far as I knew he wasn't due back until the following day. As far as his *mother* knew he wasn't due back till the following day... 'Where are you calling from?' I said anxiously.

'The airport. Just got here and I want to see you.'

I breathed a sigh of relief. For a moment I'd thought he must have got home and found our parents in a compromising situation. Then it sank in—what he *was* saying...

'What do you mean, you want to see me?'

'You haven't forgotten already, have you?' He laughed. 'I told you I'd ring you when I got back.'

'Ah, yes, well—um, when?'

'However long it takes me to get to your place.'

'I'm going out for lunch soon,' I said, panicky again, hoping that I could get hold of my dad before Marco got home.

'Can't you cancel it?'

I could, I supposed, but, hey, why should I?

'Sorry, Marco, can't do that.'

A slight hesitation, then, 'How about tonight?' He sounded so keen that I admit I was flattered.

'OK.'

'We'll make it early,' he said. 'I'll pick you up at seven.'

'Why don't I meet you outside the Corn Exchange?' I said, because I didn't want him bumping into my father.

'Fine. I've got something to tell you, and you can fill me on what's been happening while I was away.'

With a bit of judicious editing, I thought.

I put the phone down and then grabbed the telephone directory. I found Giovanna's home number and dialled, praying that she and my father hadn't gone out for a romantic brunch somewhere.

She picked up just when I was beginning to give up on her. There was a hint of discomfort when she realised who it was on the other end of the line, but I didn't have time for embarrassment.

'I've just had a call from Marco. He's on his way home.'

Nothing else needed to be said, and apart from an Italian cry of alarm nothing was.

They say women dress for men, but that lunchtime I dressed for Nicola. I pulled out all the stops and made myself look as good as I could for a pub lunch, without any apparent effort involved. I wore my best jeans, which were a bit tight—but that was OK, because they had a corset effect on my slightly protruding tummy—and I topped them with a gorgeous green fluffy jumper that Matt, bless him, had sent from the States for my last birthday. I topped the ensemble with a smart black jacket, and while I was gentle on the make-up, soft on the hair gel—bearing in mind that the last time I'd seen Nic I'd stunk of food—I slightly overdid the Poison.

I was refusing to let myself think about Dan, and Sarah, and Libby, and every other damn thing that had been troubling me. I needed a break from everything and, surprise though it was, I was actually looking forward to meeting up with Nic. I'd far rather that it had been Cass, but Cass was clearly too busy to bother with me at the moment. And Nic was better than no one.

There weren't many traditional pubs left in the area. Most had reinvented themselves as fancy eateries. Sometimes I yearned for pork scratchings instead of tapas, warm beer instead of chilled Chardonnay, and today was one of those times. There was a real fire cheerfully crackling in the grate, and Nic was beside it when I got there.

'Fab pub,' she said when I slipped into the seat next to her with my pint of best bitter. There was a bottle of red wine on the table that I noted was already half empty.

'I've ordered for us,' she said. 'Roast beef for two. Extra Yorkshire pudding.'

'Great,' I said, wishing I'd worn more comfortably fitting trousers now. Nic was wearing sensible grey jogging pants, with room for expansion. She hadn't even bothered with make-up, as far as I could tell, and I'll admit I was rather concerned for her.

'He was a twit anyway,' she said out of the blue, and it was a moment before I realised that she was talking about her ex-fiancé.

'He was always telling me off for "taking the Lord's name in vain"!' she said, doing a good impersonation of a patient but pious hospital registrar. 'Jesus Christ! It was like being a trainee nun, going out with him.'

'Then why did you?' I said, smiling at her easy way with the profane, her complete lack of suitability for the marriage she had been seriously contemplating. I was happy to let her get it out of her system, because it kept my mind off my own problems. 'Go out with him, I mean?'

She lit up a cigarette and thought about it.

'Because he was someone my mother could boast about, I think.' She shook her head. 'Sad, isn't it?' She looked at me then, closely. 'That's what I always admired about you,' she said.

'Me?' I said with surprise.

'You know—actually living with someone that your mother couldn't stand.'

I was taken aback by this.

'I didn't realise she *couldn't stand* Dan.'

Nicola shrugged. 'Well, maybe it wasn't as bad as that, but she definitely didn't approve.' She grinned at this point. 'She thought he was, and I quote, "One of those arty-farty types who never do a serious day's work in their lives and end up living off women."'

I let out a sigh. 'The trouble with both our mothers is that they don't have much imagination. They see things in clichés, never realising for a second that they are the biggest clichés of all.'

Nicola lifted her glass as if to salute me.

'Very profound,' she said, 'and the really bad thing is that I was going down the same road myself.'

'So what happened exactly?' I said. 'With you and erm...' As I said it I noticed that the crucifix and engagement ring had already been removed.

'Clive.' She laughed sourly. 'Ridiculous name, isn't it?'

Well, yes, it was. But I didn't feel it was my place to say so.

'I decided to come clean,' she said, and she said it wryly. 'I think it had something to do with our conversation the other day. I suddenly wondered why I was pretending that everything was fine when it wasn't.' She emptied her glass and topped it up again from the bottle. 'So I told him what was happening between my parents and he was so shocked it was laughable. I did laugh, in fact, and that made him angry. Well, as angry as a committed Christian will let himself get...'

I didn't say anything. I just sipped my beer while she collected her thoughts and eventually she went on.

'Of course the irony is that they're back together again now. He might never have known if I hadn't blurted it out.'

'Does that mean you're sorry you did?'

'Absolutely not,' she said. 'Any more than I'm sorry for telling the twerp to sling his hook. And at least I can smoke again now,' she said, drawing smoke deep into her lungs as if to make up for lost time. 'That was another thing he looked down his nose at.'

I couldn't help feeling rather proud of Nic. Not for taking up smoking again, but for dropping all the pretence.

'And what about your mother? Have you told her yet?'

She nodded her head wryly. 'I told her yesterday. I was all geared for a major row and I felt quite let down when she let it pass without much comment.'

'There's no pleasing some people,' I said with a grin.

Just then a waitress brought our food, and we didn't speak for a while as we tucked into the beef with a hearty disregard for any possible BSE contamination.

She looked up at me eventually, and smiled. Her bottle of wine was nearly empty by now and her cheeks were glowing.

'Just look at us,' she said. 'Anyone seeing us now would think we were the best of mates.'

I knew what she meant. It did seem odd that we were sitting there comfortably after years of mutual dislike. And all because of some silly bloke. I returned her smile and it seemed to me that she was born again *again*, this time as a normal, quite pleasant individual.

We spent the next hour reminiscing and laughing about school, and by the time we'd finished I felt as if I had a new friend.

She had a Thai massage booked at three-thirty, which was the reason for the jogging pants, I learnt. It was a regular twice-weekly event, apparently, with a genuine Thai, and she looked at me pityingly when I said I'd never even had an English massage.

'I'll ring you,' she said when she'd paid the bill and gathered up her belongings. 'We could do a club or something during the week.'

I doubted I'd be up to 'doing a club' in the middle of the week. I clearly didn't have Nicola's stamina. But I didn't turn her down there and then. I decided that if she meant what she said and came back to me, I could persuade her to leave it till the weekend. Till I'd got my first week at Pisus over and done with.

She put a blue baseball cap on her head, and when we'd donned our jackets we went outside together and both squinted at the bright daylight.

'Oh, yes,' she said, doing her mind-reading party piece. 'Good luck with Pisus and don't forget to bear me in mind for staff.'

I told her I wouldn't—forget, that was—and she turned to head off in the opposite direction from me. Then she stopped and turned around again.

'By the way—you know that creature that used to be your neighbour...?'

'Libby?' I said, guessing whom she meant straight away.

She narrowed her eyes and nodded. 'She's not to be trusted.'

'I know,' I said.

'Good,' said Nic. 'I sacked her recently and the bitch has sued the firm for unfair dismissal.'

'Was it unfair?'

She shrugged. 'That depends if you think it's unfair to sack someone you just don't happen to like very much.'

'Is she going to get anything?'

'I was all for a fight,' she practically snarled, 'but my wimpy partners have decided to pay her off to the tune of ten grand.'

She made fists with her hands, shook her head furiously, and then flounced off down the road looking very much in need of a destressing session with her Thai masseur.

I left Dad to the Sunday papers while I had a lie-down in my bedroom. I was bursting with beer and roast beef and I couldn't wait to take my jeans off. I told him about Mum's trip to sunny California and he looked like a man who'd been relieved of a huge burden. I felt like telling him that it was only temporary, that he'd have to sort things out sooner or later, but decided it was only fair to let him enjoy the moment.

I lay on the bed in my bathrobe, thinking about Libby and her forthcoming windfall, and it made me feel angry. For someone who'd caused so much trouble, she was coming off very well in the karma department. OK, so if Aisling was right her scheming had failed as far as Dan was concerned, but she had still blackened my name with him, and the more I thought about it the more I felt as if I needed to talk to someone about it.

There was only one person I could think of.

On impulse, I snatched up the phone and asked for directory enquires. I got Aisling's number at home, and dialled it, praying that she would be in.

She was.

'It's Jo,' I said. 'Jo Hurst.'

'Oh,' she said, very surprised. 'Hi!'

'Are you on your own?' I asked cautiously, worried now that Dan might be there, or Steve, who might feel it his duty to report to Dan that I had rung.

'Yes. Steve left a while ago to catch his train.'

'Can we talk in confidence?' I said.

'Do you mean that I'm not to tell Dan you called?'

'Precisely.'

'Fine by me.'

'Dan did think it was me who broke into his flat, didn't he?'

'He may have,' Aisling said cautiously, 'but not any more. And you can't blame him for thinking it because he found a scarf in his flat that he's certain is yours.'

I was dumbfounded.

'What sort of scarf?'

'A Burberry.'

My Burberry. The one that I lost the other night...

'Shit! She must have stolen it from me.' I explained about having that drink with Libby, and Aisling did not seem surprised.

'Well, that's it, then,' she said. 'Case proven.'

I was stunned as well a dumbfounded now. I'd already known that Libby was a conniving, lying cow, but this—

'You mean you think *she* broke into Dan's flat?' I said to clarify things. An idea was already taking root in my head.

'Looks like it,' she said.

I asked her the extent of the damage to Dan's CDs, and then I told her about the compensation that was heading Libby's way. Aisling agreed with me that she should be made to pay up, but the question was how we could make it happen.

'Leave it to me,' Aisling said eventually. 'I think I might have an idea.'

She disconnected immediately, as if she couldn't wait to get on the case, and—who knows what had been the trigger?—at that very moment, as I put the receiver back in its cradle, I realised what I had done. I realised that I'd sent Sarah's message to Dan from Joanna Hurst's business address. And I knew exactly what people meant now when they said that they wished that the earth would open and swallow them up.

I wrapped up warmly that evening—polo-neck sweater, smart woollen trousers, full-length coat. It was bitterly cold, and if I hadn't been so desperate to get out of the flat I'd have cancelled the arrangement I'd made with Marco.

He picked me up at the Corn Exchange, where I'd been gazing at the city's Christmas lights, switched on the day before, and thinking about this time last year when Dan and I had been together and happy. The only cloud on the horizon then was me having just agreed to spend Christmas Day with my mother. And now there were so many damn clouds I felt as if I was being crushed by them.

He drove me to a chic restaurant overlooking the river a half-mile or so from my flat. It was huge, and for a Sunday evening extremely busy. I couldn't help wondering where everyone came from. Leeds was a prospering city, all right, but there were dozens of restaurants just like this one and most of them were doing just as well. And it wasn't even the Christmas party season yet.

It was one of those places that served sausage and mash for about fifteen quid a head, and justified it by adding some fancy-sounding gravy. But it was also the sort of place where you could have a single course without raising eyebrows, and after roast beef for lunch that suited me fine.

I ordered a Caesar salad and Marco went for some kind of chicken dish. We both had a glass of house wine—him red, me white. And as we waited for the food to arrive we chatted amiably about the weather in Spain and in England.

'But if it was sun you were after,' I said, thinking about my conversation with Giovanna on just this subject, 'I'm surprised you didn't go a bit further afield.'

'It wasn't the sun I went for,' he said, looking into my eyes across the table. He left a bit of mystery hanging in the air and I asked the obvious question.

'What was it you went for, then?' I said.

'I went to visit my father.'

I stared at him in a stupefied sort of way. 'Your father?'

He nodded. 'And, yes, I know I said I never wanted to lay eyes on the man, but he wrote to me, and...' he shrugged. 'Well, I thought I'd give him a chance.'

There were so many questions I didn't know which to ask first. But I had to start somewhere. 'What's he doing in Spain?'

'He lives there now. Has done for a few years.'

'He's not a criminal, is he?' I said, for it is well known that most English gangsters eventually retire to Spain.

'Not as far as I know,' Marco said with a grin. 'But he is very rich.'

'That's not the reason you went, though, is it?'

'Of course not,' he said, sounding genuinely hurt by such a suggestion.

I took a sip of my wine.

'I presume you haven't told Giovanna yet?'

'No,' Marco said. 'I wanted to talk to you about it first. Things went well out in Spain, and I intend to keep in touch with my father, but I don't know how my mother will take the news.'

It was obvious Giovanna hadn't told him her own bit of news, and she was probably just as worried about how *he* would take *that*. It occurred to me there had probably never been a better time for both of them. But I couldn't say so, not without giving too much away.

'I think you should just be honest,' I said. 'I've got to know Giovanna quite well during the week, and I really don't think she'd be too upset, if that's what you're worried about.'

'But she thinks he's a bastard,' he said.

I shrugged. 'Well, he is, isn't he?'

'Maybe he *was*, but he's changed now. He wants to make things up to me.'

'But is it that easy?' I said, aware I was getting into dangerous territory. 'I'm only trying to think how Giovanna might feel, and I imagine her greatest fear will be that you will get hurt.'

'I know, but I'm a big bloke now. It's up to me if I want to risk it.'

'Well, that's what you should tell her, then.'

Our food arrived then, and we didn't speak again till the waiter left.

'But won't she be hurt when she finds out what I've been up to behind her back?'

I smiled at him, pleased that this was important to him.

'A bit maybe,' I said, trying to put myself in Giovanna's shoes. 'But if you don't say *too* many nice things about your father she should be OK. So long as she doesn't feel usurped by him in your affections.'

Marco shook his head emphatically. 'That could never happen.'

'Well, just make sure she knows that and it'll be fine. She's a good woman, your mother. She'll understand that knowing your father is important to you. Even if he is a rich bastard.'

He grinned again, and then told me some more about his trip. His father was divorced from the woman he'd been married to when he'd had his affair with Giovanna. He was now married to a twenty-eight-year-old former beauty queen from Essex, who was apparently as thick as the worst cliché about beauty queens, but she seemed very fond of his father.

I asked if he had any half brothers and sisters, and he said that he had but since his father was now estranged from them he didn't expect to meet them.

'Do you think that's why he contacted you?' I asked. 'Because he's lost touch with his other children?'

'I reckon so,' Marco said, without seeming to mind very much.

'I wouldn't tell Giovanna that bit,' I said. '*You* might be OK with it, but she might not like the fact that he's only showing an interest now because there's no one else.'

Marco picked up his glass and looked at me slyly over the brim. 'But if there's no one else, who do you think he'll leave all his money to?'

I was shocked. 'I thought you said you weren't interested in his money!'

He shrugged. 'I'm not—necessarily. But you can't blame me if I see it as a potential bonus.'

And if I was honest I didn't suppose that I could.

We didn't bother with coffee. I said that I had to get back early because of work in the morning, and he insisted on walking me to the entrance to my flat, when he dropped me off.

Though I didn't go into any details, I'd already mentioned that my father was staying with me, so there was no question of asking him up. With all that had happened I'd almost forgotten that he'd kissed me before he'd left for Spain—that he'd said he couldn't wait to do it again.

But now, just as I was about to put the key in the front door lock, he took hold of my shoulders, manoeuvred me into a kissing position, and did it again. And this time he groaned with pleasure.

I think I groaned with pleasure myself, as a matter of fact.

'I've been wanting to do that all night,' he said when he finally broke off for air. And, although it was one of the oldest lines in the book, although I certainly hadn't felt the same way myself, I didn't spoil things by mentioning it.

'Can we meet again soon?' he asked softly as he pecked at my nose.

And because it didn't seem too bad an idea, and because—let's face it—I'd blown it once and for all with Dan, I said, 'OK—how about Tuesday?'

He said OK as well, and that was the beginning of what was to prove a pretty wild affair between me and my father's girlfriend's son.

chapter 18

It was the last working day of our third week back in business, and although the place where we worked hadn't changed, the atmosphere was completely different now. We'd taken on eight additional employees so far and because we were all in a large open-plan office there was absolutely no sense of *them*—management—and *us*—staff—as there had been in the past. Two more would be joining the team on Monday, and although the temptation was to continue expanding that was to be it for a while. Sid was determined not to make the same mistakes as our predecessors. He wanted to keep things manageable, take it easy, step by step, and not get carried away with early success. I agreed with him wholeheartedly.

He was also very careful about choosing personnel. We had

used Nicola's recruitment firm, but Sid turned a lot more away than he took on. He was also adamant about not employing anyone who'd worked for Pisus in its former incarnation. He said they might bring old habits back with them. If this was in any way intended to be a warning to me about *my* old habits, it did the trick nicely. I'd pulled on reserves I didn't even know I had, and I'd been working far harder than I ever had before in my life. From seven in the morning till ten at night wasn't unusual, and the odd thing was that I was actually enjoying myself. I knew I wouldn't be able to keep up that kind of pace for ever, but until things were on a firmer footing, until we both felt really secure, I reckoned I'd be able to manage. I suppose it helped my motivation that I was a partner, of sorts, but I like to think that I'd have worked just as hard anyway.

It was playing havoc with my love life, however. I was having great sex with Marco, when we could find the time, but there wasn't too much time left for romance. Which I have to admit quite suited me. For the first time in my life I was having that thing I'd only read about in the past—*recreational sex*. And because Dad was still living with me, and because Marco—being a good Italian boy—still shared a house with his mother, we were doing it anywhere we could. His car being the current favourite venue.

His mother had been fine about his little secret, and he, on the whole, was OK about hers. He did seem concerned that my dad was still married, but he had to admit that my father wasn't like his, and he could see for himself how happy they were. We'd had dinner with them the previous weekend, and the way they behaved—sickening, really—it was as if *they* were the young ones in love. Giovanna was thrilled that Marco and I were together, which bothered me a bit. I think she already had us married off in her mind, and I was certain that wasn't likely ever to happen.

I'd just put the phone down on Marco, as a matter of fact. He'd called to ask to see me later, but I'd told him that I had a deadline to meet—a report to finish for Monday. He'd suggested I work on it over the weekend, and I'd said I would have to anyway, which wasn't a total lie. But mostly I just wanted some time to myself, and it was easier to blame it on the report.

'Is it still OK for tomorrow night?' I'd asked, and the receiver had felt a bit frosty against my ear. I was supposed to be taking him along to meet up with Nicola. She'd invited Sid and me, plus guests, for an all-expenses-paid night out on the town by way of a thank you for the business we'd already put her way and—more importantly, I suspect—for that which she hoped to get in the future. 'Should be fine,' he had said, moodily, annoyed with me for turning him down.

'Well, let me know if it *isn't* fine,' I'd said, and had put the phone down on him.

I wasn't in the mood for childishness, and besides, I could see Sid's sisters heading across the office towards me. Which must mean that it was getting on for four-thirty. It was becoming a habit for them to hop on a bus after school and head into the city, still dressed in their uniforms that they adjusted en route *à la* early Britney Spears.

I glanced over at Sid and saw the look of exasperation on his face. I thought it quite funny that he could start up a company but still have no control over his teenage sisters. He'd even complained to his mother about them, but she was presumably too busy with Feng Shui consultations to keep a tight rein on her girls.

He turned his back on them now, and when they saw this they pulled their tongues out at him and grinned when they realised I'd seen them.

'You should show more respect for your brother when you come here,' I told them sternly as they draped themselves over my desk. I was getting to know them pretty well now, and there was no longer any need for pussyfooting about.

There wasn't a contrite expression amongst them, however, just the odd shrug and cheeky glance in the direction of the embarrassed young man that Sid had recently taken on straight from school on account of his technical wizardry. He was an additional attraction, but the real reason they came to the office was to see little old me. Not entirely for myself, it must be admitted, but for my claim to fame—the fact that I had once been kissed by Jamie Astin. I'd mentioned it the first time they came in for a nosy around—because up until then no one else had seemed very interested—and it had taken my cred up several notches in their eyes. They were also impressed with the fact that I was going out with the 'gorgeous hunk' from the Italian, and, sad though it was, I was rather enjoying their admiration.

'We hear you're going to Zoot tomorrow night,' Darinda said wondrously. I was getting used to which one was which now.

'We're going to a club, yes,' I said, 'but I don't know which one yet.'

'Is Marco going to be there?' Belle purred.

I nodded and saved the work I was doing in case one of them started messing with my computer—which they were apt to do when they got bored.

'Can we come?' Marinda asked silkily, stroking the desk as she spoke.

'Of course you can't come,' I told her firmly.

'Is it true that Cass is going?' Darinda asked incredulously. They were getting used to the idea that Sid had a girlfriend, but they weren't that excited about his choice.

'I know she's your friend...' This was their usual start to a moan about her, and that was exactly what Belle said now. 'But she's sooo dull.'

By now Sid and Cass were like an old married couple. She'd told me that she'd decided not to join us at Pisus because she didn't think people who had a relationship should work together—which might well be prudent, but the girls were right. It did all seem a bit dull and sensible. Sometimes even I wondered what I saw in her. To be honest, since I'd become friendly with Nic I occasionally compared the two of them, and poor Cass didn't come off too favourably. But she was still my friend and I felt honour-bound to defend her.

'She was the first in our year at school to get her gold Duke of Edinburgh award,' I said, unable to come up with anything better.

When they looked at me blankly, I dug deep into my Cass-anecdote reserves and came up with absolutely nothing that could be remotely described as exciting.

'And she's very dependable,' I said in desperation, sounding the death knell for Cass's appeal value once and for all.

'They suit each other,' Marinda eventually said, though there was nothing complimentary about the remark. 'But what about you and Marco?'

'What about me and Marco?' I said carefully.

'Do you love him?' asked Darinda.

'None of your business,' I replied crisply. But I knew the answer if I'd chosen to give it. Of course I didn't love Marco. Apart from the sex, I wasn't even sure I liked him that much. Now I knew him better I could see that there was a ruthless streak in him I didn't find especially appealing. There seemed to be no disputing the fact that he loved his mother, but I was still pretty annoyed with him for arranging to go and stay with his long-lost father over the Christmas holidays. He seemed to think I was overreacting. He couldn't see any problem now that Giovanna had my dad. But I couldn't help thinking that he'd have gone anyway.

'Cass told me that you used to live with a music writer,' Marinda said in a starry-eyed sort of way, and my stomach did a little flip. 'What sort of music does he write about?'

I hadn't heard a word from him since that hugely embarrassing gaffe I'd made, when I'd blown my cover as Sarah Daly. For a while I'd hoped that the e-mail had never got to him, but that seemed less and less likely now. I was sure that he would have written to Sarah by now if it hadn't, if only to find out how things were working out with her ex.... I still couldn't think of the whole horrible nightmare without physically cringing, and I prayed each day that I wouldn't bump into him in the street.

I knew what the girls would want to hear, so I told them what I'd learnt in my Sarah Daly days.

'Last thing I heard he was doing a book on VantagePoint.'

'VantagePoint!' they squealed as one.

'How cool is that?' sighed Darinda dreamily.

'Do you think he could get their autographs for us?' asked Belle.

I was about to say that I didn't think so, but then I thought of a way for Cass to redeem herself in Sid's sisters' eyes.

'I'll speak to Cass about it,' I said. 'I'm not in touch with Dan any more, but I could get her to call him and ask, if you like.'

And they seemed to like very much.

Libby and Nigel had spent the past forty minutes loading her stuff into his car. She'd given the landlord notice that morning, and although she still had a month to vacate the flat she had been keen to make a start. A lot keener than Nigel, apparently, who seemed very worried about his car.

'It's not a removal van,' he said in exasperation as Libby tried cramming the last of the cardboard boxes onto the back seat. He shook his head firmly. 'It's not going to fit so you'll just have to take it back.'

'OK, OK,' she said with a sigh. The last thing she wanted was an argument—not now when things were going so well. Now that the cheque had arrived from her former employers, and now that Nigel had agreed to let her move into his place. He'd taken a lot of convincing to give it a go and she didn't want him regretting his decision already.

'You get in the car,' she said sweetly now, 'and I'll be back in a minute.'

She took the box back up to the flat, locked the door, and slipped quietly back down the stairs. She was anxious to avoid Dan and Aisling, neither of whom she had seen in over three weeks, and it looked as if she had succeeded. Or so she thought until she reached the hallway again and the door of Aisling's flat opened up.

'I've been getting worried about you,' she said.

Aisling moved into the hall and looked out of the open front door at Nigel's car, chock-full with boxes.

'Nice car.'

She sounded impressed, and, pleased about this, Libby dropped her guard for a moment.

Then, 'You weren't planning on moving without telling us, I hope,' Aisling said, turning to look at her.

Libby felt extremely uneasy now. It was something about Aisling's demeanour. She was usually so dizzy and silly, but right now she seemed deadly serious. Even her normally shrill voice had dropped an octave or two.

'Of course I was going to tell you,' she said. 'I only gave notice today.'

'It's all a bit sudden, though, isn't it?'

'It has been a bit whirlwind, I suppose,' said Libby as she tried to move round her. But Aisling stood firm.

'Before you rush off, maybe you can explain what happened that day in the Victoria Quarter.'

'Look, I'm really sorry about that,' Libby said with an apologetic sigh, 'but something happened and I'm afraid I'd sooner not talk about it, if you don't mind.' She tried passing Aisling again, but Aisling was definitely not to be moved.

'I know exactly what happened,' she said. 'I spoke to Baz and, darling man that he is, he gave me Paul's number.' She smiled serenely at Libby, and then looked out at Nigel again. 'I'd bet he'd be interested to know all about Paul and his vinyl collection,' she said.

'You wouldn't!'

'I *would*,' Aisling said. 'And I will if you don't cough up for the damage you did to Dan's CDs.'

Libby laughed hollowly. 'You can't pin that one on me.'

'Oh, yes, I can. I've spoken to Jo, and I know how you got hold of her scarf.'

Just then Nigel stretched round to look at the door of the house, and beeped the car horn.

'He's getting impatient,' Aisling said. 'And that makes two of us.' She took a step over the threshold of the door towards him.

Libby, shaking with anger now, caught her arm roughly.

'OK,' she said fuming. 'How much?'

'Now, let's think,' Aisling said, frowning a little. 'Approximately one hundred CDs at fourteen quid each…that would be fourteen hundred pounds.' She smiled again. 'But we'll call it a straight thousand, shall we?'

'A thousand!' Libby said, shaking her head in disbelief. 'Where am I supposed to find that sort of money?'

Aisling continued on down the path. 'Of course you can find it, Libby. Thanks to your little windfall.' She shook her head sadly. 'I've learnt so much about you lately, including the fact that your poor *deceased* father is actually alive and well and living with your mother in Tottenham. Paul was ever so helpful.'

Libby caught her arm again. She could see that Aisling wasn't bluffing, and they were only a short distance from the car now.

'All right,' she said with a deep sigh. 'You win. But I need to get my chequebook from the car.'

'That's OK,' Aisling said calmly. 'I'll come with you. You can tell him you owe me for the window cleaner, or something.'

Aisling waved happily at Nigel as she moved round to the passenger door with Libby. And Libby, who knew when she was finally beaten, mumbled quietly to herself.

'One fricking expensive window cleaner,' she seethed.

I arrived home at just after eleven o'clock and found Giovanna with my dad on the sofa. Nothing too terrible was going on, I was relieved to see, but it did make me think how less than perfect our living arrangements were.

I made some tea, and after a brief exchange of pleasantries took it off to my bedroom. I called Cass from there and told her about the girls, and the book Dan had written, and how this was a chance to make a name for herself with them. She didn't sound particularly interested, but just in case she decided to act I threatened her with her life if she mentioned my name to Dan.

'I'm not supposed to know about it,' I said when she asked me why she shouldn't do that.

There was a small suspicious pause.

'How *do* you know about it?'

'He told Sarah about it.'

'Not *recently*, I hope?'

'Ages ago,' I could truthfully tell her.

I'd woken her up, apparently, and she grunted now and put the phone down on me. And then I did what I often did when I got home late from work. I read all the e-mails that Dan and Sarah had exchanged. Then I moved on to my own Hotmail account, where I could see that a couple of messages were waiting—not from my mother, I was relieved to see, but from Matt.

I said that I'd hold you responsible if she turned out to be a nightmare, didn't I?

Which was not a promising beginning to message number one.

Well, I do and she is. She's been moving my furniture about, telling me what to eat, when to come home and how much exercise I should be taking. She's been throwing out clothes she doesn't regard as suitable for a man 'in my position', and last night she told my girlfriend it was high time she stopped dyeing her hair in order just to please men. My girlfriend (a natural blonde, by the way) now refuses to come round to my place again if my mother is there!

Wise girl, I thought.

I tell you, Jo, if I didn't know she was going home in ten days (and believe me I'm counting), I'd leave myself.
She's got a new friend, by the way. A nutty neighbour who's been filling her head with all things Californian… She took her off to a seminar two weeks ago on How To Survive Divorce and it's turned her head. She's been to several now, with different themes, but they add up to much the same thing—ALL MEN ARE BASTARDS (her darling son excepted of course!) and you should see what she's wearing! She's ditched all the things she arrived with and has replaced

*them with dungarees and cheesecloth… She looks like an aged
hippie and talks like a throwback from the women's movement.*

And he signed it *Deeply disturbed of Santa Monica.*
The second message was a follow-up to the first.

*I don't really hold you responsible. In fact I am filled with
admiration that you've managed to live in the same country
as her and stay fairly sane.*
Much love
Matt

PS Send my love to Dad.

I thought about printing the messages off and showing
them to Dad, but, apart from not wanting to disturb him and
Giovanna, it seemed rather disloyal. So I tapped a quick reply
to Matt, telling him to hang in there, and closed down for
the night.

And when I finally drifted off to sleep it wasn't my current boyfriend that I dreamt about. It was Dan.

Dan and Aisling were having a late-night beer in his flat.

'Don't you think we should warn him?' Dan said of the
unknown man Libby was moving in with.

Aisling shook her head. 'He looked as if he could take care
of himself,' she said confidently. 'And, now that you've got
some compensation, it really isn't any of our business.'

The cheque was in front of them on the coffee table and
Dan still couldn't believe it.

'There must be a lot more to you, Aisling Carter, than
meets the eye,' he said with a flick of his dark eyebrows.

'I was pretty magnificent.' She beamed. 'And my timing

was impeccable. I'm pretty damn sure she wouldn't have been quite so co-operative if lover-boy hadn't been around.'

Dan lifted his bottle by way of a toast.

'Well, however you did it I'm extremely grateful.'

Aisling tilted her head on one side and looked at him intently.

'I can't take all the credit, though. It wouldn't have happened if Jo hadn't rung me.'

Dan didn't reply. He still felt bad about ever believing that Jo was responsible, but there was something else she'd done which he found hard to forgive, let alone explain.

Aisling sipped some beer from the bottle Dan had given her and made a face.

'This stuff is as bad as your coffee and your liqueurs.'

Dan took a slug of his own beer and shrugged.

'Tastes fine to me.' He smiled at her, curled up on the sofa next to him, her feet tucked comfortably behind her. She was wearing a cosy red sweater, and now that she'd disposed of those hair extensions she looked very fetching. He found himself wondering what it would be like to kiss her.

'How are things going with Steve?' he asked.

'Things are going just fine,' she said with a gleam in her eye.

'So is it serious?' he asked casually.

'I wouldn't go that far,' she said, frowning a little now. 'And how come you've changed the subject? We were talking about Jo a moment ago.'

'You were,' he said.

Aisling looked thoughtful for a moment.

'Do you know what I think is really creepy?' she said.

He shook his head cautiously.

'I think Libby dyed her hair red so that she could look as much like Jo as possible. She's gone back to brown now.'

He sighed. That possibility had not escaped him. But what

bothered him most right now was the fact that Aisling wouldn't stop mentioning Jo.

'The book should be in the shop any day now,' he said, trying again for a change of subject.

'That's quick!' she answered, surprised. She looked at him curiously. 'You never did tell me who or what it was all about.'

He grinned. He'd had a change of heart about things of late. He'd decided there was no sense in being pretentious about his work. If the music of boy bands provided pleasure for so many people, who was he to complain? Especially if writing about one of them helped pay the rent.

'VantagePoint,' he said, only slightly embarrassed. He would have to get used to it, because he'd even agreed with the publishers to put his name on the cover now.

She smiled at him wryly. 'I can see why they want to put it out quickly,' she said, and he nodded. The band had been at the number one spot for two weeks already, and speculation had increased about them still being there at Christmas.

They sat in companionable silence for a while, and then Aisling suddenly shifted in her seat and moved closer to him. She looked at him for a moment, and he looked back at her. And then, to his surprise, she leaned closer and kissed him full on the lips. And because it was what he thought that he wanted, he kissed her back, but the truth was he could have been kissing a potato for all he felt.

'I thought so,' she said as she withdrew her mouth from his. She shook her head and sighed. 'Now, I don't care how long this takes, Dan Baxter, but I'm not moving from here until you tell me exactly why you keep avoiding talking to me about Jo.'

It took her a good twenty minutes of very hard work, but he eventually told her. And when she heard what had happened she hooted with laughter.

'But that is so cool,' she said, when she'd stopped hooting. 'And don't you see what it means?'

'It means that she wanted to make a fool out of me,' he said.

She let out a groan of exasperation. 'No, foolish man. It may have gone awry and got out of hand, but I'm sure it started because she just wanted *contact* with you any way she could. I've seen her, don't forget, and I could tell she still cared about you.'

'Strange way to show it,' he said moodily.

Aisling moved away and frowned suddenly.

'You don't suppose she sent that last message from her business address deliberately, do you? I don't mean *deliberate* deliberately, I mean *subconscious* deliberately. Like deep down she wanted to be found out.'

'Why the hell would she do that?'

Aisling shook her head, as if astonished by his stupidity.

'So you'd call her at long last, of course, and give her hell.'

Dad suggested that we had a special late breakfast together on Saturday morning. He did it all himself, including scrambling eggs to go with some very nice smoked salmon he'd bought from the local deli. He'd picked up some fresh Colombian coffee as well, and to add to the sense of occasion I manhandled the kitchen table over to the sitting room window. It was fairly dismal outside, but for the first time ever I could appreciate the value of a river view. It was all about having someone to share it with.

'I'm thinking of driving over to the house later,' he said as he poured some coffee for me. 'I need to get some more of my things.'

I looked at him dubiously over the table.

'I'm not sure there's room here for any more *things*,' I said.

I cast my eye round the room, which was beginning to fill up with cardboard boxes. Dad had been paying regular trips to his former home and always came back with several containers. It had occurred to me that he could have moved back into the house while my mother was in California, but it was as if he was trying to cut his ties from the place entirely.

'I know it's difficult,' he said with a shrug, 'but I need to do as much as I can before your mother gets back.'

'Before she finds out it's serious with Giovanna, you mean?'

He nodded sheepishly. 'I don't suppose she's going to be too happy about it.'

Neither did I, but that wasn't the point.

'We're going to have sort ourselves out,' I said, seizing the moment. I'd been trying to think of a way to tell him it was time to move on and now was my chance. 'This place is getting too small for us both and, well, there is a...er—' I hated saying it, but I couldn't stop now '—a privacy problem.'

'Exactly,' Dad said, putting down his knife and fork and giving me his full attention. 'And I've been thinking about that.'

'You have?'

He nodded. 'You've mentioned a couple of times that you don't like it much here.'

'True.'

'Well, I do, and I've been considering taking over the lease when yours runs out—if you don't choose to renew it yourself, that is.'

'Fair enough,' I said forking some overcooked scrambled egg, trying to avoid the burnt bits. 'But that's not for ages yet.'

He shifted his eyes away from me towards the window and I could sense that he was uncomfortable.

'But I could sub-let it from you in the meantime.'

I put the fork down and thought about this for a moment. Then it sank in.

'You mean you want me to move out!' My eyes scanned the pile of cardboard boxes again. 'So that's why you've been stashing so much of your stuff here!'

'It's not as bad as you're making it sound.' He managed to look at me now. 'It just seems to make sense to me.'

And, although I wasn't too keen on being evicted from my own flat, it made sense to me as well. But it didn't stop me feeling slightly peeved.

'I hope you're not planning on moving me out before Christmas.'

'Of course not,' he said with obvious relief that it had gone rather better than he'd thought. 'And as a show of good faith I'll take over the rent from the beginning of this month, if you like.'

I did like—very much, as a matter of fact.

'And I get to keep my room until I find somewhere else?'

'Of course,' he said. 'And I don't want you to feel pressured at all. You must take as long as you need to find somewhere else.'

Which sounded fine, but I was already beginning to feel as if I was the guest, overstaying my welcome. We ate on without speaking for a while and then Dad, clearly keen to break the silence, asked me if I had any plans for the day.

'Not really,' I said a bit moodily. 'Though I might dye my hair.' I'd been thinking about trying out a new image and my hair seemed the obvious place to start.

Dad looked appalled.

'Why on earth would you want to do that?'

I shrugged, and then something occurred to me.

'Mum says she has no idea where it came from,' I said, tugging at my curly red hair. 'Did anyone in your family have a mop like this?'

'Not to my knowledge,' he said thoughtfully. 'But it's beautiful hair and you should be proud of it.'

'But isn't that a bit odd?' I said, frowning as I picked up my mug of coffee.

Dad looked vague. 'Some genetic throwback, I expect.'

Then something else came into my head, completely un-invited—a picture of Brian Dick. Not because he had red hair—which he didn't—but because it suddenly occurred to me that if my mother had slept with him when she was married, she could have slept with anyone. I looked at my father across the table, and although he isn't a particularly perceptive man—in fact, he can seem incredibly thick at times—his eyes widened.

We looked at one another for a couple of seconds, and then he grinned.

'I don't think your mother would be drawing attention to the colour of your hair if she'd—well, you know...'

'Played away?' I suggested.

'Precisely,' he said.

Despite what Aisling had said, Dan still felt a fool. Whereas he could maybe accept that Jo pretending to be someone else *might* just have been about making some contact, arranging dates with 'Sarah' and then flaunting her new man in front of him was much more difficult to come to terms with.

He'd arrived at his own conclusions, as a matter of fact. As far as he was concerned, it had just been her strange way of telling him that she had finally moved on. And maybe it was high time he did as well. Which was why he'd agreed to go out with Aisling and Steve tonight. He didn't relish the idea of playing gooseberry, but he certainly felt like a break from the flat.

The phone rang while he was in the middle of drying up a backlog of dishes, and Dan wondered if it was Aisling checking up on him, making sure he was still on for tonight.

Only it wasn't.

'It's Cass,' the voice said anxiously.

'Cass?' It took a while to sink in. 'Oh, *Cass!* The one who helped Jo do her escape act, I presume?'

'I'm sorry about that,' she said.

'The same Cass I thought was my friend and have never heard from since?' He was smiling to himself as he imagined her cringing.

'I was Jo's friend first,' she said unhappily.

'And I bet she reminded you of that fact when she roped you in.'

'She did, as a matter of fact.'

Dan laughed lightly at this, and then asked Cass to what he owed the unexpected pleasure of her ringing him now.

'I understand you've written a book about some boy band or other?'

'True,' he said, 'but how did you know that?'

'Just something I heard through the grapevine,' she answered quickly.

Dan thought about this for a moment. The only people who knew what the book was about were Aisling and *Sarah Daly*, so he presumed that Jo was the 'grapevine'. He wondered if she'd told Cass about Sarah.

'I didn't know you were a VantagePoint fan,' he said.

'I'm not,' she replied indignantly. 'I couldn't even remember what their name was.'

'Well, then, why are——?'

'Because I know someone who is,' she interrupted. 'Three of them, as a matter of fact.' She briefly explained her predicament. 'They think that I'm boring, basically,' she said of her boyfriend's three younger sisters, 'and I thought if I could get hold of some autographs—'

'They'd think you were...erm...*cool?*'

'Something like that.'

'I'll have to meet this bloke some time,' Dan said, smiling.

'He must be pretty special if you're prepared to go to all this trouble.'

'It's you I'm asking to go to the trouble,' she responded stiffly.

'It's no trouble at all,' he said. 'So lighten up, will you?' He'd just been informed that the band was to do some book signings the following day, as a matter of fact, so it only required a call to their agent. 'How about I get them to sign a copy of the book? One for each of the girls?'

'That would be fantastic,' she said, sounding a lot more relaxed now.

'Well, consider it done.'

'Thanks, Dan, and I'm sorry again.'

'No problem. Now, hang on while I fetch a pen and you can give me the names of these three scary sisters.'

I put on the full slap and clubbing gear that night. I'd decided against changing my hair after that talk with Dad, but I'd chosen my skimpiest black dress, heaped on the fake tan, painted my finger and toenails scarlet, and slipped into my four-and-a-half-inch heels. I felt fantastic.

Dad wasn't quite so sure, though. He hinted that I looked like a bit of a slapper.

'But you are going to wear a coat, though, aren't you?' he said when I poo-pooed his concerns. When I told him that most young women looked like I did on a Saturday night in Leeds. 'You'll catch your death if you don't.'

'Of course I'm wearing a coat,' I said with a roll of my eyes.

'And Marco is coming to pick you up?' he said.

'Yes,' I said, 'Marco is coming to pick me up. He'll be here any minute.'

He looked at me uneasily. 'I was wondering if there's any chance that he might stay over with you tonight?'

'What *are* you suggesting, Dad?' I said as I rushed around gathering up bits and pieces to put in my bag.

'It's just that I thought it might be nice to stay with Giovanna tonight.'

I stopped rushing around and looked at him. I wasn't so sure about this. As far as Marco was concerned his mother was having a *platonic* relationship with my father. I don't think it had even occurred to him that they might want to go further. He certainly didn't know that they'd already spent at least one night together before he'd got back from Spain. I assumed it hadn't been a one-off situation, though I didn't like to think about how they'd managed things since then. It did seem a bit silly, though. With their home and ours we could easily have arranged to have one couple in each now and then. It would certainly be more comfortable for me than Marco's car. But it still didn't feel *right*.

'I dunno about that, Dad,' I said, and I suddenly realised that it wasn't just about Marco's possible reaction to discovering his mother was a sexual being. It was also about putting things on a firmer footing with Marco and me. If we started staying over at each other's place it would make us feel more of a couple, and I wasn't sure I wanted that. 'Do you think we could just leave it for a while?' I added selfishly. 'Until I know how I want things to go with Marco?'

Dad obviously misinterpreted this and assumed I meant that we hadn't yet consummated our relationship. He was very apologetic, embarrassingly so, but it seemed easier to let him believe his daughter was as pure as driven snow than explain the complexities of my current mindset.

Anyway, there wasn't time, because just at that moment Marco rang the flat bell and I grabbed my coat for the off.

The meal at the Vine had been excellent, and because Nic's firm would be putting it down to business expenses she'd insisted we chose precisely whatever we fancied and gave not a single thought to the prices on the menu. We also seemed to get through quite a few bottles of champagne.

Nic had brought along someone called Andy, who worked with her. He was a nice-looking bloke but when I asked her about him she said he was there merely to make up the numbers. She looked a lot more sophisticated than I did. She was wearing black, like me, but she wasn't showing off quite so much flesh. Cass was continuing to branch out in the fashion department and was wearing a particularly fetching strapless lemon-coloured dress. She had a cardigan on top of it, as usual, but she really was getting quite daring. The men had pushed the boat out as well, and although I say it myself I think we made quite an attractive bunch.

We'd moved on to Zoot by now, as prophesied by Sid's sister Darinda, and I kept thinking about the last time I was there, when I'd seen Dan.

I felt like dancing, but Marco didn't. He'd been in a strange mood since he picked me up. I think he was still peeved with me for refusing to see him the night before, and things were going from bad to worse. I got the impression that he didn't approve of the way I was dressed, which made me defiant and all the more determined to have a good time.

Nic seemed to sense what was going on.

'Don't worry,' she whispered, 'I'll keep an eye on old grumpy-guts, here. Off you go now and dance with Andy.' Which was very kind of her, I thought. Luckily Sid and Cass were up for some fun as well, which made a nice change, so while the four of us headed for the dance floor poor Nic had to stay and entertain boring old Marco at the bar.

It was a female DJ tonight, and she was doing her stuff from a high platform that looked out over the dance floor. She looked very young, and at twenty-six I was beginning to think my clubbing days were numbered. But I wasn't going to let it bother me that night as I swayed beneath hypnotic flashing lights to a sound that Dan insisted was not real music. At least that was what he'd used to insist, but if he was writing books about the likes of VantagePoint these days, maybe he'd revised his opinion on that as well. For some reason this notion amused me, and because I was a little bit drunk on all that champagne it made me laugh out loud.

'What's the joke?' Cass mouthed to me as she sashayed around on the dance floor.

'Did you ring Dan about those autographs?' I mouthed back at her.

She nodded. 'He was great. Really nice about it.'

Then a worrying thought struck me.

'You didn't mention me, I hope?'

'After your threats?' She grinned. 'Of course not.'

I grinned back at her and she indicated with a few deft hand signals that she was going to the cloakroom. Which left me with two men to dance with—and I made the most of it. If Marco was sulking—well, so be it. It wasn't going to stop me enjoying myself.

Dan felt someone squeezing into the gap next to him and when he looked round he was surprised to see it was Cass. He'd been leaning on the rail that surrounded the dance floor for the past few minutes, not really taking much in.

'I thought you hated this scene,' she said, straining her voice to be heard over the music.

'I do,' he yelled back. 'I was dragged here kicking and screaming.'

'You're not on your own, then?'

He pointed the bottle he was holding vaguely in the direction of Steve and Aisling.

'As good as,' he mouthed at her wryly. 'What about you? Where's the new boyfriend?'

She squinted, and then pointed at someone who didn't look old enough to be in the club.

'That's Sid,' she said proudly.'And you'll recognise who he's dancing with.'

His stomach lurched at the sight of Jo, but it was the other man, the one next to Sid, that his eyes rested upon. He wasn't the bloke she'd been with before.

'Is that who she's with?' he found himself asking.

Cass shook her head.'No, he's with Nic.'

'Nic?'

'Yes,' said Cass with a roll of her eyes. 'Nicola Dick. She and Jo are best buddies now.'

'But I thought they hated each other,' Dan said, frowning.

'So did I.' She turned round and stretched her neck, as if to look for someone over the crowd, and he followed her eyes. He could see Nicola Dick at the end of bar, and he could see some dark-haired bloke kissing her. He looked back at Cass questioningly.

'So if the bloke on the dance floor is with her, who...?'

'Precisely,' Cass said soberly, though he didn't know what she was talking about.

She started to move away from him in a purposeful manner, but he caught her arm.

'Don't tell Jo that you saw me,' he said quickly, and she paused for a moment and looked at him straight in the eye.

'OK,' she said. 'If that's what you want.'

'What the...?'

Cass had grabbed my arm and was frog-marching me through the crowd. I was trying my best to free myself, but she can be very strong when she is determined and she was very determined now to take me somewhere.

She stopped suddenly and I looked at her indignantly. She

was staring straight ahead of her, and because she was so trans-
fixed my eyes were eventually drawn that way as well.

I couldn't take it in for a moment.

Nic and Marco.

Nic and Marco kissing.

Nic and Marco eating each other's faces off.

I looked back at Cass and wondered why she was doing
this. I was actually mad with her for a moment, and then I
looked over at Nic and Marco again. This time Nic was
looking at me, over Marco's shoulder. They'd obviously
paused for breath for a moment, but instead of appearing remotely shamefaced she actually seemed very pleased with
herself.

'I'm sorry,' I heard Cass say, and I believed that she was. To
a point. Though I would not have been at all surprised if she
wasn't getting the teeniest bit of enjoyment from this. And
who could blame her? The way I'd been flaunting my so-
called friendship with Nic of late, it was only natural that she
should feel some sort of satisfaction.

'What are you going to do?' Cass asked, and she sounded
worried now.

I shrugged. 'Nothing. We're even now. She's finally got me
back for stealing her boyfriend all those years ago. Sad cow.'

Cass looked at me, and I continued to look at Nic.

'But what about Marco?' Cass asked. 'Aren't you upset
about him?'

Just then Nic released Marco from her clutches, whispered
something to him, and he turned around.

'Not in the least,' I said, though even with the distance between us I could see the blood drain from his face. And I
meant it. In fact I meant it so much that I lifted my fingers
to my mouth and blew him a cheerful farewell kiss. Then I
did it again, and this time directed the kiss towards Nic.

She didn't look so pleased about that, but before Marco could come after me and tell me how none of it had been his fault I turned on my four-and-a-half-inch heels and, with my head held high, disappeared into the crowd. I headed straight for the exit, and it was only when I was outside in my ridiculously revealing dress that I realised I'd left my coat and handbag. That took the edge off my grand gesture a little, and I was standing around feeling a little bit silly when I felt a tap on my bare shoulder.

Expecting that Marco had followed me out, I spun round and nearly collapsed in a heap when one of my heels twisted under my foot. Two sturdy arms caught me, though, just in time, and I looked into the smiling eyes of Tim Bailey.

'Are you OK?' he wanted to know, still supporting me beneath my elbows.

'Fine, fine...' I said, feeling a fully blown fool by now. He was with a short blonde who was aiming daggers at me from narrowed eyes. 'What about you?' I said, glancing back at the club entrance. 'Are you just leaving or going in?' I was talking fast, hoping he wouldn't ask any awkward questions.

'Going in,' he said, frowning, a question mark forming in his expression. Then I saw Cass in the doorway, heading my way with my coat and my bag, and I breathed a sigh of relief.

'I was just leaving,' I said. And then Sid appeared and Tim finally let go of me. They exchanged a few words and I watched the miniature blonde take hold of Tim's arm and glance disapprovingly at my dress as I slipped my coat over it.

'We should all get together some time,' Tim said, looking at me as he spoke.

'Nice-looking bloke,' Cass said as we parted from Tim and the dwarf.

'Boring, though, unfortunately,' I said, and then I felt bad. He'd been really good about what happened, about the e-mail I'd sent. He'd sent me one back saying that he understood completely.

'Boring and *engaged*,' Sid said. 'Didn't you notice that the small person was wearing a ring?'

I shook my head in despair. If someone like Tim was a two-timing toe-rag, what hope was there?

I sighed and linked arms with Cass, who in turn linked arms with Sid, and we set off down the road away from the club.

'What happened inside after I left?' I wanted to know.

'Marco tried to come after you,' Cass said as we headed down the street, 'but I told him it might be best if he left it tonight.'

'It might be best if he left it for the rest of his life,' I said.

'But what about your father and Giovanna? Marco could end up as your stepbrother, so you'll have to be civilised about it all.'

'Don't worry,' I said, 'I intend to be. I just mean that I don't want to have to listen to his excuses.' Then I looked over at Sid. 'Would it seem very small-minded of me if we looked elsewhere for staff in the future?'

'What?' he said, pretending to be shocked. 'After all the expense and trouble Nic went to tonight?'

'Exactly,' I said.

We laughed for a bit, and then Sid and Cass looked at one another.

'Are we going to tell her,' he said.

'Are you going to tell me *what?*' I said, looking at Cass. We were crossing the road on the way to the taxi rank now.

She smiled coyly, and then nodded at Sid.

'We're getting engaged,' he said solemnly.

'Engaged!' I repeated stupidly.

'Yes,' said Cass, squeezing my arm, *'engaged.'*

'And we'd like you to come to my house next Saturday night for a small celebration,' said Sid.

chapter 20

Our mother has finally gone completely off her trolley. I'm not going to tell you what she's done/doing—that's up to her—but I warn you, you're in for a shock!

No good trying to get hold of me over the next few days as I'm going away on a business trip. Thank God.

I'd been worried ever since that e-mail arrived from Matt at the beginning of the week. I'd thought about phoning my mother, but part of me didn't want to know what was going on so worrying about it was as far as I got. And what with that, and everything else that had happened during the week, I was practically pulling my mad hair out by the time I got back to the flat—thankfully early—that following Friday evening.

It had been crazy at work, in a good sort of way—hard graft and long hours, but things were going incredibly well. We'd taken on a brand-new client that would mean a phenomenal increase in our turnover if everything went according to plan. I don't think even Sid could believe our luck—and me, well, I kept trying to work out what five per cent of such a whacking great contract would mean to my bank balance. And, though I knew that things weren't really quite as simple and straightforward as all that, it was certainly very encouraging.

So it wasn't work that had got to me, but all the distractions. Marco had kept ringing the office, and although I managed to avoid him until Wednesday morning, I'd realised he wasn't going to let me off the hook until I agreed to see him.

We met during my ten-minute lunch-break, and as we walked up and down outside the office building, and I ate my cheese and pickle sandwich *al fresco*, he said exactly what I'd expected him to say all along. That it had all been Nic's fault. That she'd practically forced herself upon him. Poor thing...I was really nice about it—because I didn't want to cause any waves with our parents, and because frankly I really didn't care very much. I accepted his half-hearted apologies, but I was adamant about it being over. To put his mind at rest, however, I told him my cheesy lips were sealed as far as Giovanna was concerned. We couldn't stop her being disappointed that it hadn't worked out for us, but *I* could stop her being furious with him. And I think he was very grateful for that.

Nic was a different matter altogether, though. She'd obviously come round to the conclusion that her childish behaviour might lose her some business, and she'd kept leaving messages for me as well. I let her sweat it out till Thursday afternoon before returning her calls, only to discover that she'd taken the 'you're overreacting' route. She claimed that what had occurred had been little more than a peck on the cheek, so I said that if that was her idea of a 'peck' I shuddered to think what she did when she really got started in a public place. She laughed uneasily at that point, and suggested that we meet after work for a drink. I like to think that if she'd come clean, if she'd only been honest about what had happened, and why, I would have been as nice to her as I'd been to Marco. But she didn't, and wasn't, so I took a deep breath and told her, politely, to sling her hook. And I felt quite good about it, actually.

Dad had been pacing about the flat since I got back. He was dreading my mother coming back the following Monday, fearful of what her reaction would be when she found out about Giovanna. He hadn't been too troubled at first, but now it was looking serious between them he was getting more anxious by the day. I hadn't told him about my brother's worrying message yet. I couldn't see the point of adding to Dad's troubles when I didn't even know what Matt was talking about.

With no time for personal e-mails at work these days, I'd been checking my mail every night when I got back. I did it again now, when I went to my room. And when I saw there was a message waiting from my mother I caught my breath sharply. Until now I'd refused to let my imagination run wild, but it unleashed itself now and a variety of possibilities came into my mind—all of them extremely alarming. Which was good, in a way, because when I read what she had to say it didn't seem nearly as bad as it could have been.

I have at last found my spiritual home in California and I'm staying here.

I must say that I am very disappointed with your brother's response to my news. He has been very off hand with me and I have decided not to speak to him until he can behave more

*civilly. You'd think I'd told him I had committed mass murder
instead of informing him in an open and grown-up manner
that I have decided to stay in order to explore my sexuality.*

*I am moving in with Angelica, Matthew's neighbour. She
is a fine woman and we are very much in love.*

*I trust you will take this news rather better than your
brother did, and I would like you to inform your father that I
will soon be commencing divorce proceedings. I realise this will
come as a very great shock to him, but Angelica agrees with
me that I should move on to this next phase of my life unen-
cumbered by the past.*

*PS Why don't you come out and stay with us for Christ-
mas?*

Your Ever Loving Mother

When I got over the shock of the way she'd signed off, I
sat there in front of my screen for five full minutes while I
thought about the implications of this latest bombshell. The
first thing that struck me was that my dad was very much off
the hook, which should please him. Unfortunately, though,
it did mean that Matt was very much on it. His worst nightmare had come to pass. His mother would be living next door
to him. I think I laughed then. At the thought of poor
Matthew having to cope with our once excruciatingly bour-
geois mother who was now 'exploring her sexuality' right
under his nose.

I decided that it served him right for being the favourite!

The books had arrived that morning, and they were looking surprisingly good. Dan had been expecting the worst,
considering how quickly it had all been put together, but the
cover was pleasantly eye-catching, with a picture of the five

members of VantagePoint looking suitably roguish and yet at the same time reassuringly wholesome. And he didn't even squirm at the sight of his name writ large on the front.

The publishers had sent twenty copies for his own use, and three of them, as had been promised, were signed by each of the five band members. They'd obviously been pleased with the results themselves judging by the trouble they'd gone to, writing personal messages to each of the sisters. And, having a pretty good idea how girls of that age responded to that sort of thing, he was fairly confident that Cass's popularity would soar after this.

He'd tried calling her earlier, but she wasn't in, and now, at eight, before he cracked on with some work that had come in during the week, he tried her number again.

She was in this time, and for someone who didn't show her emotions much Cass was unusually gushing in her gratitude.

'How can I get them to you?' he interrupted in order to shut her up.

'I could come and pick them up from you,' she said, after thinking about it for a moment. 'Tomorrow some time?'

'OK,' he said, 'let's make it p.m., though, because I've got some shopping to do in the morning.'

I had to speak to someone, and to my great relief Cass was available. Sid had been ordered home to help with the preparations for the engagement celebration, and for the first time in weeks Cass was at a loose end.

Dad was relieved as well. It meant he'd have some time with Giovanna on their own in the flat. I took the smile off his face when I gave him a copy of the e-mail from my mother. I watched him as he read it, saw his mouth drop open in shock.

'My God!' he finally gasped. 'The woman's finally flipped!'

'Maybe,' I said, 'but I think you should get the divorce rolling quickly, though, before she changes her mind.'

He was sitting on the sofa, and he looked up at me now and frowned.

'Isn't it a bit unusual, this? Aren't kids supposed to try and keep their parents together?'

'Is that what you want me to do?'

'Well, no, but...'

'I'm not seven, Dad. My world isn't going to fall apart if my parents divorce now.'

Dad was quiet for a moment, and then his eyes drifted back to the e-mail.

'Barbara Dick will certainly have to go some to top this,' he said, and he actually laughed.

I left him then, and took a taxi across the city to Cass's place. The Christmas lights looked wonderful, and reminded me of Dan again. I had the sudden urge to ring him and tell him about my mother. He'd have found it hilarious that the woman who'd looked down her nose at him because he didn't have a regular income, because he didn't fit in with her stuffy friends, had now set up home with someone called Angelica.

Cass could be a very good listener when she chose to be. I'd been neglecting her lately, since I'd started my so-called friendship with Nic, but now, as we sat in her neat little flat, drinking sensible herbal tea on her flowery sofa, it was like old times.

'You seem to have overlooked something,' she said, when I'd told her about my mother's latest escapade.

I looked at her curiously.

'If she's not coming back in the foreseeable future, there's a house going begging in Staley.'

Apart from rolling her eyes, she hadn't even commented on my mother's change of sexual orientation. Typically, she seemed far more concerned with practical matters.

'I had hoped that Dad would move back there while Mum

was away,' I said, 'but he didn't seem to fancy that idea very much.'

'I was thinking of *you*,' she said. 'It's you that's looking for somewhere to live.'

'Me!' I said, shocked. 'Go and live back at home?'

'It wouldn't be like that if your parents weren't there. Think of the space and the comfort. Think of that Aga in winter.'

'But I couldn't leave Leeds.'

'I don't mean for ever. Just until you sort something else out.'

'What about work?' I said lamely.

'It's only half an hour on the train. You can take that long to cross Leeds in rush hour. It used to take you longer than that to get back to Dan's from the city centre.

'And, talking of Dan,' she said, looking at me, 'he's really has been great about everything.'

'That's nice,' I said. I wasn't sure I wanted to talk about Dan to Cass. I was afraid she might wheedle things out of me.

But she was clearly on some kind of mission, and kept mentioning him until I found myself telling her everything. About Libby, about Aisling, about the smashed CDs, and, yes, even about Sarah fixing up a date with Dan and me turning up instead with Tim.

She was wearing blue fleecy pyjamas with teddy bears printed on them, but she still managed to look sensible and wise as she listened to me pouring my heart out. I was so sure she was going to be sympathetic that it came as a shock when she eventually shook her head and told me that I was a crazy bitch who should immediately seek psychiatric help...

Dan was checking his e-mails before he switched off his computer. He occasionally still half expected to receive a message from Sarah Daly. He kind of missed her, he supposed. Which was mad now that he knew it had been Jo all the time.

There *was* an e-mail—from Jedski. And whereas he would

normally be amused by the man's harmless form of madness, tonight it made him feel depressed. He'd written to tell him about the website he was currently building, and to thank him for the brilliant idea. Trouble was, while he might well have much wider tastes than Jedski, it suddenly occurred to Dan that if he wasn't damn careful he might end up a sad old obsessive himself, with little going on in his life apart from music.

On the spur of the moment he tapped out a quick response.

Get a bloody life, for God's sake, Jedski.
Dan

We'd sat in silence for quite some time after Cass's outburst. And then, because I couldn't stand the silence any longer, and because I was peeved at being labelled a psycho, I asked her if she was sure she was doing the right thing by getting engaged to Sid.

'You've only known him a month,' I said, 'and he is a lot younger than you are.'

She looked at me for a moment, and then nodded her head.

'I'm sure, all right,' she simply said, and I kind of envied her certainty.

She sent me packing soon after that, and I was relieved to find my father alone when I got back to the flat. He was sleeping contentedly on his sofabed, snoring softly, making a sound like a single engine plane coming in to land. And as I crept around him, trying not to trip over his cardboard boxes, I realised that Cass might have a point about me moving back home for a while.

It was getting really difficult there in the flat, especially now that I was avoiding Giovanna because of Marco. It seemed easier that way than having to lie about why we'd split up. She'd been asking Dad about it, of course, and I'd told him it was a mutual thing, that we'd sooner be friends. But while Dad was a cinch with that sort of thing, I didn't think Giovanna would be. I had a feeling she'd coax the truth out of me yet. The *whole* truth—the fact that I didn't care about the break-up with Marco anywhere near as much as I cared about the break-up with Dan. I know how mothers feel about their sons, and I didn't want to hurt her feelings.

I wasn't tired at all, so I switched my computer on again and played around for a while on the Internet. With Christmas in mind I checked out a few gift sites, and when I got bored with that I clicked into my Hotmail system.

I'd been thinking about what to say to my mother on my way home in the taxi, and now that I'd made a decision about living arrangements it seemed a very good time to respond.

> *Dad is still living here at the flat, and because you're not coming back now I've decided to move into the family home for a while. I gave a copy of your e-mail to Dad, by the way, and I expect he will be in touch with you soon re the divorce.*
>
> *Thanks for the invitation, but I'm afraid I won't be able to make it for Christmas.*
>
> *Best wishes to Angelica, and good luck with your 'explorations'.*
>
> *Love*
> *Jo*

I sent it off immediately, smiling to myself as I imagined her face when she read it. How furious she'd be at not getting the reaction she'd expected to get. I knew perfectly well that she'd intended to shock us, and the cruellest thing I could do to her was to wish her well.

I tapped out a quick message to Matthew then, advising

him on a similar course. I was certain this 'new phase of her life' would lose its glamour the moment we all appeared to accept it. Which didn't mean I'd changed my mind about her and Dad. Their marriage was well and truly over, but I did think it was high time that my mother grew up.

And, yes, OK, maybe it was time that I did as well.

chapter 21

Dan got up early and went into the city. He might have been worried that music was becoming a substitute for what was missing in his life, but some of his CDs still needed replacing. And now, thanks to Aisling, he was able to indulge in an orgy of buying. By eleven o'clock he'd ticked thirty-three titles off his list and decided he'd had enough for one day.

He was just heading for the bus stop, through hordes of Christmas shoppers, when something in Waterstones' window caught his eye. He did a double take at the astonishing sight of dozens of copies of his book piled in a huge display. And he couldn't resist it. He turned round and went into the bookshop. There was another display just inside the door, and the feelings he had now were mixed. In the minute or so that he stood there he saw five copies disappear from the pile, and he had to admit to a certain amount of pride. But he thought too how ironic it was that something that had taken him a few short weeks to put together was selling like this, while the books he'd worked hard on for months had been largely overlooked by the public.

He left the shop and continued on until he turned into the Briggate, one of the main thoroughfares through the city centre. He crossed the road towards Harvey Nichols, where he intended to cut through to the Victoria Quarter. He glanced sideways and saw the store doorman, kitted out in his grey livery, and then he saw a shock of red hair. But before he realised that it belonged to Jo the doorman did what doormen do and she disappeared through the store entrance.

He still had the image of her in his mind when he got back to the flat. She'd been wearing the chunky cream sweater he'd bought her last Christmas, and remembering how good things had been then had left him shaken.

He put on a CD straight away—the very same CD that he'd been going to play the night he discovered that Libby had been there before him. He shrugged now at the memory. At least she'd left his hi-fi unharmed, he thought as he lay down on the sofa and let the soothing sound of Miles Davis's music flow over him.

For about ten seconds. Until the telephone cut through the peace he was hoping to find.

He'd forgotten that she was coming round to pick up the books, and for a moment he couldn't work out why Cass was ringing.

'I've got another favour to ask you,' she said.

I found the perfect dress in Harvey Nicks. It naturally cost me an arm and leg, but that didn't seem to matter—especially now I was earning good money again. I chose something tasteful, something very unlike what I'd worn to the club the previous weekend. I wanted to feel elegant for a change. And elegance, as everyone knows, doesn't come cheap. I didn't mind that there wouldn't be any eligible men at the party. Apart from the two families I was the only other guest, and I felt very privileged. That in itself was good enough reason to make an effort.

With the help of my flexible friend, I bought some shoes as well—medium heel in impossibly impractical ivory, to match the dress. I'd already told my dad that after tonight I would be moving back to the family home until I could find something else. He'd been surprised but, Dad being Dad, had found it hard to hide his delight that I was moving out. In fact I think he was disappointed that I wasn't leaving immediately. Tough! I'd thought as I left him to do some tentative packing, and it had suddenly occurred to me that my mother's life had not been a bed of roses either. My father could be very annoying at times—as living with him for the past few weeks had revealed.

I was obviously responding well to retail therapy, and as I toted my carrier bags around the city I bought four copies of the *Big Issue*, one from each vendor I saw, to make me feel less guilty about my Harvey Nicks purchases. And because the city was alive with Christmas promise, because the weather was bright and sunny, despite being cold, because everyone looked purposeful and happy, I felt fleetingly purposeful and happy too.

I spent another small fortune on an engagement present in a nice little specialist gift shop. I bought a beautiful set of wine glasses—six for red, six for white. They came in a fancy box, which I had giftwrapped in silver paper with matching ribbon. And I bought a congratulations card, and an expensive new lipstick, and then I went home for very long soak in the bath with a novel that had been hanging around unread for far too long.

I was a third of the way through it when the telephone rang and I had to get out of the bath to answer it.

chapter 22

I arrived fashionably late. Well, ten minutes late, to be precise, but enough to be the last to get there. Belle greeted me at the door, and she held the gift I'd brought for the happy couple while I took off my coat. She looked me up and down as I took the present back.

'You look so...er...grown up,' she said, a bit disapprovingly.

'You mean I look old?' I said, worried. I wondered if I'd overdone things by sleeking my hair up with some straightening serum.

'Not old *old*,' she said, frowning, 'but, like I say, *grown up*.'

They were all there in the sitting room when I followed Belle in—Cass's and Sid's families—and from what I could see they were getting along pretty well, considering. Considering they hadn't met before. They'd divided up into predictable groups: Sid's mother was chatting away to Cass's mother, and Sid's dad was listening to Cass's dad. He didn't seem to be saying much back, but he was nodding politely and looked fairly comfortable from where I was standing.

Marinda and Darinda were shamelessly flirting with Cass's two younger brothers, and her sisters, Mel, Sophie and Abigail, were occupying one of the huge sofas and talking animatedly amongst themselves. Sid and Cass seemed to be playing host, and were currently handing out plates of delicious-looking nibbles.

I assumed that the choice of music playing was Jennifer's. It was some sort of grand opera, I think, which seemed inappropriate for the occasion, but it was turned down quite low and nobody seemed to be objecting.

They all stopped talking when they noticed me, and while most of them waved a welcome the two mothers came over and gave me a hug. They both seemed to like my 'new look', as they called it—especially Sid's mother, surprisingly. She was looking very bohemian herself, dressed in an orange caftan with her hair flamboyantly wrapped in a matching scarf. There was no bum bag today, but her black Doc Marten boots were a bit of as surprise.

Cass's mother, who was as ever warm and affectionate, was dressed in more conservative style, and made a special fuss of me as the odd one out of the family gathering. I hadn't seen her for ages, but I got the impression she knew what had happened with my parents. I was relieved that she didn't refer to it directly, however, and when I'd exchanged my gift with Sid for a glass of champagne, I squeezed onto the sofa with Cass's three sisters. I hadn't seen them for a long time either, and I was always struck by how different they were from Cass.

They were dressed in a rainbow selection of flimsy slip dresses and were as lively and silly as most young women in their late teens and early twenties. Their conversation was a lot like Sid's sisters'—celebrities, clothes and men, in that particular order. As I quickly bored of their prattle I realised that Belle might well be right—maybe I really was growing up at last.

While they talked about the contents of the latest copy of *OK* magazine, I thought about the call I'd had from Aisling. She'd told me about getting a cheque out of Libby, about what she'd been up to in the past, about her new bloke and how she'd moved in with him. And then, I don't know why, but I got the idea she was fishing for something. I think she was trying to find out how I felt about Dan. But after my little talk with Cass the night before I thought it safest to keep my thoughts to myself.

Eventually Sid's sisters sidled over to us, and I left them all while I went to say a proper hello to Cass's younger brothers. They'd always been just kids to me in the past, and it shocked me to realise that they weren't any longer. David, I realised, must be twenty-four by now—the same age as Matt. I discovered that his girlfriend was pregnant, and that he was hoping to save enough for a deposit on a house for his new family soon. Mike, the nineteen-year-old baby of the family, was still at the local college, and a few words with him confirmed Cass's long-held suspicion that he was probably gay.

Which, all in all, no doubt explained the girls' sudden loss of interest in the two young men.

I managed a word with Sid's and Cass's fathers, and Sid himself, but despite several attempts I did not succeed in getting Cass on her own. I wanted to tell her how great she looked in her lemon dress, with her hair tousled a bit. If I didn't think I knew better I'd have suspected that she was avoiding me. And, although it couldn't possibly have been deliberate, she managed to go on avoiding me right up until Jennifer announced that food was about to be served in the dining room.

In fact it was more of a serve-yourself situation. The table had been splendidly laid out with a very extravagant cold buffet that I learnt from Sid's mother was mostly down to Sid himself. There was salmon, beef and ham, all of which had been so wonderfully decorated that it seemed a shame to spoil the effect by actually eating any of it.

Sid's father did the carving with great aplomb, while the rest of us looked on in awe at the fabulous display of colourful salads. By now the girls had taken over the music, and VantagePoint were singing their cute little hearts out in the background. We'd just got the go-ahead from Sid's mother to tuck into the buffet when the old-fashioned doorbell sounded.

There were a few puzzled glances exchanged, but Cass was hot off the mark.

'I'll get it,' she said, plainly very much at home, and proceeded to do so with considerable speed.

I was fourth in the queue for food, and with my plate in my hand and my eye on the salmon it took a moment to realise that the boy band were now doing their number one version of 'Careless Whisper'. Which, of course, made me think of Dan.

'I've got a surprise,' I heard Cass announce just as I got to the salmon. I carried on spooning it onto my plate, but when I noticed that everyone had gone a bit quiet I looked up and felt dizzy with shock. Dan saw me at about the same time, and although it was obvious that he was shocked too, he was a lot better at covering it up than me. By now my face had turned crimson, and my cutlery was rattling so much on the plate I had to put it down carefully on the table.

'This is Dan, everybody,' Cass went on. 'He has something for the girls,' she said to Sid's mother, 'and I thought it would be nice if he gave it to them himself.'

By the startled look on Jennifer's face she obviously had no idea what it was all about—but, clearly used to dealing with the unexpected, she managed a regal nod. Then Dan, prompted by Cass, opened one of the books I'd just noticed that he was holding.

'This one's for Darinda,' he said, a hint self-conscious, and Darinda, as if she was being called onto the platform to receive an unexpected school prize, slowly stepped forward and took the book. Her anxious features softened as she looked at it, and then broke into a smile when she opened it up. The other two sisters didn't need prompting. They trotted straight over to Dan in their high heels and were soon whooping with pleasure.

Because everyone wanted to know what all the fuss was about, the food was temporarily forgotten. When all was made clear someone drew attention to the music playing, and the girls got excited again and insisted on turning the sound up.

And throughout all this Cass steadfastly avoided eye contact with me.

Sid's father stepped over to Dan and shook his hand. I couldn't hear what he said, but I got the impression that he'd asked him to stay and join in the party. He seemed to hesitate for a moment, but Cass, who was still at his side, joined in the persuasion and he eventually nodded his acceptance.

As he did so he glanced over at me. I glanced elsewhere.

Of course the time inevitably arrived when I was forced to come into contact with him. I'd been snatching looks in his direction as I picked at my food, thinking how good he looked in his best black jacket, but I hadn't got as far as preparing myself for what I might say.

It was Sid's sisters who finally brought us together. They'd been clinging to him like limpets since he'd given them the books, hanging on to his every word. And he must have said something about me, because they all turned and looked at me in stunned silence. I coloured again when they let out little squeals of delight, and then Belle came and dragged me over towards the group.

'We were just telling Dan that you'd been kissed by Jamie Astin,' she said dreamily.

'And he said he knew about it,' enthused Darinda.

'His friend told him,' Marinda gasped excitedly. 'And she said that he'd asked for your telephone number!'

'Only she didn't know it.' Belle sighed tragically.

'Well, no one told me,' I said, trying to sound normal while wishing I were anywhere else at the moment. But I had to admit that I felt flattered, and I suppose I swaggered a bit. When I caught Dan's eye I saw that he was smiling wryly at me. And I felt a fool, as if I'd been caught kissing my own reflection in the mirror.

It was at that moment that I suddenly remembered I needed to visit the bathroom—and who did I meet on my way there? Why, my best friend Cass, of course.

She tried getting past me, but I wasn't going to let that happen.

'What the hell do you mean by bringing him here without at least warning me first?' I snarled as I led her roughly into the sitting room, where we could be alone.

'I thought I was doing you a favour after what you said last night.' She'd gathered herself by now and sounded defiant.

'Did he know I was going to be here?'

'No. I thought he might not come if he knew.'

'Great!' I said. 'Have you any idea how embarrassing this is?'

'Why?' she said. 'Because he knows that you have an alter ego?'

'Precisely.'

'But it's not all about you, is it? He probably feels bad as well, for thinking you broke into his flat.'

This was getting worse by the minute.

'You talked about that?'

She nodded. 'And I told him the reason you set up the date with Sarah was because you were so upset about it.'

My mind was galloping over the hurdles at some imaginary race meeting.

'And he's OK about it?'

Cass rolled her eyes. 'I wouldn't go that far, but apparently Aisling is.'

'Aisling knows! Oh, God,' I groaned.

'I wouldn't worry too much about her. I get the impression that she's on your side.'

I couldn't bear the thought of all these people discussing me as if I was a strange laboratory specimen. I just wanted out of there.

'I'm going,' I said.

'No, you're bloody well not,' Cass said crossly. She looked at me warningly. 'You're not going to spoil my party. You're going to stay here and behave like an adult for a change.'

I spent a good ten minutes in the cloakroom, and then crept back to the dining room, hopeful that Dan might have taken the initiative and headed for home.

There weren't many people left in there now. I could see the girls, huddled together in the corner, and I could hear what sounded like Irish folk music coming from the sitting room. I was about to see what was going on in there when I noticed Dan's head over the top of the girls'. I recognised the look in his eyes.

I'd seen it often enough before, at parties, when young women got wind of what he did for a living and cornered him for information about their idols.

And, because old habits really do die hard, before I realised what I was doing I dived in and rescued him.

'Your mothers are asking where you are,' I lied to all six of the girls, and when they looked about to argue with me

I lived up to my new grown-up image. 'And I want a quiet word with Dan, so do as you're told, like good girls, now, and leave us alone.'

There was a lot grumbling, but I stood my ground and within a minute the dining room had cleared. There was just Dan and me left, and we stood there looking at one another for a few seconds.

Until he reached out to me and pulled me into his arms.

And kissed me until my knees buckled.

And then, as if absolutely nothing out of the ordinary had occurred, he let go of me, smiled politely, and suggested we join the others.

chapter 23

He left it two full days, that is *forty-eight hours,* before he phoned me. During which time I went over the evening hundreds, possibly even thousands of times in my head. And the whole thing seemed—as everyone says about extraordinary events—exactly like a dream. A very strange dream in this particular case.

After that knee-buckling kiss we'd wandered into the sitting room, by which time Jennifer Perrez had kicked off her Doc Martens and was giving an Irish set-dance demonstration in her orange caftan. Which was surreal enough, but it didn't end there. Over the next couple of hours the furniture was pushed back and each and every one of us, whether we liked it or not, was expected to learn and perform several routines. It was fortunate for Jennifer that our numbers amounted to two perfect sets of eight, and—mad and unexpected as it all certainly was, and as much as most of us tried to object in the beginning—we ended up having a very good time.

Dan was a popular choice of partner, of course, and I didn't get a look-in with him. But throughout it all there he was, glancing my way once in a while as we occasionally skimmed past one another throughout that bizarre night, giving absolutely nothing away.

Afterwards, he'd gone his way and I'd gone mine. I had begun to believe that I'd imagined the whole dining room incident as I waited for the phone to ring. And as is often the case in such matters, the call finally came when I'd just about given up on him.

At ten minutes past nine on Monday evening, soon after I got back to my parents' home after work.

He spoke without any preamble.

'Have you checked your Hotmail lately, Sarah Daly?'

I felt my face colour at this reminder of my embarrassing little deception.

'No,' I said, swallowing with a gulp.

'Well, do it now,' he told me firmly, and then disconnected.

With a thumping heart I went straight to my laptop and checked into Sarah's account—something I hadn't done for quite a while. I found several messages waiting for her, but it was the last one, dated today, that I opened first.

Dear Sarah
I presume you haven't read the others, but no matter now.
I just wanted to say that I think our acquaintance with you has done us—both me and Jo—good, and I want to thank you.
And now, can you tell her to get her sad ass to the front door? Because I'm freezing my nuts off out here...
Dan

I did exactly as instructed, and when I opened the door there he was.

And then he did it again. He stepped over the threshold, pulled me towards him, and kissed me until I could no longer stand without assistance.

epilogue

I took over Libby's vacated flat after Christmas, which I had Feng Shui'd first by Sid's mother, Jennifer, to rid it of any bad vibes left by its former occupant. Dan and I both agreed that we shouldn't rush straight back into living together—and so far it's working out fine. He gets to play whatever music he wants, and I get to go out to clubs whenever I choose. Not that I *choose* too often these days. And we always get to spend the nights together.

While we were getting reacquainted again Marco and Nic started seeing each other—briefly. She rang to tell me one day at work, and I think she imagined that I'd be upset. She obviously didn't know I was back with Dan, and I didn't choose to enlighten her. Not then, anyway.

It only lasted until Marco went to Spain for Christmas—

during which time he seduced his father's beauty queen wife and brought her back to Leeds with him. Understandably, it didn't do his new relationship with his father very much good, and it all ended rather abruptly.

Nic wasn't very pleased either, apparently.

I learnt all this from Giovanna—who might have seemed fine about Marco getting in touch with his father, but who admitted to me when it was over that she hadn't been all that happy about it, really. And, although she didn't approve of his behaviour, she said that she preferred the beauty queen to Nic any day.

And at least she gets to spend more time with my father these days. Since Marco could hardly object, after what he'd done, Giovanna has moved into my old flat with my father until they can find something bigger. She still does most of the cooking for the café, but if it works out long term with Marco and the beauty queen—who seems to love working at the Italian—Giovanna is considering passing on her famous recipes.

Sid and Cass remain extremely happy—though in Sid's case you have to know him quite well to realise this. And, whereas I've always tended to think of Cass as fairly predictable, I'd never have predicted that she would marry within six months of meeting someone five years her junior. They've planned the wedding for the last week in May, and I, along with the six Foster and Perrez sisters, have agreed to wear a pale peach meringue and play my part as bridesmaid. But then I do owe her one.

Steve is going to be invited as well, I understand, and if he's still going out with Aisling then she'll be invited too. I hope so. She's become a very good friend of mine now, but I'm not so sure that Steve will be able to hold her interest that long.

One person who definitely won't be there is my mother.

Luckily for Matt, our strategy worked a treat. She soon got tired of sexual experimentation once she realised it wasn't having the desired effect. She's currently travelling around the States on Greyhound buses, and according to the last e-mail I received from her she's thinking of moving on to Australia with some people she met along the way. She has agreed to sell the house on Piper Hill, and the divorce from my dad has been set in motion.

I told Dan the other day that, despite everything, we have a lot to thank Libby for. I'd just been telling him what I'd learned through the grapevine—that she'd been thrown out of the flat by her new bloke and that she'd got her own back by trashing his car.

He seemed a bit taken aback by my comment, but *I* knew what I meant all right. I haven't forgotten his remark about me turning into my mother if I wasn't careful, even if he has. It stung bitterly at the time, but that is the way of truths, I've learnt. They hurt like hell. I'd been heading that way for certain, and I'd probably never have realised it if Dan and I had got back together too soon. If Libby hadn't lied about Aisling and kept us apart.

It isn't the only lesson I've learnt, but it is the most important.

And if it works out long term with Dan, then great. But if not it will finish for the right reasons now, because it has properly run its course. And not—most definitely not—because I've turned into my bloody mother.

That, I am certain now, is *never, ever* going to happen.

Out of the Blue

Isabel Wolff

This book is for every woman who has let a breeze of doubt turn into a full-blown hurricane!

Faith Martin, AM-U.K.!'s face of the morning weather, is used to delivering the forecast, not being told the forecast—especially when it concerns her marriage.

When Faith's ultraglam best friend plants a seed of doubt about her husband's fidelity, she begins to question everything about her comfortable life.

"Wolff handles the breakdown of marriage with warmth and humor."
—*The Times*

Spanish Disco

Erica Orloff

Prescription for heartburn:
Avoid spicy foods, alcohol, coffee and stress.

Prescription for heartache:
Avoid feeling sorry for yourself.

Too bad for editor Cassie Hayes, she's got a bad case of both. And now that her publishing company is in dire straits, she's stuck on an island with an epic poem that was supposed to be a long-awaited sequel, a cook who goes a little heavy on the cayenne, a nasty coffee addiction, a predilection for tequila and a reclusive author more than happy to ply her with beer. There's little doubt that she'll survive the adventure, but will you?

Name & Address Withheld

Jane Sigaloff

Life couldn't be better for Lizzie Ford. Not only
does she have a great job doling out advice on the
radio, but now she has a new love interest *and* a
new best friend. Unfortunately she's about to learn
that they're husband and wife. Can this expert on
social etiquette keep the man, her friend *and* her
principles? Find out in *Name & Address Withheld*,
a bittersweet comedy of morals and manners.

RED
DRESS
INK
™

Visit us at www.reddressink.com   RDI1202R-TR